THE DARK
WINTER

# THE DARK WINTER

## DAVID MARK

Quercus

First published in Great Britain in 2012 by

Quercus
55 Baker Street
7th Floor, South Block
London
W1U 8EW

A CIP catalogue record for this book is available
from the British Library

ISBN 978 0 85738 918 3 (HB)
ISBN 978 0 85738 919 0 (TPB)

10 9 8 7 6 5 4 3 2 1

Typeset by Ellipsis Digital Limited, Glasgow

Printed and bound in Great Britain by Clays Ltd, St Ives plc

To my grandparents – champion storytellers, one and all.

The quality of mercy is not strain'd,
It droppeth as the gentle rain from heaven
Upon the place beneath: it is twice bless'd;
It blesseth him that gives and him that takes.

William Shakespeare, *The Merchant of Venice*

# PROLOGUE

The old man looks up, and for a moment it feels as though he is staring through the wrong end of a telescope. The reporter is forty years away.

'Mr Stein?'

A warm, tender hand on his bony knee.

'Can you share your memories of that moment?'

It takes a physical effort of will to drag himself into the present.

He blinks.

Tells himself, with an old man's fear of losing his memories, to get it together.

*You're still here*, he tells himself. *Still living.*

'Mr Stein? Fred?'

*You're alive*, he tells himself, again. The supertanker *Carla*. Seventy miles off the Icelandic coast. One last interview, here in the galley, with its stink of fried food and burned coffee, its diesel and sea-spray; the deep, bass-note hum of unwashed men and wet wool.

So many memories . . .

He blinks again. It's becoming a habit. *There should be tears*, he thinks. Deserves tears, this.

He sees her properly. Sitting forward on the hard-backed chair like a jockey on a horse. Holding the microphone in front of his face like she's a toddler who wants him to lick her lolly.

Closes his eyes and it hits him like a wave.

For an instant, he is a young man again, starting an eighteen-hour shift, pulling on a jumper stiff with fish guts and slime. He's warming his hands on a mug of tea when he's not spooning enough porridge into his gob to fill his belly. He's hurting. Trying to convince himself his hands are his own. He's hearing the skipper's voice. The urgency of his cries. He's swinging the hook. The hatchet. Chopping at the ice. Hacking it free in lumps that could stove your skull in if you weren't quick on your feet. He's feeling the ship begin to go . . .

'The sound of the wind,' he says, and in his coat pocket he feels his fingers make the sign of the cross, genuflecting on the smooth, silky surface of the packet of Benson and Hedges. It's an old habit, the residue of a Catholic upbringing.

'Can you describe it for us?'

'It was like being in a house on a bare moor,' he says, closing one eye. 'The wind was coming from all sides. Howling. Roaring. Banging. It was like it was out to get us. I was vibrating with it. Like one of those tuning forks. I could feel the vibrations coming through the deck, and I was stood stock-still, frozen to the bloody spot.'

She nods to her cameraman, and motions to keep going. He's good value for money, this nice old chap in his charity-shop suit and Hull Kingston Rovers tie. Coping pretty well, considering. Handling the cold better than she is. Got better sea-legs, she'll give him that. Better constitution, too. She's barely kept a meal down since they hit this weather front, and it's not helping that the only room on this supposed supertanker that's big enough for her, the cameraman and the boom, is the greasy, food-spattered kitchen. Galley, she corrects herself, with a journalist's particularity.

'Go on, Mr Stein.'

'If I'm honest, love, it was the boots,' says the old man, looking away. 'My mates' boots. I could hear them on the deck. They were squeaking. They sounded all rubbery on the wood. I'd never heard it before. Eight years on the trawlers and I'd never heard the sound of footsteps. Not over the engines and the generators. Did that night, though. Wind dropped just long enough for me to hear them running. Kind of it, eh? Malicious bastard. It was like it was getting its breath back for the battering that was to come. And I was stood there, thinking: "I can hear their boots." And forty years later, that's what I remember. Their bloody boots. Can't bear to hear it now. Won't go out if it's raining. I hear a boot squeak on a wet surface and I'm on my knees. Don't even like thinking about them. That's what I wasn't sure about on this trip. It's not the waves. Not the bloody weather. It's the thought of hearing some welly boots on a wet deck and feeling like it never went away . . .'

The reporter is nodding now. Caroline. Thirty-odd. Big wooden earrings and hair like a nine-year-old boy. Nothing special to look at, but confident and bright as a button. Newsreader make-up. London accent and an expensive ring or three on fingers that had been manicured at the start of the trip, but which are beginning to look a little chipped and patched-up now.

'Then it started up again,' he says. 'It was like being in a tin shed and somebody beating on it with a cricket bat. Worse than that. Like being on a runway with a hundred planes taking off. Then the waves started rolling in on us. The spray was turning to ice when it hit the air, so it was like being stabbed with a million needles all at once. My face and hands were agony. I thought my ears were being pushed into my head. I was numb. I couldn't stand up. Couldn't take a step in the direction I wanted. Was just tumbling around on the deck, bumping and banging around. A bloody pinball, that's what I were. Rolling about, waiting for it all to stop. I must have broken a few bones during all that but I don't remember it hurting. It was like my senses couldn't take it all in. So then it was just noise and cold. And this feeling that the air was tearing itself apart.'

*She's happy*, he thinks. Loving this. And he's quite proud of himself too. It's been forty years since he told this story without a pint in his hand, and the mug of tea he's gripping in one plump, pink-marbled fist has been allowed to go cold without once reaching his lips.

'So, when was the order given to abandon ship?'

'It's all very confused. It was so dark. The lights went off the second we hit the rocks. You ever seen snow and spray in the dark? It's like being inside a busted TV. You can't stand upright, neither. Don't know which way's up . . .'

He snatches a hand to his cheek. Catches a tear. He looks at it, sitting there accusingly on a broken, cracked knuckle.

He hasn't seen his own tears in years. Not since the wife died. They'd snuck up on him then, too. After the funeral. After the wake. After they'd all gone home and he was clearing away the plates and chucking crusts and crisps in the bin. Tears had come like somebody had opened a sluice. Had fallen for so long that he was laughing by the end of it, amazed at himself, standing over the washing-up bowl and fancying he had a tap either side of his nose: emptying himself of the ocean he had given up for her.

'Mr Stein . . .'

'We'll leave it there, love. Have a break, eh?' His voice is still gravelly. Rolled in cigarettes and bitter. But he seems to be shaking, suddenly. Shaking inside his suit with its shiny sleeves and worn knees. Sweating, too.

Caroline seems about to protest. To tell him that this is why they're here. That any display of emotion will help show the viewers how deeply this has affected him. But she shuts herself up when she realises that it would sound like she was telling a sixty-three-year-old man to cry like a baby for the cameras.

'Tomorrow, love. After the whatsit.'

'OK,' she says, and indicates to her cameraman that he should stop filming. 'You know what's happening, yes?'

'I'm sure you'll keep me right.'

'Well, the captain has agreed to give us an hour at the spot where you went down. We'll be up against it, and the weather isn't going to be anything special, but we'll have time for the ceremony. Wrap up warm, eh? Like we said, there will be a simple wreath and a plaque. We'll film you passing them over the side.'

'All right, love,' he says, and his voice doesn't sound like his own. It's a squeak. Like a rubber-soled boot on wet wood.

There's a sudden tightness in his chest. He gives her the best grandfatherly smile he can muster, and says goodnight, ignoring the protests from his knees as he pushes himself out of the hard-backed chair and takes three lurching steps to the open door. He pulls himself into the narrow corridor and walks, quicker than he has in years, towards the deck. One of the crew is coming the other way. He nods a smile and starfishes himself against the wall to allow the older man to pass. He mutters something in Icelandic, and gives him a grin, but Fred can't summon up the strength to remember a language he's hardly spoken in decades, and the noise he makes as he passes the orange-overalled man is little more than a gargled cough.

He can't breathe. There's a pain in his arm and across his shoulders.

Coughing, gasping, he clatters out onto the deck like a fish spilling from a trawl, and with his eyes screwed up shut, takes great lungfuls of the icy, blustering air.

The deck is deserted. To his rear stands the man-made mountain of cargo containers that this super-container vessel will be dropping off in three days' time. Towards the bow, he can see the little squares of yellow light emanating from the bridge. Halogen lamps cast circles of pale illumina-tion on the rubbery green surface of the deck.

He stares at the waters. Wonders what his mates look like now. Whether their skeletons remain intact, or whether the motion of the sea has torn them apart and mixed them up.

He wonders whether Georgie Blanchard's legs are tangled in with Archie Cartwright's. The pair never got on.

He wonders what his own corpse should look like.

Drops his head as he considers how he has wasted forty stolen years.

He reaches into his pocket and takes out his cigarettes. It's been years since he last had to strike a match in the face of a force 5, but he remembers the art of cupping the flame inside his palm and quickly drawing in a deep gulp of cigarette smoke. He leans with his back to the gunwale and looks around, trying to steady his thoughts. Looks at the ragged thumbnail of moon, scything down into a cushion of cloud. Looks at the white ripples on the black water as the cargo ship cuts through the deep waters.

*Why you, Fred? Why did you make it back when they didn't? Why—*

Fred never finishes the thought. Never finishes the cigarette. Never gets to lay the wreath and drop the plaque, and say goodbye to eighteen crewmates who never made it back alive.

It feels for a moment as though the ship has run aground. He is thrown forward. Smashes into the gunwale with an impact that drives the air from his lungs and a single, splintered rib through the skin of his chest. Blood sprays from his lips as the strength leaves his legs. He slithers to his knees and then his belly as his hands slip on the wet deck. The shard of rib breaks off on impact with the ground and crimson agony explodes inside him, cutting through the dullness of his wits just long enough for him to open his eyes.

He tries to push himself up. To shout for help.

And then he is being scraped up in strong arms, like a flaking fillet of cod on a hot fish slice. For a moment, a solitary second, he is looking into his attacker's eyes.

Then there is the feeling of flight. Of quick, graceless descent. Of rushing, cold air. Of wind in his ears, spray at his back.

Thud.

A bone-smashing, lung-crushing impact on the deck of a small, wooden boat, bobbing on water the colour of ale.

His eyes, opening in painful stages, allow his dulled senses a glimpse of the disappearing ship. To feel the rolling, rocking motion of a too-small lifeboat in a giant ocean.

He is too tired to turn his memories into pictures, but as the cold envelops him and the moon seems to wink out, he has a vague memory of familiarity.

Of having done this before.

# PART ONE

# CHAPTER 1

2.14 p.m., Holy Trinity Square. A fortnight until Christmas.

The air smells of snow. Tastes of it. That metallic tang; a sensation at the back of the throat. Cold and menthol. Coppery, perhaps.

McAvoy breathes deeply. Fills himself up with it. This chilly, complicated Yorkshire air, laced with the salt and spray of the coast; the smoke of the oil refineries; the burned cocoa of the chocolate factory; the pungency of the animal feed unloaded from the super-container at the docks this morning; the cigarettes and fried food of a people in decline, and a city on its arse.

Here.

Hull.

Home.

McAvoy glances at the sky, ribboned with ragged strips of cloud.

Cold as the grave.

He searches for the sun. Whips his head this way and that, trying to find the source of the bright, watery light that fills up this market square and darkens the glass of the coffee shops and pubs which ring this bustling piazza. Smiles as he finds it, safe at the rear of the church, nailed to the sky like a brass plaque: obscured by the towering spire and its shroud of tarpaulin and scaffold.

'Again, Daddy. Again.'

McAvoy glances down. Pulls a face at his son. 'Sorry. Miles away.' He raises the fork and deposits another portion of chocolate cake into the boy's wide-open, grinning mouth. Watches him chew and swallow, then open his mouth again, like a baby chick awaiting a worm.

'That's what you are,' laughs McAvoy, when it occurs to him that Finlay will find this description funny. 'A baby bird asking for worms.'

'Tweet tweet,' laughs Finlay, flapping his arms like wings. 'More worms.'

McAvoy laughs, and as he scrapes the last of the cake from the plate, he leans forward and kisses the boy's head. Fin is wrapped up warm in bobble hat and fleece coat, so McAvoy is denied the delicious scent of his son's shampooed hair. He's tempted to whip off the hat and take a deep breath of the mown grass and honeycomb he associates with the boy's shaggy red head, but it is bitterly cold here, outside the trendy coffee shop, with its silver tables and metal chairs, so he contents himself with tickling the lad under the chin and enjoying his smile.

'When's Mammy coming back?' asks the boy, wiping his own face with the corner of a paper towel and licking his lips with a delightfully chocolate-smeared tongue.

'Not long,' replies McAvoy, instinctively glancing at his watch. 'She's getting prizes for Daddy.'

'Prizes. What for?'

'For being a good boy.'

'Like me?'

'Just like you.'

McAvoy leans in.

'I've been really good. Father Christmas is bringing me loads of presents. Loads and loads and loads.'

McAvoy grins. His son is right. When Christmas comes, two weeks from now, Fin will find the equivalent of a month's salary, wrapped and packaged, beneath the red tinsel and silver branches of the imitation tree. Half the living room of their nondescript new-build semi to the north of the city will be swamped with footballs, clothes and wrestling figures. They started shopping in June, just before Roisin discovered she was expecting again. They can't afford what they've spent. Can't afford the half of it, considering the expense the New Year will bring. But he knows what Christmas means to Roisin, and has given the credit card the hammering she deserves. She will find a garnet-and-platinum necklace in her own stocking on Christmas morning. A red leather jacket, sized for when she sheds the baby weight. *Sex and the City* DVDs. Tickets for the UB40 concert at Delamere Forest in March. She'll squeal and make the noises he loves. Run to the mirror and try on the coat over her baggy T-shirt and swollen, pregnant belly. Fold her pretty, delicate face into smiles, then plaster him with kisses as she forgets that it is a day for children, and that their son has yet to open any of his presents.

McAvoy feels a sudden vibration next to his chest and removes the two slimline mobile phones that reside in his inside pocket. With a slight sensation of disappointment, he realises the sound is coming from his personal phone. A message from Roisin. *You're going to love what I've got you . . . Xxxx.* He smiles. Sends her back a collection of kisses. Hears his dad's voice, calling him a soft shite. Shrugs it off.

'Your mam's silly,' he says to Fin, and the boy nods solemnly.

'Yes,' he says. 'She is.'

The mere thought of his wife is enough to make him smile. He has heard it said that to love truly is to care more for somebody else than you do for yourself. McAvoy dismisses the notion. He cares more for everybody else than he does for himself. He'd die for a stranger. His love for Roisin is as perfect and otherworldly as she is herself. Delicate, passionate, loyal, fearless . . . She keeps his heart safe for him.

McAvoy stares into space for a while. Looks at the church. He's been inside it a few times. Has been inside most of Hull's important buildings in the five years since he moved to the city. He and Roisin once saw a concert here; an hour-long set by the Cologne Philharmonic Orchestra. It had done little for him, but reduced his wife to happy tears. He'd sat and read the guidebook, clapping when prompted, pouring knowledge into his brain like a drink down a parched throat and occasionally lifting his head long enough to gaze at Roisin, wrapped up in scarf and denim jacket, wide-eyed as she became lost in the soaring strings that echoed, ghostly and majestic, from the high ceilings and vaulted columns of the church.

As the noise of the passing shoppers and nearby traffic drops to a sudden and peculiar hush, McAvoy hears the faint strains of a choirboy's voice, floating across the square. The song weaves through the pedestrians like string from a loom, causing heads to turn, footfall to slow, conversation to hush. It's a warm, Christmassy moment. McAvoy sees smiles. Sees mouths opening to form vowels of pleasure and encouragement.

For a moment, McAvoy is tempted to take his son inside. To slide in at the back of the church and listen to the service. To sing 'Once in Royal David's City' with his son's hand in his and watch the candlelight flicker on the church walls. Fin had been fascinated when they had looked up from placing their order at the coffee shop till and seen the tail end of the procession of choirboys and clergy pass through the big iron-studded double wooden doors at the mouth of the church. McAvoy, embarrassed at his inadequacy, had not been able to explain the significance of the different robes, but Fin had found the colours intoxicating. 'Why are there boys and girls?' he'd asked, pointing at the choristers in their red pepper-pot cassocks and white ruffs. McAvoy had wished he could answer. He had been raised Catholic. Had never bothered to learn the different meanings of the costumes favoured by the Church of England.

McAvoy makes a mental note to remedy his inadequacy and turns his head to look in the direction from which he assumes Roisin will appear. He can't see her among the milling shoppers, who are taking care on the slick cobbles that carpet this most historic part of town. Were this one of the nearby cities, York or Lincoln, the streets would be chock-a-block with tourists. But this is Hull. It's the last stop before the sea, on the road to nowhere, and it's falling to bloody pieces.

The tremble by his heart again. The fumble for the phones. It's the work phone this time. The on-call phone. He feels a tightening in his stomach as he answers.

'Detective Sergeant McAvoy. Serious and Organised Crime Unit.' To say that still gives him a thrill.

'Now then, Sarge. Just checking in.' It's Helen Tremberg, a tall, earnest detective constable who transferred over from Grimsby when she made the move from uniform a few months before.

'Excellent. What have we got?'

'Quiet one, given the time of year. City are playing away this weekend so all pretty basic stuff. Bit of a scrap off Beverley Road way but nobody wants to take it any further. Family party that got a bit out of control. Oh, the ACC asked if you'd give him a call when you have a moment.'

'Yes?' McAvoy tries to keep the squeak from his voice. 'Any clue?'

'Oh, I doubt it's much to worry about. Said he wanted a favour. No screaming or anything. Didn't use any rude words.'

They both give a little laugh at that. The Assistant Chief Constable is not a daunting man. Skinny, spry and softly spoken, he's more of an accountant than a thief-taker; his most telling contribution to the local force being the intro-duction of a 'data-sharing intranet matrix' and a memo warning against the use of bad language during a visit to Priory Road station by Princess Anne.

'Right. So. Nothing pressing?'

'Sorry, Sarge. I wouldn't even have called, but you asked to be notified . . .'

'No, no. You did right.'

McAvoy hangs up with a sigh. His immediate boss, Acting Detective Superintendent Trish Pharaoh, is on a course this weekend. The station's two detective inspectors are both off duty. Should anything major occur, he will be the senior officer on call, the one to take the reins. While he feels the familiar prickling of guilt in his belly at wishing for a set of circumstances that would spell misfortune and pain for some poor soul, he knows that such circumstances are inescapable. There will be crime. Same as there will be snow. It's just a question of where it falls, and how deep.

A waitress appears, goose pimples on her bare forearms. She gives a good-natured scowl at McAvoy and his son. 'You must be mad,' she says, with exaggerated shivering.

'I'm not mad,' says Fin, indignant. 'You're mad.'

McAvoy smiles down at his son, but says his name chidingly, to warn him about being rude to grown-ups. 'It's a lovely day,' he says, turning back to the waitress, who's wearing a black skirt and T-shirt and looks to be in her early thirties.

'They say it'll snow,' she says, clearing away the remnants of the chocolate cake, the glass of lemonade, the mug of hot chocolate that McAvoy had devoured in three burning, delicious gulps.

'There'll be a scattering today, but not much more. Maybe another day or two. Be a heavy fall. A good few inches at least.'

The waitress surveys him. This big, barrel-chested man in the designer double-breasted coat. Good-looking, even with the unruly hair and broad, farmer's face. He must be an easy six-foot-five, but there's a gentleness about his movements, his gestures, that suggest he is afraid of his own size; as if constantly apprehensive that he will break something more fragile than himself. She can't place his accent any more accurately than 'posh' and 'Scottish'.

'You a weatherman?' she asks, smiling.

'I grew up in the country,' he replies. 'You get a nose for these things.'

She grins at Fin and nods at his father. 'Your dad got a nose for the weather?'

Fin regards her coolly. 'We're waiting for Mammy,' he says.

'Oh yes? And where's Mammy?'

'Getting prizes for Daddy.'

'You been a good boy, have you?' she asks McAvoy, and there's a practised sauciness to her voice. She casts another glance over his well-muscled body, his thick, bullish neck, his round, square-jawed face, which, in this light, seems striped with the faintest of scars.

McAvoy smiles. 'One tries,' he says softly.

The waitress gives a last little grin then scurries back indoors.

McAvoy breathes out slowly. He plonks Fin back in his own chair and pulls out a notepad and a box of crayons from the recesses of the leather satchel at his feet. A man-bag, Roisin had called it when she'd presented him with the gift a few months before, along with the designer coat and trio of expensive suits. 'Just trust me,' she'd said, as she'd tugged down his old shiny black suit trousers and dragged his water-proofed hiking jacket from his hand. 'Try it. Just let me dress you for a little while.'

He'd relented. Let her dress him. Carried the man-bag. Grown used to the coat, which was warm and kept the rain off, and spared him too many barbs about his unruly ginger hair.

When he insisted that clothes don't make the man, she said: 'When people see you, they need to see somebody to reckon with. Somebody with confidence. Somebody with style. It's not as though you're Columbo. You're just badly dressed.'

And so Detective Sergeant Aector McAvoy had become a fashion victim. Turned up at the station that Monday morning to catcalls, wolf-whistles and a chorus of the *Rawhide* theme tune. For once, it had been good-natured banter. 'You're a scary-enough looking bugger at the best of times,' DC Ben Nielsen had said, lounging against the custody suite wall as they waited for a suspected burglar to be brought down from the cells. 'Now you're looming in the doorway with a handbag. The poor sods don't know whether they're going to get shot or bummed. It confuses them. Stick with it.'

McAvoy likes Nielsen. He's one of the half-dozen new faces brought in six months back by the brass to try and wipe out the stench of the bad old days. The era that had both made and cost McAvoy his name. Nailed him as the copper who cost a detective superintendent his job and sparked an internal investigation that scattered a crooked team of CID officers to the four winds. Who managed to glide through the whole thing without a blemish on his written record. He's the copper who did for Doug Roper, the copper who nearly died out at the woods beneath the Humber Bridge, at the hands of a man whose crimes will never be known by anybody other than a handful of senior officers who stitched his face up more expertly than the doctors at Hull Royal. He's the copper who refused to take up the offer of an easy transfer to a cosy community station. Who now finds himself on a team that doesn't trust him, working for a boss who doesn't rate him, and trying to blend into the background while carrying a Samsonite satchel with adjustable straps and waterproof bloody pockets . . .

Pharaoh has had to hit the ground running. In the wake of Doug Roper's departure the Chief Constable decided the bad-boy's old team should become an elite unit, specialising in serious crime. A unit within the greater body of CID, run by an experienced, reliable hand and staffed with the best officers from within the Humberside boundary. Nobody had expected the job to go to Trish Pharaoh, the sassy, deter- mined 'token woman' from across the Humber. Detective Chief Inspector Colin Ray had been the bookies' choice for promotion, with his protégée Sharon Archer as his number two. Instead, Trish Pharoah had been hand-picked by the Chief Constable, who needed something attention-grabbing to put in a press release. Brought her over from Grimsby and told her to make waves. Ray and Archer were drafted into the team as Pharaoh's deputies, and neither took to the roll with good grace. Rumour had it the top brass told them on their first day that their new boss was a mere figurehead – a light- ning conductor positioned to take the heat when it all went wrong. Told them that, in reality, they were the unit's leaders. Pharaoh had different ideas, though; saw a chance to build something special and set about picking her team. But for every officer she recruited, Ray brought in one of his own. The unit was soon laced with intrigue and duplicity, split between Ray's old campaigners and Pharaoh's more forward-thinking, hand-picked specialists.

McAvoy falls into neither camp. His business cards declare him a member of the Serious and Organised Crime Unit, but he is nobody's blue-eyed boy. He requested the transfer himself. Used up his thank-you from the top brass. Slid into the unit as a muted reward for nearly getting himself killed in the line of a duty that nobody had asked him to burden himself with.

In truth, he is somewhere between an ambassador and a mascot; an educated, well-spoken, physically imposing emblem of the brave new world of Humberside Police – tailor-made for giving talks to the Women's Institute and local schools, and a valuable asset when putting together year-end reports on the force's new software requirements.

'What's going on, Daddy?'

As McAvoy stares out across the square, the smell of snow grows suddenly stronger. He's heard it said that it can be too cold for snow, but a childhood spent in the harsh and unforgiving embrace of the Western Highlands has taught him that it is never too cold for flakes to fall. This sudden plunging in temperature will harden the ground. Catch the snowfall without letting it settle. Cause the wind to rebound. Build a blizzard that will blind his young eyes and turn his fingers to blue stone . . .

In the back of his throat he tastes the metallic tang again, and for an instant wonders at the eerie similarity between the flavour of changing weather and the sharp, bitter taste of blood.

And then he hears screaming. Loud. Piercing. Multi-voiced. This is no drunken reveller, tickled by a boyfriend, chased by a pal. This is terror, unleashed.

McAvoy's head snaps towards the direction of the sound. The movement in the square stops suddenly, as if the men, the women, the families moving on its surface are mere music-box ballerinas, spinning to a graceless, abrupt halt.

He stands, extricating his frame from the cramped confines of the table, and stares into the mouth of the church. He takes two steps and finds the table legs still blocking his thick shins. He kicks out. Knocks the table to the floor. Begins to run.

McAvoy sprints across the square, sensing movement on all sides. 'Get back,' he shouts, motioning with his arms as curious shoppers begin to jog towards Holy Trinity. His breathing becomes shallow, as adrenalin begins to pump into his veins. He feels the blood fill his cheeks. It is only as he runs through the open metal gates and into the shadow of the double doors that he remembers his son. He pulls up like a lame horse, all arms and legs and knotted, tumbling limbs. He stares back across the square. Sees a four-year-old boy sitting in front of an upended table, mouth open, crying for his daddy.

And for a moment, he is torn. Truly motionless with uncertainty.

A figure bursts from the doors. It is clad in black, head to toe.

There are fresh shrieks as this shadow springs forth from the open-mouthed House of God: a streak of silver in its left hand, stains upon its handle, damp upon its breast . . .

McAvoy has no time to raise his hands. He sees the blade rise. Fall. And then he is on his back, staring at the darkening sky, hearing running footsteps. Distant sirens. A voice. Feeling hands upon him.

*'You'll be all right. Stay with me. Stay with me, lad.'*

And harsher, stronger, like a firm black pencil stroke among shading and blurs, another voice, drenched in anguish . . .

'He's killed her. She's dead. She's dead!'

Staring wide-eyed into the sky, he is the first to see the snow begin to fall.

# CHAPTER 2

She lies where she fell, crumpled and folded on the altar steps: one leg drawn up, bent the wrong way at the knee – a dislodged training shoe hanging precariously from stockinged toes.

She is a black girl, her face and hands a rich mahogany: her upturned palms soft, the colour of churned milk. She's young. Still in the throes of adolescence. Not old enough to buy cigarettes. Not old enough to have sex. Not old enough to die.

Nobody has tried to restart her heart. There are too many holes in her. Pressing on her chest would be like squeezing a wet sponge.

Her pure white cassock has been pulled up behind her back, creased beneath her corpse. Its thick white material hugs tight to the curve of one small, firm breast.

The girl's blood has made her robe sodden and crimson down one side. It remains pristine on the other. Were it not for the twisted expression that enfolds the entirety of her face, it would seem as though this hideous indignity had only been visited on one side of her small frame.

It is clear she died in agony. The blood that streaks her cheeks, neck, chin and lips looks as though it was hurled at her in great wet handfuls. It settled on her in a hazy red rain as she lay here, dead and staring, gaze fixed on a distant ceiling of curving columns and hand-drawn stars.

'You poor, poor girl.'

McAvoy stands by the altar, one big pink hand gripping the wooden back-rest of the front pew. He feels sick and dizzy and there's a haziness to his vision where the swelling above his eye is disrupting the edges of his sight. The paramedic had wanted to take him straight to casualty for an X-ray, but McAvoy, no stranger to injury, knows that this wound brings nothing more harmful than pain. Pain can be endured.

'Got lucky, eh Sarge?'

McAvoy turns too quickly as the voice rings out in the echoing cavern of the empty church. There is a fresh explosion of pain in his skull and he sinks into the pew as DC Helen Tremberg makes her way up the central aisle. A sickness hits him in the gut.

'I'm sorry, Detective Constable Tremberg?'

'They said he almost filleted you as well. Lucky break.'

Her cheeks are flushed. She's excited. For the past hour she's been marshalling the uniformed officers from their makeshift HQ in the verger's office and one of the younger constables had called her 'ma'am', thinking her a senior officer. She had enjoyed the feeling. Enjoyed telling people what to do, and seeing it done. Already the dozen uniforms have taken the first batch of statements from the congregation, as well as the names and addresses of those currently too deeply in shock to be able to explain what they saw.

'He hit me with the handle, not the blade.'

'Must have liked the look of you, eh? Must have been more difficult to knock you out than to kill you. Heat of the moment, machete in your hand. Million to one that he decides to crack you one rather than slash you.'

McAvoy stares at his feet, waiting for the thudding pain to cease.

He knows how this story will be told. He has a reputation as a desk jockey; a master of spreadsheets and databases, computing and technology. To be knocked out cold at a crime scene by the prime suspect? He can hear the jokes already.

'Your boy get home OK?'

McAvoy nods. Swallows. Coughs some gravel into his voice.

'Roisin came and got him. The waitress from the coffee shop was looking after him. I think I'm in the doghouse with both of them.'

'The waitress?'

McAvoy smiles. 'Yeah, probably her as well.'

They fall silent for a moment, Tremberg letting herself look at the girl's corpse for the first time. She shakes her head and looks away. Focuses on her notebook. Tries to get this right. She's never had any worries about organising a crime scene or giving a report, but there's something about McAvoy that she finds strangely disconcerting. It's more than just his size. There's a sadness to him. A quiet, brooding intensity that makes him difficult company. She gets on fine with the blokes at the station. She's perfectly at ease telling jokes with the lads and can drink most of her male colleagues under the table, but there is a quality to her sergeant that makes her unsure how to impress him. He seems to take

18

it all so personally. And he's obsessed with getting things done by the book. With filling in forms and quoting the right sections and sub-sections, and using the politically correct references for every scumbag they come into contact with.

She knows he has his secrets. Something happened a year ago, up at the Country Park, and it cost a well-known copper his job and put McAvoy on the shelf for months. He was injured, she knows that. The faintest of scars are on his face. There are rumours of more beneath the expensive clothes he seems to wear so inelegantly. Tremberg had only joined Trish Pharaoh's team a few weeks before McAvoy returned from sick leave, and she had been excited about having a chance to get to know him. But the first meeting was a disappointment. She'd found a small man trapped in a giant's body. He had the personality of an unassuming, bespectacled accountant, but it was rattling around inside a colossal frame. And then there were the eyes. Those big, sad cow-eyes that seemed to be forever questioning, assessing, disapproving, judging. At times, he put her in mind of an old Scottish king, his sword across his knees and a blanket round his shoulders, coughing, wheezing, but still able to wield a claymore with enough force to decapitate a bull.

She looks at him now. Hopes to God that they make a start on this before Detective Chief Inspector Colin Ray and his trained seal can steam in and spoil the party.

McAvoy stands. Steadies himself and sees that his hand, supporting his weight on the pew, is resting on a leather-bound Bible.

'So little mercy,' he says, half to himself.

'Sarge?'

'Just makes you wonder,' he mutters, and a disloyal blush climbs from his shirt and up his broad face. 'Why her? Why here? Why now?' He waves a huge, shovel-like hand. 'Why any of it?'

'Horrible world,' says Tremberg with a shrug.

McAvoy looks at his feet and strokes the cover of the Bible. 'Chapter and verse,' he says softly, and closes his eyes.

'She's called Daphne Cotton,' says Tremberg, her voice suddenly softer and less abrasive, as if, after the viewing of the corpse, her earlier bombast has been diluted by the sheer brutal sadness of the scene. 'Fifteen years old. She's been part of this church for four years. Adopted.'

'Stop there,' says McAvoy, already dizzy with ideas and questions. He has a logical mind, but things make more sense to him when they are written down and neatly ordered. He likes the process of detection. Likes the orderliness of logging things properly. With his aching head and dulled wits, he wonders how much of this will go in. 'Daphne Cotton,' he repeats. 'Fifteen. Adopted. Local?'

Tremberg looks confused. 'Sarge?'

'She's a black girl, DC Tremberg. Was she adopted from overseas?'

'Oh, right. Don't know.'

'Right.'

They fall into silence, both disappointed in the other and themselves. McAvoy finds himself worrying about his use of the word 'black'. Would it be more appropriate to use the procedural moniker? Is it wrong to notice her colour? Is he being a good detective or a bigot? He knows few other officers concern themselves with such subtleties, but McAvoy would give

himself an ulcer fretting about such things were it not for
Roisin's ability to calm him down.

'So,' says McAvoy, looking back at the girl's body and then
up to the ceiling. 'What did they tell you, the witnesses?'

Tremberg glances at her notebook. 'She's an altar server,
Sarge. An acolyte. They hold the candles in the procession. Sit
in front of the altar during the service. Take the stuff the
priest hands them and put it away. Lots of ceremony and
pomp. It's a big honour, apparently. She's been doing it since
she was twelve.' There is enough scepticism and eyebrow-
raising in Tremberg's speech to hint at a set of religious
beliefs somewhere south of agnostic.

'You're not a regular at Sunday service?' asks McAvoy with
a faint smile.

Tremberg gives a snort of derisory laughter. 'In my family,
Sundays were for the Grand Prix. We followed F1 religiously
though.'

At the far end of the central aisle a door bangs open with
a sudden gust of wind, and for a moment McAvoy sees grave-
stones and gates, Christmas lights and uniforms, as a blue
light flashes rhythmically, illuminating the darkness in
sweeping circles. He can imagine the scene out there. Police
constables in yellow coats fixing blue-and-white striped
police tape around the wrought-iron gates. Drinkers from the
nearby pubs peering over half-empty pint glasses as cars do
battle in the forecourt, screeching to a halt, inches from col-
lision; anxious drivers leaping out to pick up loved ones who
had been in the congregation and who are now emerging
into the cold, snow-blown square, to be led away from the
horror of what they have witnessed.

'So whoever did this knew she would be here?'

'If she's who he was after, Sarge. We don't know it wasn't random.'

'True. Do we have anything to that effect?'

'Not yet. I've got a statement here from a Euan Leech who reckons the bloke pushed aside two other servers to get at her, but in all the confusion . . .'

'And the other statements?'

'Couldn't say. Just saw a figure suddenly appear by the altar and the next thing he was hacking her down and it was all screams. It might become clearer when they have time to get their minds straight.'

'Nothing from the patrols yet? No sign of him?'

'Not a sausage. Too windy to get the chopper up, and too late now anyway. But with the amount of blood he's covered in, somebody will have spotted him . . .'

'OK,' says McAvoy. He turns away from the girl's body and looks into Tremberg's face. She's a very average-looking woman, compared to his Roisin, but she has a face that he reckons an artist would enjoy. Thin, elfin features sit in the centre of a round, broad head, like a gourmet meal in the middle of a large, plain plate. She's tall and athletic, perhaps thirty years old, and dresses in an inoffensive, nondescript fashion that makes her neither a sex object to the male officers nor a threat to the more Machiavellian women. She's funny, energetic and easy to get along with, and although there's a slight tremble to her lips that betrays the adrenalin running through her body at the thought of being involved in the hunt for this killer, she is otherwise masking it with an aplomb McAvoy finds admirable.

'The family,' he says. 'Were they here?'

'No. They usually are. The verger said they were friends of the church, whatever you think that means. But no, she was here on her own. They dropped her off and she was going to make her own way back. That's according to one of the other acolytes. An older lad. Wants to be a priest. Or a vicar. Don't know the difference.'

'But they've been informed, her parents. They know?'

'Yes, sir. Family liaison have been contacted. I thought you'd want it to be our first port of call, soon as you got your faculties together.'

McAvoy gives a thin smile. He's pleased he is standing up. Were he sitting down, his legs would be jiggling up and down with a feeling that a less specific man would call excitement. McAvoy does not think of it as such. It is not even nervousness. It is a feeling he associates with the beginning of things. The potential of the blank page. He wants to know about Daphne Cotton. Wants to know who killed her, and why. Wants to know why he, Aector McAvoy, was spared the blade. Why there were tears in the man's eyes. Wants to show that he can do this. That he's more than the copper who brought down Doug Roper.

He looks at his surroundings, at this majestic, awe-inspiring place.

Will it be the same? he wonders. Can the faithful sit in their pews and praise the Lord and not remember the time a killer leapt from the congregation and slaughtered one of the acolytes as she held her candle and attended the priest? He screws up his eyes. Rubs a palm over his features. When he opens them again he is staring at a great golden eagle, its wings folded in repose. He wonders at its significance. Why it stands here, on a tiled floor, at the top of the nave, facing the gothic stairs that lead to the lectern. Wonders who chose this bird, for this place. Feels his mind beginning to race. To analyse. This murder in a church, less than two weeks before Christmas. He contorts his features, as he remembers that moment, not yet two hours ago, when the song of the choir flooded across the square and warmed the hearts of those who heard it. Thinks of how Daphne Cotton must have felt in those awful moments, when the protective embrace of her faith, of her congregation, was punctured by a blade.

'The car's outside, Sarge,' says Tremberg eagerly, gesturing to the door with her head. 'Ben Nielsen's on his way here to oversee interviews. We've got child specialists en route to interview the choirboys. They probably had the best views, poor sods . . .'

As McAvoy starts walking towards the door, the phone rings in his inside pocket. A tremor of anxiety floods him. He should have called in. Should have logged this straightaway with the top brass. Stamped his brand on the case. But he was lying on a stretcher in the back of an ambulance, letting an inexperienced DC run the show.

'Detective Sergeant McAvoy,' he says, and stops walking, already letting his head drop.

'McAvoy. This is ACC Everett. What's going on down there?' The voice of the Assistant Chief Constable is tense and stern.

'We're on top of things, sir. We're on our way to see the family now . . .'

'We?'

'DC Helen Tremberg and myself, sir . . .'

'Not Pharaoh?'

McAvoy hears himself gulp. It feels as though he's swallowed ice water on an empty stomach. His guts start to cramp.

'Detective Superintendent Pharaoh is on a course this weekend, sir. I'm duty senior officer . . .'

'Pharaoh phoned in, McAvoy. Cancelled the course the second she heard. This is a murder, Sergeant. In the city's biggest, most historic church. The church where William Wilberforce was baptised. A teenage girl, hacked up by a lunatic in front of the congregation? This is all-hands-to-the-pump time, man.'

'So do you want me to fill her in after I've spoken to the girl's family?'

'No.' There is a finality to Everett's voice that makes a mockery of his own belief that this could be his investigation.

'Yes, sir,' he says defeatedly, like a schoolboy told he has not made the team. Beside him, Tremberg turns away, popping two pieces of gum into her mouth and chewing angrily as she realises what is happening.

'No, I was ringing about the other matter, McAvoy. The one I telephoned about earlier,' Everett continues with barely a pause.

'Yes, sir, I got the message but—'

'Well, never mind that now. Other things have come up. But now you're free of having to lead the investigation you can do something else for me. A favour, actually.'

McAvoy's eyes are closed now. He's barely listening.

'If I can, sir.'

'Excellent. I've had a call from a pal of mine at Southampton. It seems an old chap from their neck of the woods has had an accident while making some documentary out at sea. Terrible. Terrible. He's from this area originally. Still got family. A sister, out at Beeford. Normally, a uniform would drive by and break the news, but this lady, well . . .' Everett starts to stumble over his words. He sounds like a shy man making a speech at a wedding. 'Well, look, she's the wife of the Police Authority vice-chair. A very important lady. She and her husband are big supporters of a lot of the initiatives the community policing programme are hoping to see through over the next few years. And you always have such a fine way with people . . .'

There is a rushing sound in McAvoy's ears. His heart is thudding. He can smell his own blood in his nostrils. He opens his eyes to see Tremberg walking away from him, an air of contempt to her gait. She'll find her way into Pharaoh's team.

*Do what you do best, McAvoy. Be the gentle, decent soul. Do Everett's bidding. Keep your head down. Get on with your job. Earn a wage. Love your wife . . .*

'Yes, sir.'

# CHAPTER 3

McAvoy slows down to 20mph. Squints into the darkness as the wheels of the boxy saloon throw up muddy streaks against the spray-jewelled glass. His eyes are eerily keen, but the December gloom enfolds him in a damp fist. Concentrating, he glimpses the eyes of song thrushes roosting in the lower reaches of the hedgerows. Can see the dead, rotting stems of cow-parsley and flaxweed sticking out like broken spears from the muddy, tyre-worn boundary of the road. Fancies that a rabbit is streaking across the wet gravel to his rear; a moment of fur and exclamation mark of tail, glimpsed in the foggy glass.

It is already 6 p.m. The drive back from Beeford, twenty miles up the coast from his North Hull home, will take an hour in these conditions. He will have to pass his own front door on his journey back to the central police station, and the thought makes him irritable, but a recent order from the Chief Constable's office forbade the overnight use of pool cars without prior written approval, and McAvoy assumes there must be a good reason for the directive, and will ensure it is enforced.

A gap suddenly opens up in the hedgerows to McAvoy's right and he gently swings the lumbering vehicle into the space for which he has been searching. In daylight, in spring, he imagines the scene around him will be a watercolour of ploughed brown soil and swaying blonde corn; but in this Stygian dark, this feels a lonely place, and it is with relief that he spies the brooding hulk of the tall, slate-grey farmhouse as the car grinds over firm, reassuring gravel and up the private drive.

A security light blinks on as McAvoy ramps up next to a muddy 4x4 in the oval parking area. An elderly woman is standing at an open back door. Despite the quizzical expression on her face, she has an attractiveness about her that the years have not diluted. She is straight-backed and slim. Subtle adornments – designer reading glasses, Swarovski crystal earrings, the softest trace of blush-coloured lipstick – gild soft, neatly composed features. Her short bobbed hair looks as though it is drawn in pencil. She is wearing a sleeveless body warmer over a burnt-orange sweater, with navy-blue, neatly pressed slacks tucked into thick walking socks. In her hand she holds a wine glass, containing just the faintest puddle of red.

McAvoy opens the car door into a gust of wind that threatens to pull his tie from around his neck.

'This is private property,' the woman says as she reaches down for a pair of wellington boots that stand by the door. 'Are you lost? Were you looking for the Driffield road?'

McAvoy feels colour rising in his cheeks. He slams the car door shut before his notes, loose on the passenger seat, can start playing games with the wind. Quickly, he calls up her name from memory.

'Mrs Stein-Collinson? Barbara Stein-Collinson?'

The woman is halfway out into the driveway, but her name stops her short. A look of concern freezes her face. 'Yes. What's wrong?'

'Mrs Stein-Collinson, my name is Detective Sergeant Aector McAvoy. Might we go inside? I'm afraid I have—'

She shakes her head, but her denial is not directed at the policeman. It is as though she is aiming the gesture at a vision. A memory. Her face softens, and she closes her eyes.

'Fred,' she says, and her next words do not sound like a question. 'The silly sod's dead.'

McAvoy tries to catch her eye, to hold her gaze in the earnest, comforting way he does so well, but she is not paying him any attention. He turns away, oddly embarrassed, though it is more at the cack-handed way he has handled this, the only mission for which his superiors feel he is suited. He watches the snow fall inconsequentially onto the gravel. Sniffs politely as the cold makes his nose run.

'Found him, have they?' she asks at last.

'Perhaps we could—'

Her sudden glare cuts him dead. She stands there, snarling, her head shaking, her glasses slipping down her nose as her countenance turns hard and cold. She spits out her words, as if taking bites out of the air.

'Forty years too bloody late.'

'Would you mind taking your boots off? We have a cream carpet in the kitchen.'

McAvoy bends down and starts unfastening the soggy, triple-knotted laces. Lets his eyes sweep the little cloakroom from his vantage point at knee height. No wellingtons. No dog baskets. No rubbish bags or newspapers waiting for the next bonfire or tip-trip. *Incomers*, he thinks instinctively.

'So,' she says, standing above him like a monarch preparing to bestow a knighthood. 'Where did they find him?'

McAvoy looks up, but can't make eye contact without straining his neck, and can't unpick his laces without looking at them. 'If you'll just give me a moment, Mrs Stein-Collinson . . .'

She responds with an irritated sigh. He imagines her face becoming stern. Tries to decide if it will do more harm to give her the details from this most inappropriate of positions, or to make the poor lady wait until he's removed his boots.

'He was about seventy miles off the coast of Iceland,' McAvoy says, trying to inject as much empathy and compassion into his voice as he can. 'Still in the lifeboat. A cargo ship saw the vessel and the search teams went straight to the scene.'

With a tug, he pulls off one boot, coating his thumb and forefinger in thick mud. He surreptitiously wipes his hand on the seat of his trousers as he begins work on the other.

'Exposure, I assume,' she says thoughtfully. 'He won't have taken any pills. Won't have wanted to numb himself to it, our Fred. Will have wanted to feel what they did. I never guessed this was what he was planning. I mean, who would? Not when he's laughing and telling stories and buying everybody a drink . . .'

McAvoy wrestles the other boot free and stands up quickly. She's already halfway through the open door, and it's with relief that he leaves the cloakroom and steps into the large, open kitchen. He's surprised by what he finds. The kitchen is as unruly as a student bedsit. There are dirty dishes stacked high around the deep porcelain sink which sits beneath a large, curtainless window. Splashes of grease and what looks like pasta sauce are welded to the rings of the double-oven at the far end. Newspapers and assorted household bills are scattered across the rectangular oak table that fills the centre of the room, and laundry sits in crumpled islands all over the precious carpet, which has not been cream in many a year. His policeman's eye takes in the dribbles of wine that sit at the bottom of the dirty glasses on the draining board. Even the pint glasses, embossed with pub logos, seem to have been used for the slugging of claret.

'That's him,' she says, nodding at the wall behind McAvoy. He turns and is greeted with a stadium of faces; a gallery of higgledy-piggledy photographs stuck or Sellotaped to a dozen cork boards. The photos are from each of the last five decades. Black and white and colour.

'There,' she says again. 'Next to our Alice. Peter's grand-niece, if that's a word. There he is. Looking like the cat that got the cream.'

McAvoy focuses on the image that she is pointing to. A good-looking man with luscious black hair, swept back in a rocker's quiff, holding a pint of beer and grinning at the camera. The fashion of the man in the foreground suggests it was taken in the mid-eighties. He'd have been thirty-something. McAvoy's age. In his prime.

'Handsome man,' he says.

'He knew it, too,' she says, and her face softens. She reaches out and strokes the photo with a pale, bejewelled hand. 'Poor Fred,' she says, and then turns to look at McAvoy, as if seeing him for the first time. 'I'm pleased you came. It wouldn't have been nice to hear it in a phone call. Not with Peter away.'

'Peter?'

'My husband. He does a lot of work with the police, actually. You might know him. He's on the authority. Was a councillor for many a year until it got a bit much for him. He's not as young as he was.'

The mention of the Police Authority comes as a slap to the jaw. McAvoy takes a breath. Tries to do what he came for. 'Yes, I'm aware of your husband and all the hard work and dedication he put in to campaign for the police service. As soon as we heard the sad news about Mr Stein, Assistant Chief Constable Everett asked me to come and speak to you personally. We're in a position to be able to offer you the services of a highly qualified family liaison officer and—'

She stops him with a smile that makes her look suddenly pretty. Somehow vital and colourful. 'There's no need for that now.' She frowns. 'I'm sorry, what was your name?'

'Detective Sergeant McAvoy.'

'No, your real name.'

McAvoy screws up his face. 'Aector,' he says. 'Hector, to the English. Not that there's much difference in how you say it. It's the spelling that matters.'

'Heads will be rolling for this, won't they?' she asks suddenly, as if remembering why this man is standing, in stockinged feet, in her kitchen. 'I mean, we didn't want him to go, but he said they would take care of him. He must have been planning it from the moment they got in touch with him. I mean, we knew the tragedy had affected him, deep down, but it still came as a surprise. I didn't expect them to find him, but . . .'

McAvoy frowns and, without thinking about it, pulls one of the chairs from under the table and sits down. He is suddenly intrigued by Mrs Stein-Collinson. By her brother, the dead rocker. By the lady from the TV and the Norwegian tanker that plucked the inflatable from the grey sea.

'I'm sorry, Mrs Stein-Collinson, but I'm only familiar with the vaguest of details about this case. Would you perhaps be able to clarify the nature of the tragedy that your brother was party to . . .'

Mrs Stein-Collinson lets out a sigh, refills her glass and comes across to the table, where she removes a pile of laundry from a chair and sits down opposite McAvoy.

'If you're not from around here, you won't have heard of the *Yarborough*,' she says softly. 'It was the fourth trawler. The one that went down last. Three others went down in 1968. So many lives. So many good lads. The papers were full of it. Catching on to what we already knew. It was bleeding dangerous work.'

She picks a pen from a pile of paperwork and holds it like a cigarette. Her gaze settles on the middle distance, and McAvoy suddenly sees the East Hull girl in this middle-class lady of a certain age. Sees a youngster raised in a fishing family, brought up amid the smog of smokehouses and the stink of unwashed overalls. Barbara Stein. Babs to her mates. Married well and got herself a pad in the country. Never really settled. Never felt comfortable. Had to stay close enough to Hull to be able to phone her mam.

'Please,' he says softly, and there is suddenly no affectation or falsehood in his voice. He will tell himself later that it is presumptuous, but in this moment, he feels he knows her. 'Carry on.'

'By the time the *Yarborough* went down the papers had had a bellyful of it. We all had. It didn't make the front page. Not until later. Eighteen men and boys, pulled down by ice and wind and tides seventy miles off Iceland.' She shakes her head. Takes a drink. 'But our Fred was the one who survived. Worst storm in a century and Fred walked out of it. Managed to get himself into a lifeboat and woke up in the back of beyond. Three days before we heard from him. So I suppose that's why I'm not crying now, you see? I got him back. Sarah, his wife. She got him back. Papers tried their damnedest to get him to talk about it. He wouldn't have a bit of it. Didn't want to answer any questions. He's only a couple of years older than me and we were always close, though we knocked lumps out of each other as bairns. It was me that took the phone call to say he was alive. The British consul in Iceland hadn't been able to get Sarah so he called our house. I thought it were a joke at first. Then Fred came on the line. Said hello, clear as day, like he was just in the next room.' Her face lights up as she speaks, as if she is reliving that moment. McAvoy notices her eyes dart to the telephone on the wall by the cooker.

'I can't even imagine it,' he says. He is not serving her an idle platitude. He truly cannot imagine how it would feel to lose one that he loved, and then to have them restored.

'So, we got him back. The hubbub died down soon after. Sarah asked him to give up the sea and he agreed. I don't think he took much persuading. Took a job at the docks. Worked there for nigh-on thirty years. Retired with a bad chest. Every once in a while he'd get a phone call from a writer or a journalist asking him for his story, but he'd always say no. Then when Sarah died, I think he got a glimpse of his own mortality. They only had one daughter, and she upped and left when she was a teenager. He suddenly had itchy feet. I honestly think if somebody had been willing to take him on he'd have gone back to trawling, though there's none of that these days.'

She begins to stand, but a pain in her knee makes her reconsider. McAvoy, without being asked, returns to the work-surface and grabs the wine bottle. He refills her glass, and she says thank you without a word passing between them.

'Anyway, not so long back he rings me up, telling me this TV company's been in touch with him. That they're doing a documentary on the Black Winter. That he's going out with them on this cargo ship to lay a wreath and say goodbye to his old mates. Of course it was completely out of the blue. I'd barely thought about all that in years, and I think to him it had just become a story. He said once he felt like it had happened to somebody else. But I suppose he must have kept it all inside. For him to go and do this.' Her bottom lip trembles and she pulls a tissue from her sleeve.

'Perhaps they were paying him for his story?'

'Oh, I'd say that's guaranteed,' she says, suddenly smiling and giving the photo-wall a quick glance. 'He always knew how to make money, our Fred. Knew how to spend it too, mind. That's trawling for you, though. A month away grafting then three days home. A wodge in your pocket and a few hours to spend it. The three-day millionaires, they called them.'

'So that was the last you heard?'

'From him, yes. We got a phone call from the woman at the TV company three days ago. We must have been listed as his emergency contacts. Said he'd disappeared. That one of the lifeboats was missing and that Fred had got himself a bit upset talking about it all. That they were looking for him. That she'd keep us informed. That was the end of it. All seems bloody silly to me. After all those years. To end up dead in the sea, just like his mates.' She stops and looks at him, her blue eyes suddenly intense and probing. 'It sounds awful, Hector, but why didn't he just take pills? Why do all this song and dance? Do you think he felt guilty? Wanted to go like his mates from 'sixty-eight? That's what the telly lady seemed to be hinting at, but it doesn't seem like the sort of thing he'd do. He'd do it quiet. No fuss. He liked to tell a story and spin a yarn and charm a lady, but he wouldn't even talk to the papers when all this happened, so why would he want a dramatic bloody exit now?'

'Perhaps that's why he agreed to be filmed? Because they would be passing the area where the trawler went down?'

She breathes out, and the sigh seems to come from deep within her. It is as though she is deflating. 'Perhaps,' she says, and drains her drink.

'I'm terribly sorry, Mrs Stein-Collinson.'

She nods. Smiles. 'Barbara.'

He extends a hand, which she takes with a cold, soft palm.

'So what happens next?' she asks. 'Like I said, I don't think he's been taken care of particularly well. He's an old man, and they let him wander off and do this! I've got plenty of questions . . .'

McAvoy finds himself nodding. He has questions of his own. There is something scratching weakly at the inside of his skull. He wants to know more. Wants it to make sense. Wants to be able to tell this nice lady why her brother died, forty years after he should have done, in the exact way that nearly claimed him as a young man.

He knows he shouldn't promise that he will stay in touch. That he will find out what happened. Knows he shouldn't give her his home phone number and tell her to call if she has any more information. Any questions. Just to talk.

But he does.

37

# CHAPTER 4

McAvoy pulls his phone out of his inside pocket and replays the last voicemail. Even distorted as it is by the tinny loud-speaker, the anger in the woman's voice is unmistakable.

'McAvoy. Me again. How many times is this? I've got better things to do with my time than chase after you. We need you here. Get a fucking move on.'

The voice is Trish Pharaoh's. The most recent message had been left only forty-five minutes after the first, but there had been six in between, including a mumbled, whispered heads-up from Ben Nielsen, suggesting that whatever McAvoy was doing, he should drop it immediately and head for Queen's Gardens or risk losing important body parts.

There are a dozen reporters milling around the front of the station, but they pay him little heed and he makes it through the large double doors and into the lobby of the squat glass-and-brick building without being questioned.

'Incident room?' he asks, panting.

'Pharaoh's?' asks the portly, pale-skinned desk sergeant. He is sitting on a swivel chair with a mug of coffee and a hard-back book. Muscly and middle-aged, he carries the look of somebody who has worked the night shift for a long time, and isn't going to let anything come between him and his routine. He is wearing a short-sleeved shirt which seems too tight at the collar, giving his large, round head a curiously disembodied look.

'Indeed.'

'Still setting up. Try Roper's old office. Know the way?'

McAvoy locks eyes with the desk sergeant. Tries to work out whether there is an accusation in the way the man says it. Feels his blush begin.

'I'm sure I can find it,' he says, trying a smile.

'I'm sure you fucking can,' says the uniformed officer, and runs his tongue over his lips with the faintest of sneers.

McAvoy turns away. He has grown used to this. Grown used to contempt and venom, to distrust and outright loathing, among the cadre of officers who rode Doug Roper's coat-tails.

Knows that if it weren't for his size half of his colleagues would spit in his face.

He walks as quickly as dignity will allow until he is out of sight, then breaks into a semi-run. He takes the steps three at a time. Down another corridor. Pictures and posters and warnings and appeals whizzing past in a blur from notice-boards and unhealthy magnolia walls.

Voices. Shouts. Clatters. Bangs. Through double mahogany doors and into the lion's den.

He is raising his hand to knock on the door when it suddenly swings inwards. Trish Pharaoh storms angrily out, deep in rushed conversation.

'. . . high time they realised that, Ben.'

She's a handsome woman in her early forties, and looks more like a cleaner than a senior detective. Barely regulation height, she's plump, with long black hair that is expertly styled about once every six months, and left to grow wild the rest of the time. She has four children, and treats her officers with the same mix of tenderness, pride and aggressive disappointment as she does her offspring. Tactile and flirty, she scares the hell out of the younger male officers, to whom she exudes a certain best-mate's-mum kind of sexiness. She wears a wedding ring, though the photos on her desk do not include a man's picture.

She stops suddenly when she notices McAvoy, and DC Nielsen clatters into her back. She spins round and glares at him before turning to snarl at McAvoy.

'The wanderer returns,' she says.

'Ma'am, I was in a radio black spot on a goodwill assignment from ACC Everett and—'

'Shush.'

She places her finger to her own lips, and then holds her palms out in front of her, her eyes closed, as if counting to ten. The three of them stand in silence in the corridor for a moment. DC Nielsen and Sergeant McAvoy, naughty, clumsy, absentee schoolboys who've gravely disappointed a favourite teacher.

Eventually, she sighs. 'Anyway, you're here now. I'm sure you had your reasons. Ben will bring you up to speed and you can start working the database. It's a bit late to get much done on the phones, but we need the congregation loading into that matrix you came up with. I'm right in thinking that it was for this kind of case, yes? Lots of witnesses. Disparate backgrounds? Links between—'

'Yes, yes,' says McAvoy, suddenly enthusiastic. 'It's like a Venn diagram. We find out everything about a certain group of people, then load that into the system and see where there are parallels, or, in particular, overlaps, and—'

'Fascinating,' she says with a bright smile. 'Like I said, Ben can bring you up to speed and get your statement.'

'Ma'am?'

'You were a witness, McAvoy. You saw who did this. They hit you in the bloody face with the murder weapon. Quite what you and ACC Everett were thinking . . .'

'I was following orders, ma'am.'

'Well, follow mine. There'll be a briefing at eight,' she says, looking at her watch, then clip-clops down the corridor in heeled biker boots.

DC Nielsen raises an eyebrow at McAvoy. They both look like teenagers who've just got away with something, and there is an impish smile on both their faces as the junior officer steps back into the office and McAvoy follows him into the brightly lit room.

DCs Helen Tremberg and Sophie Kirkland are sitting side by side at the same desk, staring an open laptop computer. Sophie is eating a slice of pizza and using it to gesture at something on the screen. It is the only computer in the room. The rest of the office is empty, save for some spilled and battered old files, and a firing squad of assorted bin-bags, which look like they've been sitting there by the wall for months.

'Given us the presidential suite,' says Ben, leading McAvoy to a semi-circle of plastic chairs by the window.

'Looks like it. Why here? Why not back at Priory?'

'Convenience, they said. Order came down from on high. I think they were imagining headlines.'

'Like what?'

'Usual shit. Us being eight miles from the scene, when there's a station three hundred yards from where it happened.'

'But there's facilities at Priory,' says McAvoy, confused. 'This can't have been Pharaoh's call.'

'No, she thought it was bloody stupid as well. But she's had to hit the ground running. By the time she got up to speed, the ACC had put out a press release saying this would be co-ordinated from our city-centre local policing team.'

'So we're running uphill?' he asks.

'In fucking treacle, Sarge.'

He sighs. Plonks himself down in the hard-backed chair. He looks at his watch.

'What do we know?'

'Right,' says Nielsen, jabbing a finger on the page. 'Daphne Cotton. Fifteen. Residing with Tamara and Paul Cotton at Fergus Grove, Hessle. Nice little place, Sarge. Off a main road. Terraced. Three-bedroomed. Big front garden and a back yard. You know the ones? Back to front houses near the cemetery?'

McAvoy nods. He and Roisin had been to view a house in the area when she was pregnant with Fin. Had decided against it. Too little parking and the kitchen was too small. Nice neighbourhood, though.

'Brothers? Sisters?'

'The family liaison is trying to get all that, but I don't think so. Her parents are an older couple. White, obviously.'

McAvoy screws up his face. 'What?'

'She's adopted, Sarge,' says Nielsen quickly.

'She could have been adopted by black people, Constable,' he says softly.

Nielsen looks to the ceiling, as if considering this for the first time. 'Yes,' he concedes. 'She could have been.'

They sit in silence for a moment, both brooding over the point. Behind them, they can hear the two female officers. Helen Tremberg is reading out names from a list of members of the congregation and Sophie Kirkland is dividing them up between CID officers.

'She wasn't, though,' says Nielsen.

'No,' says McAvoy, and tells himself to just let some things go. To shut his mouth until he has a point worth making.

Nielsen leaves another respectful pause. Then, after a bright smile, ploughs on. 'Anyway, as you can imagine, the parents are broken up. They weren't there, you see. Normally, the mum goes to the service with Daphne, but she was planning some big Christmas shindig and was busy preparing the food. Dad was at work.'

'On a Saturday? What does he do?'

'They run a haulage firm, of sorts.' He suddenly stops and shouts over at Helen Tremberg. 'What is it the dad does, Hell's Bells?'

Helen pushes herself back from the desk and walks over to where the two men are sitting. She gives McAvoy a smile. 'Joining us, eh?'

McAvoy tries not to grin. He feels a sudden sensation of warmth towards her. Towards Ben, also. He doesn't like to admit it, but he is feeling excited. Alive.

'Logistics, is it?' asks McAvoy, trying to keep his voice even.

'According to their website, they take a lot of charity stuff to inaccessible locations. They have the contract for a lot of the different aid agencies. You know when you give your old jumpers and whatnot to the women with the bin-bags? Well, this is one of the companies that gets it to places where it's needed. Some freight, sometimes container ships, sometimes air.'

'Right,' says McAvoy, making a note in his own pad. 'Carry on.'

'Well, long and the short of it is that this couple have a child of their own who died a few years ago. Leukaemia. Anyway, they adopted Daphne through an international agency when she was ten. They had a year of paperwork but it's all above board. She's from Sierra Leone, by birth. Lost her family in the genocide. Tragic stuff.'

McAvoy nods. He remembers little about the politics of the disagreement. Can only summon up hazy television footage of atrocities and brutality. Innocents, sprayed with bullets and chopped down with blades.

'Is the machete significant?' asks McAvoy. 'That's the weapon of choice out there, isn't it?'

'The boss asked the same thing,' says Nielsen. 'We're looking into it.'

'And are they are a church-going family? How did she become a server?'

'Apparently she was that way inclined when she arrived. Her family were very religious. She had seen some horrors over there but it hadn't put her off. Her mum, her new mum, took her to Holy Trinity just for a day out when she first arrived, and she thought it was the most beautiful thing she had ever seen. It became a big part of her life. Her mum says she'd never been so proud as the day she became an acolyte.'

McAvoy tries to get a mental picture of Daphne Cotton. Of a young girl, plucked from horror, decked out in a white robe and allowed to hold the candle during the honouring of her God.

'Have we got a picture?' he asks softly.

Helen jogs back to her desk and returns almost instantly with a colour photocopy of a family snap. It shows a smiling Daphne, sandwiched between her two short, plump, greying adoptive parents. The background shows Bridlington sea front. The skies are eerily and unusually blue. The image seems almost too glossy and perfect. McAvoy wonders who took the snap. Which poor passer-by captured the image that would come to define this tragic girl. McAvoy takes his own mental picture. Memorises the snap. Makes this smiling, happy girl his vision of Daphne Cotton. Superimposes it onto the bloodied, broken corpse. Makes her human. Makes her death the tragedy it needs to be.

'So, she was a regular at church, yes?'

'Three nights a week and twice on Sundays.'

'Big commitment.'

'Huge, but she was a clever girl. Never let it get in the way of her homework. She was a straight-A student, according to her mum. We haven't spoken to her teachers yet.'

'Which school?'

'Hessle High. Walking distance from home. She's due to break up on Tuesday for the Christmas holidays.'

'We need to speak to her friends. Her teachers. Everybody who knew her.'

'That's what Sophie and me are dividing up, Sarge,' says Tremberg, pulling an appeasing face. It is as if she is trying to tell an ageing father not to worry – that it's been taken care of.

'Right, right,' says McAvoy, trying to slow himself down. To restore order in his mind.

'Shall we get your statement down, now, Sarge? Best get it out of the way. Tomorrow will be a nightmare.'

McAvoy nods. He knows that in reality, the only thing he is bringing to this investigation is a witness statement and a glorified filing system. But he's got a foot in the door. A chance to do some good. To catch a killer. He lets his mind drift back to this afternoon. To the chaos and bloodshed in the square. To that moment when the masked man appeared from the doorway of the church, and looked into his eyes.

'Is there anything distinctive, Sarge?' asks Nielsen, although there is no real hope in his voice. 'Anything you'd recognise again?'

McAvoy closes his eyes. Lets the masked face swim in his vision. Blocks out the cold, snow-filled air and the screams of the passers-by. Lets his memory focus in on one moment. One picture. One scene.

'Yes,' he says, with the sudden sense that the memory is important. 'There were tears in his eyes.'

He stares into the blue irises of the mental image. Fancies he can see his own reflection on the wet lenses. His voice, when it emerges from his dry mouth, is but a breath.

'Why were you crying? Who were you weeping for?'

# CHAPTER 5

It sits to the north of the city, the east of everything else – three left turns and a right from the edge of the new estate; thrown up for first-time buyers by builders following plans that could have been designed by a child with a page of graph paper and a box of Monopoly houses.

Three bedrooms. Chessboard tiles. A back yard, with a nine-slab patio propped up on reclaimed railway sleepers. All decorated to the drab, lifeless taste of a landlord who made the purchase through an agent, and has yet to visit.

*Home*, thinks McAvoy, bones weary, drowsily parking the people-carrier on the kerb and watching his wife, framed like a film star through the square front window, swaying with his son in her arms, and waving to Daddy.

It's late. Too late for Fin to still be up. He must have taken his nap around tea-time. He'll be awake all night, eager to bounce on Mummy and Daddy's bed, to try on Daddy's shoes and stomp around on the lino in the kitchen, squashing imaginary monsters.

She's done this for him. Settled the lad for a nap so that he'll be awake and fresh and ready to make Daddy feel better when he finally gets home from the station, thoughts made heavy and dull by the relentlessness of the assault with which they have battered his skull.

Roisin opens the door for him and McAvoy doesn't know who to kiss first. He opens his arms and takes them both in. Feels the hard pressure of Fin's head on one cheek. Roisin's lips, soft and warm and perfect, on the other. Holds them both. Feels her hand stroke his back. Takes their warmth inside himself. Senses her breathing him in, in return.

'I'm sorry,' he says, and whether it's addressed to her or the boy or the universe in general, he would not be able to say.

Eventually he pulls away. Roisin takes a step backwards to allow him into the little lobby at the foot of the stairs. As he pushes the door closed behind him, he turns and knocks the same picture from the wall that he has dislodged almost nightly since they moved into this, their first proper home, two years ago. They giggle, sharing the joke, as he stoops to pick it up, and awkwardly hangs it back on the hook. It's a pencil sketch of a hillside, done in a shaky hand. It meant a lot to McAvoy once, back when images of his childhood had been the emblem of his happy times. It doesn't matter so much now. Not since Fin. Not since her.

She's beautiful, of course. Slim and dark-haired, her skin an almost sand-blown tan that betrays her heritage. Mucky, his dad had said when he first saw her, but he hadn't meant it in a bad way.

She's wearing a tracksuit that hugs her figure and her hair tumbles to her shoulders. She's only wearing a small pair of hoops in her ears today. She used to have row upon row, climbing up both ears, but Fin developed a liking for pulling at them and so she has limited her adornment in recent months. It is the same with the gold that dazzles at her throat. She wears two chains. One bears her name in copperplate: a gift from her father when she turned sixteen. The other is a simple pearl, a captured raindrop, that McAvoy presented her with on their wedding night as an extra present, in case his heart hadn't been enough.

Without being asked, she hands Fin to his father. The child beams, opens his mouth like a capital O and then begins aping McAvoy's facial expressions. They frown, grin, pretend to cry, aim monster-like bites at one another, until they are laughing and Fin is wriggling with excitement. McAvoy puts him down and the child runs off with his bow-legged cowboy gait, adorable in his blue jeans, white shirt and tiny waistcoat, chattering to himself in the made-up language that McAvoy wishes he better understood.

'You waited,' he says to his wife as he looks around the living room. Roisin had been planning to put up the Christmas decorations today. They have a plastic tree and a box of baubles, half a dozen cards to stretch on a wire over the fake-coal fireplace, but they remain in the cardboard container by the kitchen door.

'It wouldn't have been any fun without you,' she says. 'We'll do it another day. As a family.'

McAvoy takes off his coat and throws it over the back of an armchair. Roisin comes forward for another hug, the better to feel his body without the impediment of his bulky waterproof. The top of her head comes up to his chin, and he leans forward to kiss it. Her hair smells of baking. Something sweet and festive. Mince pies, perhaps.

'I'm sorry I'm later than I said,' he begins, but she shushes him and pulls his mouth to hers. He tastes cherries and cinnamon in her kisses, and they stand, framed in the window, mouth on mouth, until Fin runs back into the living room and begins whacking his father on the leg with a wooden cow.

'Grandpa sent it for me,' says Fin, holding up the toy as his father peers down. 'Cow. Cow.'

McAvoy takes it from his son's grip. Examines it. He recognises the workmanship. Can picture his father, wood shavings on his glasses, knife and rock-hammer held by white hands sheathed in fingerless gloves, sitting at the table, mouth ajar, concentrating on every minute detail, breathing life into wooden toys.

'Was there a letter?'

'Just the usual,' says Roisin, not looking up. 'Hopes he's getting big and strong. Eating his vegetables. Being a good boy. Hopes to meet him one day soon.'

McAvoy's father addresses all of his correspondence to the boy. He has not spoken to his only son since a falling out around the time Roisin fell pregnant, and McAvoy knows him to be stubborn enough to go to his grave without ever making amends. Were he to think unkindly of his father, he would wonder who the daft old sod thought was going to read the letters to his four-year-old grandson, but he has trained himself to blink such traitorous thoughts away.

McAvoy feels the toy's smooth edges. Tries to soak up some of the wisdom and experience of the old man through the things he holds in his hand, but no answers come. He hands it back to his son, who runs away again. McAvoy watches him go, then turns to Roisin, his eyes full of guilt.

'You went towards the screams, Aector. You did what you would always do.'

'But what does it say about me? That I would seek out a stranger rather than protect my son?'

'It says you're a good man.'

He stares around his living room. It's all he wants. His wife in his arms, his child playing at his feet. He breathes heavily and slowly, savouring every mouthful of these moments. And then he catches the scent. The tang. Faint. Almost imperceptible among the spices and soap of his family, his home. It's like a moth fluttering at the very edge of vision. That whiff. Of blood. For an instant he imagines Daphne Cotton. Tries to get an image of what her father will be enduring. Lets his heart reach out. To feel a connection and offer up warmth.

He raises his arm and pulls Roisin back down into an embrace.

Hates himself for the warmth that spreads through him: for being damnably happy, as an innocent girl lies dead on a slab.

# CHAPTER 6

8.04 a.m. Roper's old room at Queen's Gardens.

*A commotion of cops.*

Buttocks perched on desks; feet on swivel chairs, backs lounging against bare walls. A collection of untucked shirts and two-for-one supermarket ties. Nobody's smoking, but the room smells of nicotine and beer.

McAvoy, in the middle, sitting properly on a hard-backed seat, notebook on his lap, tie tight at a throat scrubbed pink and raw by vigorous, punishing hands.

Trying to keep his feet still on the threadbare carpet. Listening to a dozen conversations at once and finding none he would know how to join.

Six hours' sleep and a good breakfast that wouldn't go down.

It's still sitting there; a weight in his chest; every breath a wheeze that tastes of scrambled egg and granary bread. There's a flask of hot water and peppermint leaves in the bag at his feet, but he's afraid to unscrew it in this cramped, busy room, for fear of releasing the aroma. He could not stomach the comments. Could not stand to be remarkable. Not here. Not now.

DAVID MARK

He glances at his watch. *Late*, he thinks.

'Right, boys and girls,' says Pharaoh, clapping her hands as she enters the room. 'I've been up since five, I've had no fucking breakfast and in a minute I've got a press conference with a bunch of wankers who want to know how we've allowed a teenage girl to be killed at Christmas. I would like to be able to tell them that the person who did it is a nutter and that we've caught him, but I can't. We haven't caught him, so that's not going to happen. Nor do we know that he's a nutter.'

'Well, I know I wouldn't ask him to babysit, ma'am.' This from Ben Nielsen, to laughs and nods.

'Nor would I, Ben, but I'd pick him before you. Remember, I've got a teenage daughter.'

Laughs and whoops. A polystyrene cup chucked at a grinning Ben Nielsen.

'What I mean,' continues Pharaoh, pushing her hair out of her eyes, 'is that we don't know this was random. We don't know if it's somebody who hates the church, somebody with a grudge against the clergy. We don't know if Daphne Cotton was the intended victim. Why did he wear a balaclava? Why disguise himself if he were just a random attacker? And the weapon. What's the significance of the machete?'

'Are we thinking race hate?' This from Helen Tremberg, to an accompanying chorus of moans.

'We're thinking everything, my love. We haven't flagged it as race hate, but the very fact that it was a black girl means that it has to be considered.'

'Fucking hell.'

Colin Ray speaks for all of them. They know what this means. Race crimes are a recipe for headlines and headaches. It's kid gloves and placards all the way; the clamour for a resolution comes not just from the public and the pressure groups, but from the top brass, still sensitive about a decade of bad publicity spawned when a black prisoner died in the custody suite. The video footage aired at the subsequent investigation – and replayed almost constantly across the news channels – showed four officers standing around chatting while the lad took his last, rasping breaths on the cold, tiled floor at Queen's Gardens nick.

'So, this is goldfish-bowl time,' concludes Pharaoh. 'We need this solved quickly, but we need to remember we're being watched. We're talking national news. People don't like having their Christmases ruined by murder, and they need us to make them feel safe again. This happened about nineteen hours ago, and that gives this murderous fucker a good head start. The public appeal will be on the news by nine, which means a lot of you will have the fun and games of answering the phones. The calls will be coming through to this room. And yes, the tech monkeys will be wiring them up within the next half hour. There'll be no shortage of nutters, people, but every piece of information is important. Every name needs to be checked.'

She stops her flow momentarily, and her eyes seek out McAvoy. She gives him a nod.

'Now I know you're all technical wizards, but on the off-chance that you're not, McAvoy here is going to show you how his brand-spanking-new database works.'

There are groans. A chorus of swear words.

'Now now, children,' she smiles. 'I've been on inquiries where the floor has caved in under the weight of paperwork, so if McAvoy's system helps us keep a better track of what we're doing, then it's something we need to be using. Personally, I feel like I've got something of a head start, given that I once got to level three on Sonic the Hedgehog, but the rest of you might need a catch-up course.'

McAvoy joins in the laughter. Looks up and gets a grin and the tiniest of winks from Pharaoh.

'Don't forget,' she adds, 'McAvoy has seen this bloke. He could have been a victim himself, if he hadn't used his forehead to block the blow.'

There are more laughs, but they feel somehow more warm and inclusive, and McAvoy is almost tempted to take a bow and add a witticism of his own. Pharaoh interrupts before he can.

'Right, you should all know what you're doing for the next couple of hours. We need witness statements. We need CCTV footage of every inch of that square. Where did he go when he left the church? And most important, we need to know everything there is about Daphne Cotton. We need to unpick her life. We'll have the PME results by lunchtime, toxicology by tonight. Just bring your A-game, people. None of us want to live in a city where you can chop up a girl in church and get away with it. It's Christmas, after all.'

She gives the troops a grin. And then she's barging back out of the room, a dervish of perfume and jangling jewellery, her soft palms touching shoulders and forearms, investing faith and belief in her team.

They sit in silence for a moment, each officer lost in his or her own thoughts.

Eventually, DCI Colin Ray turns and opens the blinds. It's night-time black beyond the glass, and the window reflects a shambolic semi-circle of squatting, lounging, disordered men and women; scratching heads and blowing through steepled palms.

The officers get a glimpse of themselves; a sharp, unexpected vision of who and what they are. Each sees the truth of themselves: their imperfections, their one-dimensional, cold, crumpled, actuality.

Of all the men and women staring into their own faces, only Aector McAvoy feels no compulsion to look away.

They have been answering phones for six hours now. Beyond the dusty, grime-encrusted windows, the sky has almost completed its subtle transition from deep grey to soft black. Above, the clouds continue to hang low and fat, but the worst of the snow is another few days away. They might get a white Christmas this year, though McAvoy, who experienced nothing else in his youth, is only excited by the prospect because he knows it will make his wife and child smile.

He and Helen Tremberg are the only two actual police officers in the room. A community support officer is sitting at one of the spare desks and Gemma Tang, the pretty Chinese press officer, is leaning over the large table by the window, crossing out large sections of a press release. She's model-beautiful, with a backside that Ben Nielsen has frequently imagined bouncing coins off. McAvoy is giving himself eye-strain trying not to look.

In ones and twos, the officers have drifted away from the major incident room. Trish Pharaoh and Ben Nielsen are at the morgue, witnessing the post-mortem exam. The two most junior detectives are collecting witness statements from those members of the congregation too shaken up to speak coherently yesterday. Sophie Kirkland took a phone call just before lunch from a pub landlady whose security cameras had captured a fleeting image of a man in black roughly five minutes after the attack took place. She's taken two uniformed officers with her to search the local area for clues.

Colin Ray and Shaz Archer have gone to speak to an informant. A telephone call to his bedsit home has already produced one lead. One of the punters at the Kingston Hotel has been letting his mouth run away with him. According to the snout, the bloke has always had strong opinions about foreigners and incomers, but recently lost his wife to the attentions of an Iranian pizza chef, and has been talking more and more about making somebody pay. It would be dismissed as idle gossip, were it not for the fact that a quick check on the Police National Computer showed that he'd been nicked twice for possessing illegal weaponry, and once for wounding. Even though Colin Ray is supposed to be managing the office, he's decided that he's best placed to follow this particular line of inquiry, and made himself scarce. Inspector Archer, never far behind, has tagged along, leaving only McAvoy and Helen Tremberg to answer the phones.

McAvoy looks back through his notes. He's written pages of names, numbers, details and theories on his lined pad. The script is unintelligible to anybody but him. He's the only officer who knows Teeline shorthand. He learned it in his spare time while in training, after being impressed by the speed at which a journalist had taken down the quotes of the senior officer he'd been shadowing that day. It has proven a useful six months of his time, even if it has left him open to the occasional moment of open-mouthed scorn from colleagues who wonder if he's having a mental breakdown and filling his notebook with hieroglyphics.

The phone calls so far have been pretty weak. Despite the television appeal this morning, they're suffering from Sunday syndrome. People are enjoying days out with their families or relaxing down the pub, and the idea of ringing a police station with information about a murder feels much more like a nine-to-five, Monday-to-Friday kind of activity, so the flurry of calls that the team had expected has not materialised. It's barely proving worth the overtime.

If nothing else, at least the incident room is taking shape; this is largely thanks to McAvoy and the relative inactivity the day has delivered. He's brought a whiteboard in from another office and begun sketching a brief outline of the previous day's sequence of events. His own description of the suspect has been written in the centre of the board in red marker pen. *Medium build. Medium height. Dark clothes. Balaclava. Wet, blue eyes.* It's not much to go on, and they all know it. And although there is nothing more McAvoy could have done, he feels achingly guilty that he did not glimpse more of his attacker.

A map of the city has been stapled to another wall. On it, drawing pins of different colours denote the definite and possible sightings of the suspect as he made his escape from Trinity Square. It is a composite of witness statements, CCTV footage, and guesswork. With it, they can surmise that the suspect travelled east through the city and past the river, before disappearing from the map somewhere near Drypool Bridge. A team of uniformed officers have walked the route, but found nothing save a footprint in the snow that matched the location given by one of the more believable witnesses. There was no sign of the murder weapon. The uniforms' best guess was that he'd ditched it in the Hull. When Pharaoh had heard that snippet of information she had slammed her hands down so hard that one of her bangles had snapped.

The phone on his desk begins to ring. He picks up the beige, Bakelite receiver.

'CID. Major Incident Room.'

A woman's voice is at the other end of the line. 'I'd like to speak to somebody about Daphne. About Daphne Cotton,' she says. And then, unnecessarily, even more shakily, adds: 'The girl who was killed.'

'You can talk to me. My name is Detective Sergeant Aector McAvoy—'

'That's fine,' she says, cutting him off. With the tremble in her voice it's hard to place her, but McAvoy would class the speaker as around his own age.

'Do you have information . . . ?'

She takes a breath, and McAvoy can tell she has been rehearsing this. She wants to get it out in one go. He lets her speak.

'I'm a supply teacher. A year or so ago I did some shifts at Hessle High. Daphne's school. We hit it off. She was a lovely girl. Very intelligent and thoughtful. She was a very keen writer, you know. That's what I teach. English. She showed me some of her short stories. She had real talent.'

She pauses. Her voice cracks.

'Take your time,' says McAvoy softly.

A breath. A sniff. A clearing of a throat blocked with tears.

'I've done some voluntary work in the part of the world she's from. Seen some of the things she's seen. We got talking. I don't know, but I suppose I became a sort of outlet for her. She told me things that she kept hidden. There were things in her stories. Things a young girl shouldn't know about. She was very shy when I questioned her about it, so I started setting her writing assignments. Helping to get out the stuff that was inside her.'

McAvoy waits for more. When nothing else is forthcoming, he clears his throat to speak.

Then she blurts it out.

'This has happened to her before.'

# CHAPTER 7

He spots her as soon as he pushes open the glass doors of the trendy pub and steps into the warm blue-black light. She is seated on her own at a small round table by the radiator near the bar. There are empty sofas and loungers near by, but she seems to have chosen the seat nearest the heater, and is all but pressing herself against its white-painted surface. She is staring at the wall, ignoring the other customers. McAvoy cannot see her features, but there is something that makes her seated form seem burdened and sad.

'Miss Mountford?' asks Aector, as he approaches her table.

She looks up. Her deep brown eyes are framed with red and seem to float in darkness. The bags beneath her eyes are dark, almost bruised black by tiredness. There is a silver stud in her left nostril, but her other features do not match the mental picture McAvoy had painted when he had arranged to meet her here, in this most inappropriate setting. She is short and plump, with frizzy brown hair that has been inexpertly pushed behind her ears to leave two misshapen curls running down her cheeks. She is not wearing make-up, and her short, fat fingers end in nails that are bitten almost to nothing, while her clothes – a black cardigan over a white vest – speak of a need for comfort over style. She wears no rings, though a large, ethnic wooden bangle has been wedged onto a chunky freckled wrist.

Vicki Mountford nods timidly and makes to stand, but McAvoy gestures that she should remain seated. He takes the chair opposite her and, with some ceremony, removes his coat. He notices her glass. It is a straight tumbler and contains the dwindling remains of half a dozen ice-cubes, melted to the size and shape of sucked sweets.

'Why here, Miss Mountford? Are you sure there's nowhere more comfortable we could go?'

She rubs a hand across her round features and looks at her glass, and then towards the bar. Then she shrugs. 'I share a house, like I said. My housemate's got the living room tonight. I don't like police stations. This is where I always am at this time on a Sunday. It doesn't bother me.' She looks at her glass again. 'I need a drink to talk about her,' she adds softly.

'It must have been very difficult,' says McAvoy, as tenderly as he can over the hubbub of the half-full bar. 'We break the news to family, but people sometimes forget about the friends. To hear something so terrible on the radio. To read it in the newspapers. I can't imagine.'

Vicki nods, and McAvoy sees gratitude in the gesture. Then her eyes fall to the glass again. He is wondering whether he should offer to buy her a drink when a waitress, clad in black T-shirt and leggings, approaches the table.

'Double vodka and tonic,' says Vicki gratefully, then raises her eyebrows at McAvoy. 'And you?'

McAvoy doesn't know what to ask for. He should perhaps order coffee or a soft drink, but to do so might alienate a potential lead, who so clearly has a taste for something stronger.

'Same for me,' he says.

They do not speak until the waitress returns. She is back inside a minute, placing the drinks on neat white napkins on the black-varnished table. Vicki drains half of hers in one swallow. McAvoy takes only the merest sip before placing the drink back on the surface. He wishes he'd ordered a pint.

'I forgot it was Sunday,' says McAvoy. 'Was expecting office workers and people in designer suits.'

Vicki manages a smile. 'I only come in on Sundays. You can't get a table on a week night and people look at you strangely when you're on your own. It's music night in here on a Sunday. There'll be a jazz band on in an hour or two.'

'Any good? I don't mind a bit of jazz.'

'Different ones each week. They've got a South American group on tonight. All right, apparently.'

McAvoy sticks out his lower lip – his own elaborate gesture of interest. He had policed the Beverley Jazz Festival during his last days as a uniformed constable and been blown away by some of the ethnic jazz groups that had made their way to the East Yorkshire town to play a dozen intermingling tunes for drunk students and the occasional true aficionado.

'Expensive, is it?'

'If you're here before six, it's free. A fiver after that, I think. I've never paid.'

'No? Must save you a bob or two.'

'On a supply-teacher's wages every penny counts.'

Her words seem to steer them back to the reason for their meeting. McAvoy positions himself straighter in his chair. Looks pointedly at his notebook. Softens his face as he prepares to let her tell the story in her own words.

'She must have meant a great deal to you,' he says encouragingly.

Vicki nods. Then gives what is little more than a shrug. 'It's just the wastefulness of it all,' she says, and it seems as though some of the anguish leaves her voice, to be replaced by a weary resignation. 'For her to go through all that and to get her life in some kind of order . . .'

'Yes?'

She stops. Tips the empty glass to her mouth and inserts her tongue, draining it of the last dribbles of watery alcohol. Closing her eyes, she appears to make a decision, and then ducks down below the level of the table. McAvoy hears a bag being unzipped and a moment later she is handing him some folded sheets of white paper.

'That's what she wrote,' she says. 'That's what I'm talking about.'

'And this is?'

'It's her story. A bit of it, anyway. A snippet of how it felt to be her. Like I said, she had a talent. I would have liked to have taught her all the time but there was no permanent position at the school. We just got chatting. I've done some voluntary work in Sierra Leone. Building schools, a bit of teaching here and there. I knew some of the places she was familiar with. It was enough for us to become friends.'

McAvoy cocks his head. A fourteen-year-old girl, and a woman perhaps two decades her senior?

'She had friends her own age, of course,' says Vicki, as if reading his thoughts. She moves her empty glass in slow, steady circles. 'She was an ordinary girl, inasmuch as there is such a thing. She liked pop music. Watched *Skins* and *Big Brother*, like they all do. I never saw her room but I don't doubt there were some Take That posters on the wall. It was her writing that set her apart. That and her faith, although that wasn't something we ever really discussed. I'm not really that way inclined. I put "creature of light" on official forms when they ask my religion. That or "Jedi".'

McAvoy smiles. Without thinking, he takes a large swallow of his drink and feels the pleasing warmth of its passage down his throat.

'I just leave it blank.'

'Not a believer?'

'Nobody's business,' he says, and hopes she will leave it at that.

'You're probably right. Daphne certainly never shoved it down anybody's throat. She wore a crucifix but she was quite literally a buttoned-up sort of girl in her school uniform, so she couldn't be accused of flaunting her beliefs. We only got talking because I'd been intrigued by some of the answers she'd given in class. It must have been about a year ago. I was on a three-week posting at the school. We were doing *Macbeth*.'

McAvoy screws up his face and tries to remember the passage that he had memorised for performance day at school. 'And oftentimes, to win us to our harm, The instruments of darkness tell us truths, Win us with honest trifles, to betray, in deepest consequence—' He stops, embarrassed.

'I'm impressed,' says Vicki and as her face breaks into a grin, McAvoy is dazzled by the transformation that the simple act of smiling has upon her looks. She is casually cool enough to sit alone in a jazz club, rather than too unremarkable to attract a companion.

'I did it when I was thirteen,' says McAvoy. 'I had to recite that in front of a room full of parents and teachers. I still shudder when I think about it. I don't think I've ever been as scared.'

'Really? It's never bothered me,' she says, as the interview evolves into a chat between friends. 'You couldn't get me off the stage when I was a kid. I've never been the shy type.'

'I envy you,' says McAvoy, and means it.

'I didn't think you could be a policeman if you were shy,' she says, crinkling her suddenly pretty eyes.

'You just have to learn how to hide it,' he says with a shrug. 'How am I doing?'

'You had me fooled,' she whispers. 'I won't tell.'

McAvoy wonders if he is playing this right.

'So,' he says, trying to get them back on track. '*Macbeth*?'

'Well, long story short, I was asking some questions of the class. Something about evil. I wanted to know which of the characters in the play could be called truly good and which truly bad. All the other kids had Banquo and Macduff down as heroes. Daphne disagreed. She put just about everybody down the middle. She said you couldn't be one thing or another. That good people did evil things. That evil people were capable of kindness. That people weren't always one thing. She can't have been more than twelve or thirteen when she was saying this, and the way she said it just

66

intrigued me. I asked her to stay back after class and we just got talking. My contract with the school eventually became a six-month thing, so I got to know Daphne pretty well. Obviously, the other teachers knew she had been adopted and that she must have seen some hellish things, but how much was in her official record I couldn't say.'

'So how and when did she tell you about her time in Sierra Leone? About what happened to her?'

'I think I just asked her one day,' says Vicki, turning in her seat to try and catch the waitress's eye. Without thinking about it, McAvoy pushes his own glass across the table and, wordlessly, Vicki takes it in her palm. 'Like I told you, I've done quite a lot of work in countries that have seen conflict and poverty. I was walking between classes with her and she just came out with it. Told me that all of her family had been killed. She was the only one who survived.'

For a whole minute they sit in silence. McAvoy's mind is full of this murdered girl. He has investigated lost lives before. But there is something about the butchering of Daphne Cotton that smacks of futility. Of a cruel end to a life that had been unexpectedly reprieved, and which could per- haps have offered so much.

'Read it,' says Vicki eventually, nodding at the papers on the table in front of McAvoy. 'She wrote that about three months ago. We'd been talking about drawing on your own experiences to become a better writer. Putting parts of your- self into your work. I'm not sure if she fully understood, but what she wrote just tore me up. Read it.'

McAvoy unfolds the pages. Looks at Daphne Cotton's words.

*They say that three years old is too young to form memories, so perhaps what follows is the product of what I have been told, and what I have read. I truly cannot say.*

*I cannot smell blood when I think of my family. I do not smell the bodies or remember the touch of their dead skin. I know it happened. I know I was plucked from the pile of bodies like a baby from a collapsed building. But I do not remember it. And yet I know that it happened.*

*I was three years old. I was the second youngest child in a large family. My oldest brother was fourteen. My oldest sister a year younger. My youngest brother was perhaps ten months old. I had two more brothers and one sister. My youngest brother was called Ishmael. I think we were a happy family. In the three photographs I have, we are all smiling. The photographs were gifts from the sisters as I left to meet my new parents. I do not know where they came from.*

*We lived in Freetown, where my father worked as a tailor. I was born into a time of violence and warfare, but my parents kept us cocooned from the troubles. They were God-fearing Christians, as were their parents, my grandparents. We lived together in a large apartment in the city, and I think I remember saying prayers of gratitude for our good fortune. From history books and the internet, I know that people were dying in their thousands at a time when we were living a happy life, but my parents never allowed this horror to penetrate our lives.*

*In January of 1999, the fighting reached Freetown. When I ask my memory for pictures of our flight from the bloodshed and carnage of that day, there is nothing. Perhaps we left before the soldiers arrived. I know that we went north with a group* of other families from our church. How we reached Songo, the region of my mother's people, I cannot say.

I remember dry grass and a white building. I think I remember songs and prayers. I remember Ishmael's cough. We may have been there for days or weeks. I sometimes feel I have let my family down by not remembering. I pray to God the Father that I remedy this sin. I ask for the memories, no matter how much they will hurt.

When I was old enough, the sisters at the orphanage told me that the rebels had come. That it had been a bright, sunny day. That the fighting was beginning to die down elsewhere in the country, and that the men who passed our church were fleeing defeat. They were drunk and they were angry.

They herded my family and their friends into the church. Nobody else came out alive, so nobody can say what happened. Some of the bodies had bullet holes in the backs of their heads. Others had died from the cuts of machetes.

I do not know why I was spared. I was found among the bodies. I was bleeding from a cut to my shoulder. I think I remember white people in blue uniforms, but this could be my imaginings.

I tell myself that I have forgiven these men for what they did. I know that I am lying. I pray to God each day that this lie becomes truth. He has granted me a new family. I have a good life, now. I feared at first that the city with which Freetown is twinned would be its mirror image. That the pages of its history would be written in blood. But this city has welcomed me. My new parents never ask me to forget. And I have never felt as close to God. His temple embraces me. Holy Trinity has become His warm and loving arms. I felt content in its *embrace. I pray that I will find the strength to please Him and be worthy of His love . . .*

There is a lump in McAvoy's throat and cold grit in his eyes. When he looks up, Vicki's eyes are waiting to meet his.

'See what I mean,' she says, biting her lip. 'The waste.'

McAvoy nods slowly.

'You spoke to her about it?' he asks, his voice hoarse and gravelly.

'Of course. She never knew much about what happened. Just what the nuns at the orphanage told her. She'd been rounded up with her family and shepherded into the church. Some were hacked down with machetes. Others shot. Some raped. Daphne was found by a United Nations force, in among the bodies. She'd been hacked with a machete but survived.'

McAvoy balls his fists. He is struggling to take this in.

'Who else knew about this?'

'The details? Not many. I don't even know how much she told her adoptive parents. They know her family were killed, but as for what happened to Daphne . . .'

'Have you shown this to anybody else?'

Vicki purses her lips and breathes out. 'Maybe one or two,' she says, and her eyes dart away again. It is the first time that she has looked as if she has something to hide.

McAvoy nods. His thoughts are a storm.

'Do you think it's connected?' asks Vicki. 'I mean, it's too big a coincidence, isn't it? A church. A knife. It was a machete, wasn't it?'

Without thinking, McAvoy nods. He realises he does not know if the information has been made available to the public, and then back-pedals. 'It could be,' he says.

Vicki looks torn between the desire to cry and to spit. She is enraged and grief-stricken. 'Bastard,' she says.

Again, McAvoy nods. He's unsure what to do next. He wants to ring Trish Pharaoh and tell her, as procedure dictates. But procedure dictated he stay in the office and man the phones, and he had side-stepped that the second he had answered Vicki's call.

'It's like somebody was trying to finish off what was started all those years ago,' says Vicki, staring into her latest empty glass. She glances up and stares at him, hard. 'Who would do that?'

In her eyes, he is a policeman. A man who can offer explanations. To make sense of it.

He wishes he were worthy of such respect.

His thoughts are consumed by Daphne Cotton's words. By the simple, beautiful, untouched innocence of a mind that had not been contorted by the indignities witnessed by her body.

Suddenly, he wants to hurt whoever did this. He hates himself immediately, but he knows it to be true. That this crime is unforgivable. He takes comfort in the acknowledgement. The acceptance that, if he is hunting evil, he must be on the side of good.

# CHAPTER 8

About three car lengths away, on the opposite side of the car park, Trish Pharaoh is leaning on the bonnet of a silver Mercedes, her face cupped in her hands. She looks like a teenage girl watching TV. Her face is set in a playful smirk, and despite the harsh weather, her make-up is perfect.

'Get in the car,' she says. She pulls open the passenger door and then walks the long way round to the driver's side. She climbs inside, flashing fleshy thigh and a toned calf that disappears into tight biker boots.

For a moment, McAvoy doesn't know what to do. He doesn't know why she's here. Was she checking up on him? Is he going to get booted off the case? He rubs a hand over his face and crosses the car park with the most dignified walk he can muster.

He slips inside the Mercedes and the scent of expensive perfume takes him in a claustrophobic embrace. He smells mandarin oranges and lavender.

'Comfy?' she asks, but he detects no malice.

He catches sight of himself in the darkened glass of the

driver's door and realises how ridiculous he looks, crammed into this tiny car.

'I got your message,' she says, pulling down the vanity mirror above the steering wheel so she can check her eye make-up as she talks. 'Gave Helen Tremberg a ring. She said you were meeting the informant here. I thought I'd tag along.'

McAvoy has to work hard to stop himself from pushing all the air out of his lungs. Relief floods him.

'I, I just concluded the interview, actually, ma'am,' he says apologetically. 'She's at a jazz night inside and will still be there—'

She waves a hand to stop him, gives a shrug. 'I love that accent,' she says, half to herself. 'I did a stint in Edinburgh, you know. Best Practice initiative or some such nonsense. Some idea my old boss had about a prostitute tolerance area. Never got off the ground. Maybe ten years ago now. I was a detective sergeant. That your era?'

McAvoy scratches his forehead, miming thinking. 'Erm . . .'

'My son does that,' laughs Pharaoh, looking at him. 'Or he strokes his chin. It's so sweet.'

Another blush explodes in McAvoy's cheeks. 'How old is he?'

'Ten,' she says, and takes her eyes off the mirror. She stares into the middle distance, looking at nothing.

'Still got the terrible teens ahead,' says Pharaoh, picking a piece of fluff off her tights and blowing it off her palm with pursed, wet lips. 'The things we see in this job, they're going to have a hard time getting out of the house, let alone getting into trouble. Can't wait.'

'I'm sure it won't be that bad,' he replies, uncertain what else to say. He doesn't know whether she has any help from a husband. Finds himself marvelling at the way she has juggled life and career. 'My boy's a few years away from all that.'

She turns her head and looks at him. 'You've got another on the way, haven't you?'

He can't help but let the smile split his face. 'Two months to go,' he says. 'She's bigger than she was with Fin, but the pregnancy hasn't been so hard. It was hellish before . . .' he stops himself, sensing a trap ahead. 'I won't be taking any paternity time, ma'am. If this looks like being a lengthy investigation, you've got me for as long as you need.'

She rolls her eyes and shakes her head.

'Hector,' she says, and then gives a soft laugh. 'Sorry. It's Aector, isn't it? With a cough in the middle? I'm not sure I've got the slaver to be able to say it the Gaelic way every day. Can you handle Hector?'

'It's fine,' he says.

'Hector, if you don't take paternity leave I'll wring your bloody neck. You're entitled to it, you take it.'

'But—'

'But nothing, you wally.' She laughs again. 'Hector, can I ask you a question?'

'Of course, ma'am.'

She squeezes his thigh in a friendly, comforting way as she looks up into his eyes. 'What's the matter with you?'

'Ma'am?'

'McAvoy, we like a gentle giant but there's a fine line between not using your size to take advantage, and being a complete bloody pansy.'

McAvoy blinks a few times.

'A pansy?'

'Say it,' she says.

He looks away, trying to keep his voice even. 'Say what?'

'Tell me what you've been itching to tell us all since we got here.'

He forces himself to look into her eyes.

'I don't know . . .'

'Yes you do, Hector. You want to tell me to read your file. To ask around. To find out what you did.'

'I . . .'

'Hector, I've known you for, what, six months? Maybe a bit longer? How many conversations have we had?'

He shrugs.

'Hector, every time I give you a job to do you look at me with this expression somewhere between an eager-to-please puppy and a bloody serial killer. You look at me like you'll do whatever I ask, and you'll do it better than everybody else. And that's a very endearing quality. But there's this other bit peering out from behind all that which says, "Don't you know who I am? Don't you know what I did?"'

'I'm sorry if that's the impression I give, ma'am, but—'

'I met Doug Roper, Hector.'

McAvoy visibly flinches at the name.

'He was a sexist, vicious bastard, and for every hanger-on who wanted to be part of his gang or ride his coat-tails, there were a dozen more who thought he was a total prick.'

'I'm not allowed . . .'

'. . . to talk about it? I know, Hector. We all know. We know that Doug did something very bad, and that you were the one who found out about it. We know that you took it to the brass. That you were promised the earth, and that Roper would swing. And we know that they lost their nerve, let him swan off without a stink, and that you were left as the poor bastard in the middle, in a CID team that was disintegrating faster than a snowball in a microwave. How am I doing so far?'

McAvoy stays silent.

'I don't know what they promised you, Hector. I very much doubt it's what you've got. It must be hard, eh? Must eat away at you, people knowing, but not knowing.' She makes a claw of her hand and presses it to her heart. 'Must get you here.'

'You've no idea,' he says softly, and when he looks up, her face is close to his. He sees his own reflection swim on her eyes. Overcome by this moment, he finds himself leaning in . . .

She pulls back abruptly and looks back up at the mirror, withdrawing her hand from McAvoy's thigh to flick away an invisible eyelash from her cheek.

'So,' she says, smiling brightly. 'That's about enough of that. I was going to have this chat with you a few months ago, but you know how it is, finding the time . . .'

'Well I appreciate it, ma'am.' His heart is thundering.

She eases down the electric window and a pleasing cold draught fills the car. She closes her eyes and seems to enjoy its sensation on her skin as she angles her face towards the fresh, cool air.

McAvoy does the same with his own window. Feels his damp fringe flutter on the breeze.

They sit in silence for a moment. McAvoy tries to find something to do with his hands. He reaches into his pocket and pulls out his phone. Realises it's been switched off since before he interviewed Vicki Mountford. He turns it on, and the tinkling sound that accompanies its welcome screen sounds irritatingly loud in the confines of the car. Immediately, the voicemail begins to ring. He holds it to his ear. Two messages. One, from Helen Tremberg, warning him that Trish Pharaoh has been asking about his whereabouts and might be tagging along on the Mountford interview. And one from Barbara Stein-Collinson. The sister of the dead trawlerman:

*Hello, Sergeant. I'm sorry to ring you on a Sunday. I just thought you should be aware that I've heard from the TV people who were with Fred when he died. It all seems, I don't know, a bit wrong, somehow. Maybe it's nothing. Could you perhaps give me a call, if you find a moment? Many thanks.*

McAvoy closes his phone. He knows he'll call her back. Will listen to her concerns. Make the right noises. Tell her he'll do what he can.

'Anything?' asks Pharaoh.

'Maybe,' he says, and truly isn't sure. 'A favour I did for the ACC. Wife of one of the Police Authority faces. Her brother's been found dead. Old trawlerman. Was busy making a documentary about the trawler tragedies of 1968. Looks like he chucked himself over the side, seventy miles off Iceland. They found him in a lifeboat. I had to break the news.'

'Poor bugger,' she says thoughtfully. It's the police officer's mantra.

'I'll follow it up in my own time . . .'

'Oh, McAvoy, give it a rest.' Her voice has absorbed a touch of steel.

'Ma'am?'

'Look, McAvoy,' she says, and she seems suddenly short-tempered. 'People don't know what to make of you. You're either going to be a future chief constable or end up under a bridge drinking Special Brew. They can't read you. They just know you're a big softie who could break them in half and who cost Humberside's most notorious copper his job. Those are facts that require some qualification, do you understand?'

McAvoy's thought are fireworks, exploding in his vision. He can smell the blood rushing in his head.

'Why now?' he manages. 'Why are you telling me this?'

'I got your message about this witness. At the time, I was fielding calls from the press, from the top brass, from the DCs and uniform. I was trying to get something out of Daphne's mum, and trying not to get tears on the family album. Then I listened to my messages, and the only one that was calm, precise, unemotional and bloody interesting was yours. So I felt a surge of warmth for you, my boy. I decided to show you a little love.' She smiles again. 'Enjoy it while it lasts.'

McAvoy realises he's been holding his breath. When he lets it out, he fancies that he feels himself growing lighter. He is overcome with affection for Pharaoh. Filled with a desire to repay her faith.

'It was worth the trip,' he says enthusiastically. 'Vicki Mountford, I mean.'

'Enlighten me,' she says.

Without thinking about it, McAvoy removes his hat and begins to unhook his bag from his shoulder. Midway, he stops and cocks his head, looking at his superior officer with a half-smile of his own. And for the first time in as long as he can remember, he decides to act on impulse.

'Do you like jazz?' he asks.

The notice is a mess of faded black on white, tagged with purple scrawls and unfinished signatures.

THE PLAYING OF BALL GAMES IS NOT ALLOWED

Visitors to Hull's Orchard Park estate might wonder who will enforce the order. Rows of houses stand empty, boarded up for demolition. Many are darkened to the colour of bruised fruit by smoke and demolition dust. Others are doorless. Windowless. Standing sentry over front lawns of mud and broken brick made into minefields of broken glass.

Few of the homes are inhabited.

This was the place to be, once upon a time. The old Hull Corporation had a waiting list of families desperate to move into this new community of solid houses, friendly shopkeepers and neatly tended lawns. Even when the high-rises started to climb into the skies in the sixties, it was still an address that smacked of honest, hard-working men and house-proud women. Poor, but with a front step you could eat your dinner off.

Not now. Thirty-odd years ago, the fishing industry died. The government gave it up. Handed it over to the Europeans and told them to have a ball. Told the Brits to be grateful they'd had it for so long. Told thousands of fishermen to fuck off home.

During the 1970s, the sons of the East Coast's trawlermen, of its fish merchants, of its market traders and seamen, became the first generation in three centuries to find there was no living to be made from the ocean. No living to be made anywhere, unless you had the O levels and a Surrey accent. They signed on. Drank away their benefit cheques. Spawned children who followed Mam and Dad's example as they grew into teenagers who spent their evenings stealing cars and trashing bus shelters, breaking into pharmacies and knocking-up teenage girls in the petrol-stinking lock-ups. Orchard Park began to die.

Ten years ago, Hull Council accepted what its people already knew. The city was on the bones of its arse. Its population was shrinking. Anybody with the cash moved to the surrounding towns and villages. Its graduates simply passed through on their way to more prosperous cities. Mortgage companies started offering easy cash to council tenants, who bought themselves two-up-two-down semis in any one of the new, identikit estates that were cropping up on the outskirts of the city. By the year 2000, there were 10,000 empty homes in Hull, and most of them were on Orchard Park. Wholesale demolition began.

There are still proud homeowners here and there. Amid the black teeth and rotted gums of the burned-out and vandalised houses stands the occasional white-painted molar. The lawns are rich green. The earth, coffee-brown. Hanging baskets dangle next to double-glazed doors curtained with lace. These are the homes of the people who will not leave. Who believe Orchard Park will be saved. That the bad element will move on. That the high-rises will fall. That the properties they spent their life savings to purchase will soon become a steal.

Across a rutted stretch of tarmac, surrounded on all sides by iron shutters, and blackened bricks, they face one another. Perfect little seaside chalets.

Though there are lights on at number 59, its owners are not home. Warren Epworth suffered an angina attack last night and was taken to Hull Royal Infirmary as a precautionary measure. His wife, Joyce, is staying with her daughter in Kirk Ella. It is a move her daughter hopes will become a permanent measure when her father is discharged. She hopes, too, that while the house is unattended, it will be robbed. Vandalised. Burned to the bloody ground. Her parents need proof that that their community is irredeemable. They need to leave.

Tonight, the living room of the house where the Epworths have lived for forty-two years is occupied by two men.

One wears a black balaclava. A dark sweater. Black combat boots.

He has wet, blue eyes.

The other man lies on a floral print sofa. He's dressed in an old Manchester United shirt, jogging pants and trainers. He is scrawny and unkempt, with scabbed, goose-pimpled arms and an unshaven, ratty face. There is sticky, clotted red around his lips and one of his teeth points inwards, showing a rotten, bloodied gum.

His eyes are closed.

He reeks of alcohol.

The man in the balaclava looks around the living room. At the ornate picture frames on the mantelpiece. At the smiling portraits. The newborn babies and dressed-up grandchildren. At school photos. A ruby wedding snap showing an elderly couple holding hands and nuzzling foreheads at the head of a table strewn with presents.

The man nods, as if making a decision. Sweeps his arm along the mantelpiece and grabs the snaps. Bundles them into a black holdall at his feet.

Then he turns back to the figure on the sofa.

From his inside pocket he withdraws a yellow metal container. He closes his eyes. Breathes through his nose.

Sprays the lighter fuel on the unconscious man.

He stands back, his gloved hands balled into fists.

Watches the other man cough and splutter into wakefulness.

Sees him look up. Stare at him.

Know.

Know that he's been living on borrowed time.

That he escaped when he should have been taken.

That the debt must be repaid.

He sees the other man's eyes widen and shrink. Sees the panic and fury contort the muscles in his face.

'What . . . where . . . ?'

The man is trying to stand, but his mind is foggy with alcohol. His memories are smudged and edgeless. He remembers the pub. The scrap with the other punter. The car park. The first few steps of his long walk back to his flat above the bookie's. Then a fist in his hair. The cold, hard neck of a bottle forced into his mouth. The sudden taste of blood and vodka. The fading sight of a black-clad man.

'Is this . . . ?'

The layout of the house seems familiar. Horribly similar to the place he once called home. The place he set aflame because he was pissed and liked the sound of fire engines.

The place that slow-cooked his wife and children.

'Why . . . ?'

The man in the balaclava holds up a hand, as if urging a speeding car to slow. He shakes his head. Conveys, in one gesture, that there is no point in struggling. That this has already been decided upon.

In one swift motion he pulls a cheap yellow lighter from his pocket. He drops to a crouch, like a sprinter on the blocks, and presses the flame to the patterned carpet.

Then he turns away.

The flame runs both left and right, growing and gathering pace as the twin streams of fire encircle the sofa.

The man in the balaclava steps back and shields his eyes.

As the man on the sofa draws breath to scream, it is as if he is inhaling the flame. With a gasping gulp of air, the spitting blaze leaps towards him.

Wraps him in its embrace.

The black-clad man does not look at the burning creature. Does not pause to watch him thrash and fight against the angry cloak of red and gold that engulfs him. That fuses his polyester shirt to his skin. Fills the room with the smell of sour meat.

He picks up the holdall and walks to the door.

Leaves the burning man to wonder if this is how his family felt when the flames ate into their skin.

# CHAPTER 9

McAvoy lathers shaving foam upon his face and begins scraping at the bristles with his cut-throat razor. Roisin had bought it for him in a fancy boutique near Harrods during one of the frequent trips to London they had taken during their early courtship. It is a lethal-looking object, with a blade that could rob a ladybird of its wings mid-flight. She likes to watch him sharpen it on the wet leather strop that hangs by the mirror.

'Can you see OK? Do you want to open a window?'

He turns from the mirror. Roisin is poking her head out from behind the shower curtain. He can see the shadow of her belly and breasts behind the patterned material, and feels a familiar tightening in his gut. *So beautiful*, he thinks, and the thought is so powerful he has to dig his fingernails into his palms to contain it.

'Yes,' he says, nodding as well in case she can't hear his voice over the sound of the gushing water. 'It's OK.'

She pulls her head back behind the curtain and he watches her silhouette change shape as she tips her head back and rinses her hair. Watches her slowly turn, play with the shower-head and direct the stream of water at her shoulders. Watches her reach for the posh soap and lather her arms. Her belly. Sees her soap her thighs. Between her legs. Her small, tender breasts.

McAvoy is still deciding whether to reach behind the curtain and stroke the curve of her hips when she abruptly cuts the water off. She whisks the curtain back and stands there in the bathtub, dripping water. So unaware of her own beauty.

'I'm sorry I fell asleep,' she says, shaking her hair like a wet dog and holding out her hand so he can help her from the bath. 'What time did you get in?'

McAvoy can't meet her eyes. She has to nod her head and raise her eyebrows before he crosses the lino floor and encloses her small, wet hand in his. Takes her weight as she climbs from the tub.

McAvoy leans in and kisses her wet face, catching her at the corner of her mouth. She smiles, pleased, and kisses him back, her damp body rubbing against his chest. 'You should have joined me in there,' she whispers, nodding at the bathtub. 'I could have made up for last night.'

'It's better in theory,' he says, as relief floods through him.

'Oh yes?' Her voice is flirty. Playful.

'The shower, I mean,' he says between kisses. 'We end up slipping, remember?'

They share a laugh at the memory of their last attempt to share a cubicle. The difference in their height meant that while Roisin nearly drowned, McAvoy was bone-dry from the chest up.

Her hands move down his body. Her lips move to his neck.

She sniffs.

'Dolly Girl by Anna Sui?'

She pulls away, looking at him quizzically. There is shaving foam on her face.

'I . . .'

She sniffs again, and grins, then smears the shaving foam across her upper lip so that it looks like a moustache. She leans up on tiptoes, and kisses his soap-lathered mouth.

'Whoever she is, she has good taste.'

Then she returns her lips to his skin.

'Roisin, it was work, I couldn't . . .'

She shushes him. Pulls his head down so that she's looking up into his eyes. 'Aector, the day you cheat on me is the day the world turns into a Malteser. Not a giant Malteser, just a regular-sized one that we all have to try and balance on. Now, I can't see that happening any time soon. So shut up. Kiss me.'

'But . . .'

Her tongue slithers between his cracked, dry lips.

'Daddy! Telephone!'

The door flies open and Fin bursts into the bathroom. He slips on the wet lino and lands on his bottom, dropping the phone, which skids away like a hockey puck. Fin giggles, making no attempt to get up, even as his Buzz Lightyear pyjamas start to absorb the water.

McAvoy reaches down and picks up the mobile from the floor.

'Aector McAvoy,' he says into the receiver.

'Is this a bad time, Sergeant?'

It takes him a moment to place the voice. It is tremulous

but unmistakably middle class. 'Mrs Stein-Collinson?' he asks, and screws his eyes closed, chiding himself for failing to call her back last night.

'That's right,' she says, relieved to have been recognised. 'You sound busy. Who was that who answered?'

'My boy,' he says.

'He sounds a character,' she says, and her voice is full of smiles.

'I'm terribly sorry I didn't call back last night . . .'

'Oh, I understand,' she says, and he imagines her waving away his protests with a wrinkled, manicured hand. 'That poor girl. Have you made any progress? The radio has been so vague.'

McAvoy wonders how much he can say. Finds solace in 'We're following up some useful lines of inquiry.'

'Good, good,' she says distractedly, then pauses.

'Have there been any developments?' he prompts.

'Well, that's the funny thing,' she says, and her voice becomes excited and conspiratorial. 'I got a call tea-time yesterday from the lady who was making the documentary with our Fred. She's back in this country and felt she should get in touch.'

'Do you remember the lady's name?'

She stops, as if unsure whether to go on. McAvoy, practised in nudging conversations along, lets her take the breath she needs.

'The lifeboat,' she says suddenly, with a voice like a finger jabbing at a map. 'The lifeboat they found him in. It shouldn't have been there. The TV lady got talking to the captain when they docked and he didn't know where it came from. Somebody had brought it with them. And it wasn't Fred. The TV crew were with him the whole time. I'm sure there's a simple explanation, but it just seems . . .'

'Odd,' he finishes, and he can hear relief in her accompanying exhalation.

'Do you think there might be more to this?' she asks, and her voice is a mixture of excited curiosity and puzzled sadness. 'I mean, nobody would want to hurt Fred, would they? It's just, what with him surviving all those years ago. I don't know, but . . .'

McAvoy is no longer listening. He's staring at himself in the mirror. All he can see through the steam and the mist is the scar upon his shoulder. It is the shape of a blade.

Thinking of a church. Of bloodied bodies and a crying baby, nestled in the arm of a butchered parent.

The inequity of it all burning in his chest.

He cannot help but remember. Despite all he has done to bury the image, he cannot help but let the picture flash in his mind. Cannot help but see himself, months before, stumbling backwards, feet slipping on the mud and dead leaves, as Tony Halthwaite, the killer nobody believed in, swung a blade towards his throat.

Cannot help but shudder, now; seeing the steel again, arcing down towards an exposed jugular with practised precision.

Remembers seeing Roisin's face. Fin's. Finding one last gasp of instinct and energy.

Throwing himself out of the way.

Feeling his skin of his shoulder open up and the blood spray and then lashing out with his boot.

Surviving. Ducking the blade, where others had fallen . . .

# PART TWO

# CHAPTER 10

'You only had three pints, Hector,' Pharaoh had chided, standing in the doorway of the incident room like a head teacher on the lookout for truants and laughing as McAvoy had raced up the stairs, red-faced and panting, his bag tangling on the banister and yanking him backwards as if lassoed. 'I'd love to see you after a session at my place sometime. You wouldn't get out of bed for a fortnight.'

She had been wearing a knee-length red leather skirt and a tight black cardigan that accentuated her impressive chest. She was heavily made-up and her hair was perfect. She had outdrunk McAvoy by a ratio of 3:1 last night, but were it not for the dark semi-circles beneath her eyes, she might have just returned from a holiday on a sugar daddy's yacht.

'Ma'am, I'm so sorry, the traffic and Fin, and . . .'

'Don't fret,' she'd said with a smile. 'We muddled through without you.'

'On the radio,' he panted. 'House fire? Orchard Park.'

She nodded. 'Given it to the lads at Greenwood. We can't spare the manpower. Sergeant Knaggs is taking it on. I think he was a bit upset when he took my phone call and realised there still wasn't room for him on Daphne's case.'

*Daphne*, noted McAvoy. Not *the Cotton case*. Pharaoh was really feeling this one.

'Straightforward, is it?'

'Not sure. Whoever got roasted, it isn't the homeowner. He's in hospital already. One of the decent ones from the estate. Nice old boy. His wife's staying with their daughter out in Toryville. Kirk Ella, I think. Apparently she sounded over the moon when she heard the house had gone up in smoke. Less so when the uniforms mentioned they'd found a barbecued human being on the sofa. No bloody idea who it might be. I very much doubt we'll ever get a chat with him, anyway. Ninety per cent burns. No face left. Internal organs all but cooked. There was definitely an accelerant used, but forensics can't say much more. He's in the new unit at Hull Royal Infirmary but they're probably going to move him over to Wakefield. Don't know why. Unless they've got a wetsuit made of skin to zip him into, he's had it.'

McAvoy nodded. He was vaguely interested in the Orchard Park fire, but if he was honest with himself, he had dismissed the victim as a drug addict or a burglar the second he heard the story on the radio. A shame, but not a tragedy. Worth somebody's time. But not necessarily his.

'So I missed the post mortem?'

'Count your blessings,' she said. 'Even Colin Ray kept his trap shut.'

'Upshot?'

Pharaoh hadn't needed to look at her notes. Just reeled it off, emotionless, staring into his eyes without really looking at him. 'Eight separate slash wounds, each to the bone. The first severed her clavicle and collar bone. An overhand hacking motion with the right hand. Six more slashes in the same area, splintering the clavicle. One spar of bone punctured her thorax. A final thrust, as she lay on the floor, right to the heart. She'll have been dead by the time he pulled the blade out.'

McAvoy closed his eyes. Steadied his breathing. 'He meant to kill her, then? The final thrust, that's just so . . .'

'Final,' Pharaoh nodded. 'He wanted her dead. We don't know who he is, why he wanted to kill her or why he chose to do it in a packed fucking church, but we know he was pretty bloody determined.'

McAvoy watched as she pressed her forehead into her knuckles. Worked her jaw in circles. Screwed her eyes shut. She was getting angry.

'What else?'

'Proof of what your young lady told you last night. Evidence of old scarring to her collarbone. Same side. Pathologist could barely see it under the mess of new wounds, but it was there. This had happened to her before.'

'What are we going to do with that information, ma'am? Have you alerted the team?'

She nodded. 'We don't know what it means, but it's something to look into. Such a tiny number of people knew about it, it could be a horrible coincidence, but I find that hard to believe. Colin Ray gobbled it up like a pork-pie. As soon as I mentioned it, he'd made up his mind. This was some African refugee, finishing what they started. Went out of here grumbling about foreigners finishing their dirty business in

Yorkshire. I don't think he really got the right end of the stick.'

McAvoy kept quiet. The same idea had occurred to him.

'According to the toxicology reports, she had no more alcohol in her system than a sip of communion wine. She had a bit of a cold. And she was a virgin.'

She'd turned away, then, unable to keep it up. 'It's incident room phones for you,' she said over her shoulder, heading for the stairs. 'Call yourself office manager if you like. Just make sure the PCs and the support staff don't say anything stupid. I've got to go back and see the family, then the *Hull Daily Mail* want a chat. Chief Constable wants a briefing at three. Like I've got anything to fucking tell him. There's a load of CCTV to go through, if you get five minutes.' Then, more like a wife than a superior, she'd turned, given him a smile and said: 'You got compliments on the info. Thought you might like to know.'

That had been two hours ago, and the morning has been dire. The first three phone calls he's taken have done little to lift his spirits.

His thoughts drift to Fred Stein. There is something about all this that seems not just peculiar but almost eerie. He understands guilt. Knows how it feels to survive an attack when others have been less fortunate. But to redress the balance in such a dramatic, almost contrived manner? To tag along with a film crew? To bring your own lifeboat? He doesn't know enough about Fred Stein to assess his personality, his capacity for self-hatred, but in his experience ex-trawlermen are not usually given to such extravagance.

He slips out into the corridor and leaves a message for

Caroline Wills – the documentary-maker who had managed to lose the star of her show seventy miles off the Icelandic coast.

He walks back to his desk. The incident room is taking shape. The filing cabinets have been lined up against the far wall, the desks arranged in neat twos, like seats on a bus, and the map stapled to the board by the grimy window has more pins in it than yesterday. Definite sightings, possible sightings and best-guesses. One uniformed officer is talking softly into a telephone but from his body language, it doesn't look like an exciting lead. McAvoy has received a dozen texts from Tremberg, Kirkland and Nielsen keeping him apprised of their movements. Nielsen is finishing off the witness list, and losing patience. They saw, but didn't see. Heard, but weren't really listening. Witnessed the aftermath, but couldn't say where the killer had come from, or where he went.

Sophie Kirkland is up at the tech lab, working her way through Daphne Cotton's hard drive. So far, she's found that she liked to visit websites featuring Christian doctrine and Justin Timberlake.

He'd be loath to admit it, but McAvoy is bored. He can't get on with any of his usual workload because the files are back at Priory Road, and despite his reservations, the officers are using the database in the manner he had hoped, so there's not even any cleaning up to be done on the system.

The mobile phone rings. It's a withheld number. McAvoy sinks into his chair and answers with a palpable air of relief.

'Detective Sergeant Aector McAvoy,' he says.

'I know, son. I just rang you.' It's DCI Ray.

'Yes, sir.' He sits up straight. Adjusts his tie.

'I take it Pharaoh's still busy?'

'I think she'll be preparing for her interview with the *Hull Mail* at the moment . . .'

'Ready for her close-up, is she?'

McAvoy says nothing. The polite thing to do is to make a small laughing noise, so as not to upset the senior officer. But he just insulted Trish Pharaoh, and McAvoy is taking it to heart.

'Was there something you wanted, sir?'

Colin Ray's voice changes. Becomes aggressive. 'Yeah, there is, son. You can tell her that me and Shaz are bringing somebody in. Neville the Racist. Drinks in Kingston. He's agreed to a chat, so don't be worrying about issuing a press release. Just going to let him have a look at an interview room and see if it jogs his memory.'

McAvoy's heart is racing. He stands up, too quickly, and drags the phone off his desk. 'What's the link?' he stammers.

'He don't like the foreigners, our Neville,' says Ray. 'Hates the buggers, truth be told. And he's got a nasty temper. Your teacher lady got me thinking. I reckon our Neville wanted to teach one of them a lesson so figured he'd bump one off and pin it on another. Make it look like unfinished business from Africa or wherever. It's a hundred yards from Kingston to Holy Trinity and Terry the barman reckons Nev was missing for a good hour on Saturday afternoon. That's not his normal routine at all. Normally stays for the duration. Neville reckons he went to buy a present for his granddaughter, but . . .'

'Granddaughter?' Incredulity creeps into McAvoy's tone. 'How old is he?'

'Late fifties. Fit as an ox, mind.'

'Chief Inspector, I saw this man. He was in good shape. Fast. I don't think—'

'Just tell Pharaoh when she finishes preening.'

The line goes dead.

McAvoy rests his forehead on his hand. He hears blood rushing in his head. Could it be that easy? Could it be a simple race hate crime? An old bigot venting his frustrations? McAvoy wonders what such a result would mean. Whether his own contribution, however peremptory, would be noted. Whether Colin Ray would leapfrog Trish Pharaoh in the chain of command.

He looks up. There's a hard breeze shaking the bare branches of the charcoal-sketch trees beyond the dusty glass. There's a storm coming. When the snow falls, it will be a blizzard.

McAvoy's phone rings again.

'McAvoy,' he says dejectedly.

'Sergeant? Hello, this is Caroline Wills. From Wagtail Productions? I've just got clear. What can I do for you?'

McAvoy drags his notepad closer to himself and pulls the top off his biro with his teeth.

Focuses on Fred Stein.

'Thanks for returning my call, Miss Wills. It's regarding Fred Stein.'

'Really?' She sounds disappointed. 'I had rather hoped it might be the Daphne Cotton case.'

McAvoy places his pen between his teeth, as some kind of physical reminder to watch what he says.

'You're aware of the ongoing murder investigation?'

'Just what I've heard,' she says breezily. 'Horrible business, isn't it? Poor girl.'

'Indeed. Anyway, Fred Stein.'

'Yes, yes, sad stuff. Nice old boy. We were getting on well. You're Hull CID though, aren't you? What's the connection?'

'Mr Stein's sister lives in this part of the world. She simply has some concerns about the facts regarding his death and I said I would do what I can to fill in the gaps.'

'Wife of the Chief Constable, is she?' She laughs again; a high, pleasant sound. She sounds middle-class. Definitely Southern. He has her pegged as early thirties and savvy.

McAvoy decides to play along.

'Member of the Police Authority, actually. Tipped to be chairman before he's sixty.'

'Ah. All makes sense now.'

'So, what can you tell me?'

'Well, I gave a statement to the Icelandic authorities and am due to provide one for the coroner when he opens the inquest, but I know so little about what happened it's not going to be a killer to go over it again. Basically, I run a little TV company specialising in documentaries. We've been involved in some stuff for terrestrial TV but largely you'll find our work on the documentary channels. About five years ago I did a programme on the sinking of the *Dunbar*. Spent some time in Hull. My goodness, what a place.'

McAvoy hears himself laughing. 'That's one way of describing it.'

'Yeah, yeah. Down to earth. Proper Northern, if that doesn't sound too silly.'

'Oh yes. A whippet down each trouser leg and a bag of chips on their shoulder.'

'You know what I mean,' she giggles.

'What was the interest in the *Dunbar*?'

The vessel in question was a brand-new supertrawler that sank in the late seventies during a ferocious storm off the coast of Norway. For years, the fishing community in Hull had voiced their doubts about its loss. There was talk of it being a spy ship, sailing into Russian waters to photograph enemy vessels during the Cold War. The gossip mongers reckoned the crew were all still alive, holed in some Russian gulag. Even when the local fishing industry went belly up, the rumours about the *Dunbar* persisted until, eventually, a city MP had to make good on a pre-election promise and lobby for a public inquiry. When it came, the results were inconclusive. The *Dunbar* had indeed sunk to the bottom of the Barents Sea. Bodies were indeed found on board. But were there spies among their number? Nobody could say. It was tabloid and conspiracy theorist heaven.

'The Yanks love anything that reminds them of the Cold War. We pitched the idea to a channel in the US. You know the kind of thing; were these plucky Yorkshiremen really spies against the Soviets? Were they silenced by the Reds? I think they miss the good old days. Anyway, they went for it and I attended the last few days of the inquiry. Good crowd. One chap, Tony something-or-other, smelled like an ashtray. As it happened the programme never saw the light of day. We still got paid for it but there was no room in the schedules.

'So. Last year I was going through some old footage. Things that never aired. I was watching the *Dunbar* programme and realised what an interesting little story it was. Not the Cold War nonsense. Just the people involved. Their lives. Their stories. Long story short, I did some research and realised it was coming up for forty years since the Black Winter. Four trawlers in a few days. Terrible stuff. I went through the old contacts book and tried to get in touch with some of the old hacks I met during the inquiry. Well, you know how these things are. People move on. But after a bit of graft I found Russ Chandler. More of a writer than a journalist but knows his stuff. Certainly knows the fishing industry. He told me all about Fred Stein. The one who got away. It seemed tailor-made for what we wanted. A programme about the Black Winter with a modern twist. When we heard Fred had never spoken about what happened to him, we got the chequebook out. Set Russ the job of tracking him down. Made the offer, did the deal and bish-bash-bosh – next thing we're trying to find a container ship we can hitch a ride with to Iceland.'

McAvoy nods. He's stopped making notes. He finds himself liking the way this lady talks.

'So, that was that. We sent transport. Made the arrangements. Met him at the gangplank, or whatever you call them. Real nice old boy. Full of stories. Real charmer. We planned to do a series of interviews during the journey and then he was going to lay a wreath over the spot where it happened. Would have made a wonderful closing scene. But after what should have been the last interview he got really emotional. Went to get a breath of fresh air and didn't come back. Two days later, while we were going bloody frantic, we heard over the radio his body had been found in a lifeboat. Died of exposure and injuries to his ribs . . .'

She pauses.

'Emotional, you said. Emotional enough to kill himself?'

'I wouldn't have said so. But if he brought his own lifeboat he must have planned it from the start. I don't remember seeing him unload it, and I've checked with the taxi firm that brought him to the dock and they don't remember him having it with him, but people make mistakes and forget the silliest things. Apparently, with this style of lifeboat, before you inflate it it's not much bigger than a medium-sized suitcase. You just flip open the switches, pull the lever and it inflates. Got a rigid mid-section, so it's possible that the impact on that is what did his ribs in. Hard to say. I've got to be honest, the captain was never really keen on us even being there and most of the conversation was in Icelandic, so trying to find out what happened was a nightmare.'

McAvoy nods. None of this makes sense. 'What do you think happened?'

'Me? I think he probably did himself in. I don't know if it was guilt or just the fact he was getting old and it seemed like the right time. He'd had forty years that, in his head, he didn't deserve. Maybe he didn't think he'd used them right. Either way, it's a shame. At least he'll be remembered.'

'What do you mean?'

'The documentary. The interviews are extraordinary. So moving. I can send you them if you're interested.'

McAvoy nods, then realises she can't see him. 'Yes, thank you.'

They both stay silent for a moment. 'It's Russ you could really do with speaking to, if you want to fill in some of the gaps,' she says lightly. 'He's the bloodhound who found him. Knew chapter and verse on the story. He's a cracking writer, is Russ. I miss him.'

'Why, where is he?'

'He wanted to come on the tanker with us but there was no way we could get insurance for him.'

'No?'

'No, he's a bit . . .'

'What?'

She gives a little laugh, unsure of the best way to say it. 'Unhinged,' she says. 'He drinks. In fact, no, Oliver Reed used to drink. Amy Winehouse used to drink. Russ really, really drinks. You've never seen anything like it. Smokes more than your sixty a day as well. Already cost him one leg and it's probably going to cost him the other.'

'Sounds like he knows his vices.'

'Vices, yes. But it's the voices that do Russ the most harm. He's in a private clinic in Lincolnshire at the moment. Halfway between drying out and being sectioned. Real character, but he's had one of those lives. It's made him bitter, and everybody likes bitter with a whisky chaser. You should talk to him, though. He can tell you more about Fred than anyone. We wouldn't have even found him if it wasn't for Russ. It's a shame he's having to use his cheque to pay for treatment.'

McAvoy looks around the room. The officers have gone back to writing up telephone interviews and logging calls. There is nothing for him to do. Something inside him is screaming. That this is important. That this conversation, this information, somehow matters.

He lowers his voice. Closes his eyes. Already regretting his decision.

'Is he accepting visitors?'

# CHAPTER 11

3.22 p.m. Linwood Manor.

Deepest, darkest Lincolnshire.

Two hours from home.

*Pretty swish*, thinks McAvoy, as his tyres slide to an elegant halt on the shingled forecourt and he looks up at the imposing, red-brick building. He takes in the giant oak double doors, standing open to reveal a neatly tiled floor.

'A converted Victorian manor house set in four acres of landscaped woodland'; McAvoy thought he had clicked on the wrong link and arrived at an upmarket country hotel when he first navigated his way through a maze of mental health websites and spotted the address he was looking for.

Run by an international company specialising in detox treatments, borderline personality disorders and alcohol dependence, the home page boasted a 90 per cent success rate, and made what could have been viewed as a month of agonising withdrawal seem like a vacation in paradise.

Although it's only mid-afternoon, the sky is already darkening, and the grey cloud of ferocious snow that will soon split and engulf Hull has already been torn open here.

A confetti of plump white flakes tumbles from the sky, and McAvoy is grateful for his knee-length coat as he trots up the steps and through the doors, feeling the wind tug at the hems of his trousers and almost slipping on the wet tiles.

A smiling, middle-aged woman in a white blouse and believably dyed black hair is sitting behind a mahogany reception desk. A vase of gerbera and gypsophila stands on its polished, gleaming surface. Glossy brochures and price lists stand in a rack to her left. It would be impossible to pop in for a leaflet without having to walk past her. Impossible, too, not to nod a hello in response to her wide, gleaming grin. Difficult to get out again without engaging her in conversation and being persuaded within twenty minutes that Linwood Manor is the best place to put yourself, your loved ones, and your cash.

'Hello there. Awful day, isn't it? Looks like you're dressed for the conditions. Do you think it'll lie? We might get a white Christmas after all. Haven't had one of them in years. I think our guests will appreciate it. We had a hoot last year. Can I help you, m'duck?'

McAvoy has to make a mental effort not to recoil from the sheer force of her jolliness. Although she's slim, she puts him in mind of a fat and happy Victorian cook, with big, floury arms and a red face. He pities the poor shambling drunks who must deal with her on their way to begin their detox programmes. *Another twenty seconds in her company*, McAvoy thinks, *and I'll be needing a bottle of brandy.*

'I'm Detective Sergeant Aector McAvoy. Humberside Police CID Serious and Organised Crime Unit. I was wondering . . .'

'Serious crime, is it? Isn't all crime serious? I mean, it's not as though having your bike nicked isn't serious to somebody. That's what happened to my nephew and he was so upset . . .'

She rattles on until he wants to reach across the desk and physically press her lips together. The smile never leaves her face, although it never quite reaches her eyes, which puts him in mind of lights left on in the upstairs windows of a deserted house.

'It's about one of your patients,' he says, jumping in when she pauses for breath. 'Russell Chandler. I did call ahead, but I had difficulty getting through.'

'Ooh, we've had no end of problems. It's probably the weather. Email and internet have been playing up as well.'

McAvoy runs his tongue around his mouth and twitches his face to reveal a hint of teeth. He has had quite enough of today. Although he covered his own back by contacting ACC Everett and telling him that Barbara Stein-Collinson had requested his help in tying up some loose ends regarding her brother's death, he'd still received an angry call from Trish Pharaoh when the message had been relayed that her office manager had been sent on an errand for the top brass. 'Say no, you silly sod,' she'd shouted down the line. 'We're in the middle of a murder investigation, for God's sake. This is where you let yourself down, McAvoy. Trying to do too many things for too many people and ending up pissing everybody off.'

She'd only hung up when he gave her something bigger to worry about, and relayed Colin Ray's message about bringing in a suspect.

'Russell Chandler,' he says firmly. 'I understand he's a patient here?'

The receptionist switches off her grin. 'I'm afraid that's confidential.'

McAvoy doesn't speak. Just looks at her for a moment with an expression that could melt a computer screen. 'It's important,' he says eventually, and although he's not sure if the statement is true, discovers that he is starting to believe it.

'House rules,' she says, and there's an air of smugness about her now. Despite the cold wind blowing in through the open doors, McAvoy feels sweat trickling down his neck. He's pretty sure that if he made a big enough fuss, he could gain access to Chandler, but what if they were to complain? What would be his defence? Chandler is not a suspect in any investigation. Not even a witness in any real sense. It's just a bit of background info on a case from another patch. And besides, he wonders, would it be ethical to speak to somebody in a place like this? At a time when they're seeking help to combat their problems? *Oh Christ, Aector, what have you bloody done?*

He steps back from the desk, suddenly unsure of himself.

'Excuse me, did I hear my name?'

McAvoy turns. Standing in the doorway are two men. One is dressed in athletics gear . . . Hooded sweatshirt, zipped up to his chin, woolly hat pulled down tight and jogging trousers tucked into football socks. He's jogging on the spot and the small window of face that peeks out from between the hat and the hoodie is flushed and red. The other man is shorter and almost skeletally thin. He's wearing baggy corduroy trousers, plimsolls, and a padded lumberjack shirt over a V-neck T-shirt. His head is shaven, but the light from the hall reveals that he would be bald on top even without the ministrations of the razor, and his dark goatee beard is flecked with grey. He wears glasses that, even from a distance of some yards, appear filthy with dust and grime.

'Was the gatekeeper here making life difficult?' he asks with a smile and nodding at the receptionist. McAvoy hears a trace of Liverpudlian in his accent. 'She's ferocious, is our Margaret,' he says. 'Isn't that right, sweetie?'

McAvoy turns to look at the receptionist but she's rolled her eyes and turned to her screen and is trying to ignore the exchange. When McAvoy turns back, Chandler has crossed the floor and is holding out his hand.

'Russ Chandler,' he says, and as McAvoy takes his hand in his, he feels like he's closing his palm around a collection of dried twigs.

'Detective Sergeant Aector McAvoy.'

'I know,' says Chandler, grinning warmly. 'I used to do a bit of work in your part of the world. Knew Tony Halthwaite pretty well. Doug Roper, too. All got shushed up, eh?'

McAvoy thinks, *Does everybody bloody know?*

'I'd rather not . . .'

'Don't fret, mate. My lips are sealed. Unless you happen to have a bottle of whisky on you, in which case they'll bloody open.' He looks past McAvoy and grins at the receptionist. 'Just kidding, sweetheart.'

In the doorway, the man in the running gear has upped the pace of his stationary sprinting. His knees are getting higher. He looks like he knows what he's doing.

Chandler notices McAvoy staring and spins back to his companion. 'You just get going, son. Usual route. Keep your arms up. We'll see you by the bench.'

With barely more than a nod, the other man disappears from the doorway. McAvoy hears fast footsteps on the shingle. He looks at Chandler inquisitively.

'Room-mate,' he says, by way of explanation. 'They put us in twos in here so there's somebody there during the night to make sure we don't top ourselves.'

'This your game, is it? You a boxing man?'

'I wrote a book a few years back. Chap from Scunthorpe who'd had something like 200 pro fights. *Diary of a Journeyman* sort of thing. Good read, actually. Got into it then. You like a fight?'

'I boxed a bit at school. Bit more at university. Was hard getting people to get in the ring with me. I've always been the biggest in the gym.'

'I can see that,' smiles Chandler, without malice. 'Anyway, what can I do for you?'

'Is there somewhere we can talk, Mr Chandler? It's regarding Fred Stein.'

Chandler sticks his lower lip out playfully and raises his eyebrows in a show of surprise. 'Fred? I'm not sure . . .'

'It won't take long.'

Chandler nods, seemingly unfazed at the prospect. 'You mind walking and talking? I've promised my young lad I'll time him.'

McAvoy nods gratefully, happy that this is working out.

As they leave the foyer and trot down the stairs into the

darkening air and billowing snow, McAvoy notices his companion is limping on his right leg. Remembers what Caroline
told him. Glances down. Chandler turns and looks up at the
bigger man as they walk. 'Amputated,' he says simply. 'Price
you pay for loving the ciggies and living on bacon. Got a falsie
under these trousers. I'd recommend them to anybody who
goes to Weight Watchers. You just slip your lower leg off and
you've lost half a stone.'

McAvoy isn't sure whether to pat him on the shoulder or
give him an encouraging smile, so just brushes over it. 'Fred
Stein,' he says, as they begin following a neatly tended gravel
path towards a line of evergreens. 'You heard what happened?'

'Did indeed,' he says, with a sigh that becomes a cough. It's
a hacking sound. Unhealthy. 'Poor bugger.'

'Caroline Wills told me that you were the one that managed to get him to talk. Tracked him down. Brokered the deal.'

'Something like that.'

'Was there anything in his manner when you met him that
suggested he was thinking of taking his own life?'

Chandler stops. They're perhaps 500 yards from the
building. He cranes his neck to see if anybody's poking their
head out of the front door, then reaches down and hitches
up his trouser leg. He takes hold of the limb at the knee and
with a swift jerk, snaps off his leg just below the joint.
Absent-mindedly, he reaches inside the false limb and pulls
out a cigarette and lighter. He sparks up, and draws the
smoke deep into his lungs. It seems an almost religious experience. Without saying another word, he leans down and
fastens the leg back in place. He looks up with a grin that

tries to be impish but instead looks strangely gruesome, splitting so unhealthy a face.

'Frowned upon?' asks McAvoy, smiling, despite himself.

'You've got to sign an agreement when you check in,' he says contemptuously. 'No fags. No chocolate. No bloody sugar. All part of the programme, apparently. Can't detox you when you're still putting toxins in yourself.'

'And you don't think perhaps you should listen?'

'Oh, there's no doubt they're right, Sergeant. But that's the thing with addictions. Rather hard to drop.'

'But the money you're spending to be here, surely it's worth trying . . .'

'I'm giving it my best shot,' he says, looking away and blowing out a lungful of smoke. 'I've been in places like this three times before. I come out full of hope and within a day I'm in a boozer, knocking back whisky. I know I'll do it even before I'm out the gates. It's the finality I struggle with. The idea of never having another cig. Never having another drink. What's the bloody point?'

'Your health, surely . . .'

'Who am I staying healthy for? There's just me, mate. No kids. No missus. No adoring fans desperate to sleep with me. Got to pay to publish my own bloody work.' He says the last with a sudden rush of venom, and McAvoy notices the way his jaw locks around the cigarette.

McAvoy quickly runs through in his mind the brief details he had pulled off the internet about this man. He'd found his byline on several features on various special-interest websites and national newspapers, but the majority of hits had come from a Surrey-based publishing house. Russ Chandler had written several self-published books. Some were about the glory days of the fishing industry, others on local history and a couple of tomes on unsolved crimes in various Northern cities. They came with an author profile that revealed Russell Chandler was born in Chester in 1966 and spent some time in the army before becoming a full-time writer. He had worked as an insurance salesman and as office manager for a haulage firm. He had lived in Oxford, East Yorkshire and London, and now made his home in East Anglia. His last book had been published four years earlier, a biography of three of the RAF Bomber Command pilots who had taken part in the raid on Dresden in World War Two. McAvoy had read the extract. He'd been impressed.

'I won't tell,' says McAvoy, watching the writer take a contented drag.

'Thank you,' he replies, making a small, theatrical bow. Then he offers him the packet. 'You smoke?'

'No,' says McAvoy, shaking his head. Then, conversationally: 'My wife does.'

Chandler looks at him with the faintest smirk on his lips. 'You want to take one home for her?'

McAvoy wonders if he's being laughed at. Feels the prickling of temper in his chest.

'No thanks. She's seven months pregnant. Got her down to three a day by way of compromise. One glass of wine . . .' He stops. Looks at the ground.

'She like a drink?'

McAvoy looks up to see Chandler staring at him hard. He tries to dismiss the moment with a wave of his hand, but Chandler is already intrigued.

'The way you said that . . .'

McAvoy shrugs. Figures it can't hurt. 'We've lost babies before now,' he says. 'This will be our fourth attempt at a second child.'

Chandler reaches out. Puts a hand on McAvoy's broad shoulder.

'I'd pray for you, if I believed any of that bollocks. But I don't. So I'll just wish you the best.'

McAvoy finds himself half-smiling. He nods in appreciation, then feels his lips begin to tremble and his eyes fog like glass as he realises he has made Roisin sound as if she were to blame for the children that never were. 'It wasn't the smoking,' he begins defensively. 'And they're just little glasses of wine. She knows her limits . . .'

'I wouldn't know,' says Chandler quietly, and McAvoy wonders if he has just made this interview more difficult for himself than it need be.

'My dad always said willpower was the way,' says McAvoy hurriedly. 'Decide whether you're a smoker or a non-smoker, and just be that. I'm a non-smoker. My wife's a smoker. Just one of those things.'

'Sounds a bright chap.'

'He was. Is.'

'He a cop too?'

'No,' says McAvoy, looking away. 'Crofter. Up near Loch Ewe. Western Highlands to you. His family have farmed the same patch of land for more than one hundred years.'

'Yeah?' Chandler sounds interested. 'I've read about them, crofters. Hard life, from what I've heard.'

'Oh aye,' says McAvoy, now torn between talking more

about his childhood, of testing the edges of that damp scab, and getting back to Fred Stein. 'Dying way of life, too.'

'So I hear. All the crofts being turned into tourist lodges nowadays, from what I read in *The Times*. Your dad not fancy that?'

'He'd rather bite his own arms off,' says McAvoy, more to himself than to his companion. 'He and my brother work the land.'

'Not you, though?' Chandler's voice is subtle. Soft. Inviting.

'I gave it ten years,' he says. 'Then went to live with my mother. City life. Or at least, as much of a city life as you can get in Inverness. Gave that a year. Then off to boarding school, paid for by my stepdad. Bit of a culture shock. University in Edinburgh. Three years of a five-year degree. Then this. Policeman. Yorkshire. Hull. Husband and father. I wouldn't be any use to my dad up there now. Don't think I ever really was.'

'Shame,' says Chandler, and seems to mean it.

McAvoy nods. Wishes he were capable of thinking about his old life, his old family, with anything other than sadness.

They stand in silence for a moment, until they remember what has brought them together.

'So?'

'Yeah, Fred. Was big news in his day. Before my time, of course. Was just a baby when it happened. But I did a bit of work in Hull and it was impossible not to hear about the Black Winter. Anyways, I heard the story about Fred Stein years ago. The *Yorkshire Post* used to have an office on Ferensway and they had framed front pages on the wall. I was in there one day, having a can of ale with an old boy from the

*Sun* who used to share an office with them, and I started reading this front page from the sixties. All about this one bloke who survived. Made it to the lifeboats with two of his crewmates and drifted to some remote bloody hell-hole in Iceland. Tramped cross-country until some local farmer found him. Media frenzy, there was, when it turned out he was alive. Everybody had given him up for dead, see? I just logged the info in the back of my brain. It's getting cramped back there, like.'

'Did you know him personally at this point?'

'No, no. He was just a story. I had it in my mind that one day I might try and get him to talk about it. There might be a book in it. That's what I do, see? I publish at least a book a year. You can buy them in the bookshops under local interest or get them from the publishing house website. Sell pretty well, considering. Fred seemed ideal, but I never really got round to it.'

'Until?'

'Well, that Caroline, from Wagtail. Met her during the *Dunbar* inquiry. Nice girl, if a bit fond of herself. Didn't know a damn thing about the fishing industry and was willing to pay for background. That's my line. Did her chapter and verse on the history of the local fleet; the characters, the names. Theories, contacts. She was made up with it. That's when Fred Stein came back into my mind. I told her about it, thought no more, and then last year she got back in touch and said she thought there could be a documentary in it.'

They've reached the tree line now and the darkness suddenly becomes harder to penetrate. Chandler points to a wrought-iron bench and they both take a seat. McAvoy is hunched up inside his coat but the wind is still bitter on the few inches of exposed skin. He wonders how Chandler, just skin and bone in a shirt and vest, can stand it. He seems so fragile, and there's a pestilence about him, a suggestion that even without cigarettes, his breath would be a plume of grey smoke.

'So where do you start with something like that? Tracking him down?'

'It's not difficult,' he says dismissively. 'Start with a last known address and just start working the phones and writing letters. Fishing community's a small one with a long memory. Found him in Southampton within a week. Put the phone down on me the first three times, so wrote him a nice letter with my details and he got in touch. Gave him the spiel. Chance to close that chapter in his life. To honour his crew-mates. Say goodbye. Tell his side of the story. I really don't think he was that interested, to be honest, but when I men-tioned what they were willing to pay, he changed his tune. I'm not saying he was mercenary or anything. There's nothing wrong with greed. He wanted a few quid in his old age, that was all.'

'And you met in person?'

'Just the once. Caroline was in the US and she needed the deal signed, sealed and delivered. I went down there on expenses and we had a few beers down his local. Nice old boy, really. Would have made a better book than a TV programme but my pockets aren't deep enough. That's the way of the world now. You try getting a book deal and you'll see nobody gives a damn. It's all celebrity biographies and misery fucking memoirs.'

The venom is back in Chandler's voice. McAvoy notices that he has started rooting about beneath the bench with his left hand, and he suddenly pulls out a bottle of single malt.

'Good lad,' he says, as he unplugs the bottle and takes a giant swig.

McAvoy watches Chandler in the gathering gloom, wide-eyed and strangely impressed. Sees the smaller man's silhouette change shape as the bottle tips up and stays there at the end of a long, bony arm.

'Website said it costs five thousand a week to stay here,' says McAvoy, shaking his head. 'Money well spent, eh?'

'I don't know if I get more pleasure from the drink, or from being naughty,' he says, smiling.

'I don't suppose you just found that bottle by accident?'

'My young room-mate,' he laughs. 'He'll do anything for me.'

'I'll bloody bet.'

They sit for another twenty minutes. The afternoon dusk turns midnight black. The snow lays half-heartedly on the wet gravel, then disappears into nothingness. They talk about Hull. McAvoy shivers and puts his hands in his pockets.

Eventually, the conversation returns to Stein.

'You haven't asked why this is a Hull CID matter,' says McAvoy as he watches Chandler finish off the last of the whisky and notes that he hasn't been offered a drop.

'His sister's got a husband on the Police Authority,' Chandler says with a wave of his hand. 'I'd imagine you're doing somebody a favour.'

McAvoy looks at his feet, wishing he were as shrewd or well-informed as an alcoholic hack.

'So what do I tell her?' he asks.

'Tell her that Fred was a good bloke. A nice chap full of stories. That he didn't mind talking about what happened to him when he had a pint in his hand, and that he was shit-scared of going on that bloody great cargo ship with a TV crew who wanted to make him dance like a monkey.'

The irritation is there again. The bitterness. It might almost be called rage.

'You don't seem to have a great deal of time for TV journalism.'

'Get that, did you?' Chandler spits. Lights his final cigarette. 'Vultures with cheque books.'

'You've worked for them, though,' points out McAvoy, as diplomatically as he dares.

'What fucking choice have I got? I was born with one bloody talent, son. I can write. Two, if you count getting people to talk. I should be on every bloody bookshelf in the land. But I'm not. I've got a bedsit in East Anglia and even if I still had my licence, I couldn't afford a car. I use what little royalties I get from one book to pay for the publishing run on the next.'

'Mr Chandler, I—'

'No, son, you've hit the nail on the head. I'm a fucking failure as a writer. I've had more rejection letters from publishers than I can fucking stomach. But put Caroline Wills in front of the camera and put a fat cheque in an old boy's hand and you get TV bloody gold. My graft. My idea!'

McAvoy waves his hands, urging Chandler to slow down.

'Your idea? I though Miss Wills contacted you . . .'

Chandler dismisses him with an angry grunt. 'I have a mil-lion bloody ideas. I've got a notebook full of them. If I come up with enough outlines, maybe one day a publishing house will like one of them. Fred was in there. An idea I had. A book about people who survived. The ones that got away. The indi-viduals who escaped when nobody else got out alive. I hadn't even started looking for him, nor for any of the others, by the time the rejection letters hit the doormat. That's my life, son. That's why I'm here. That's why I'm fucking here!'

Chandler is standing now. In the darkness, McAvoy can see the glowing tip of his cigarette moving from side to side, up and down, rolling around his mouth as if wedged in the lips of a cow chewing grass.

'Mr Chandler, if you would just calm down a moment . . .'

Chandler extinguishes his cigarette on the palm of his hand. He places the stub in his pocket. 'Are we done?'

McAvoy, red-faced, bewildered, angry and confused, doesn't know what to say. He just nods. Dismisses Chandler by turning his away and sits back down on the bench. He listens to his footsteps limp away. His brain hurts. His mind is a fog of good intentions, guilt and an intuition he doesn't fully trust.

*Why did I come here?* he asks himself. *What have I bloody learned?*

As he walks back to his car, he feels a hundred years old. He wants to upload his mind into the database and delete the bits that aren't important. Look for connections. See what it is that his subconscious is telling him.

He closes the door on the swirling, angry snow. Closes his eyes.

Switches on his mobile phone.

Listens to his messages.

The bollocking from Pharaoh.

The instruction to call Helen Tremberg as soon as he can.

# CHAPTER 12

McAvoy plays with the car radio.

6.58 p.m. Two minutes to the next news bulletin.

Outside lane on the A15, downhill to approaching the harp strings and tangled metal of the Humber Bridge. It was an impressive sight the first few times he'd driven across this mile and a half of rigid tarmac and pristine steel that stitches Yorkshire to Lincolnshire, but the novelty has worn off, and he simply resents the £3 it costs for the privilege of not having to drive through Goole.

He feels the car swerve as the road becomes the bridge. Feels the buffeting of the ferocious wind that whips down the estuary as if it's in a rush to get inland.

Slows down, so he can listen to the bulletin in full before he reaches the kiosk and has to pay his fare.

*Good evening. Members of Humberside Fire and Rescue Service are attending a blaze at a recently opened specialist burns unit at Hull Royal Infirmary. The fire was reported shortly after 6 p.m. and is thought to have been confined to just one room occupied by a single male patient. His condition is said to be critical. In other news, the detective leading the murder enquiry following the death of a teenage girl at Hull's Holy Trinity Church has denied reports that a city man has been arrested in connection with the investigation. Acting Detective Superintendent Patricia Pharaoh told reporters that no arrests have been made, and that the man in question was merely assisting with inquiries. She repeated earlier calls for witnesses to the horrific stabbing to come forward . . .*

'Fuck,' says McAvoy, and, without giving a damn about who sees, reaches for his phone. Pulls over on the inside lane of the bridge and switches on his hazard lights. Hears the blare of horns as drivers of the vehicles behind him let him know he's a wanker.

Helen Tremberg answers on the third ring.

'Speak of the devil,' she says, and there's not much humour in her voice.

'Really?' he asks, and winces.

'You bet. Me and Ben are having a little wager as to who's going to kill you first. Pharaoh, Colin Ray, or ACC Everett.'

'Everett? Why?'

'Wouldn't like to say. Just came stomping into the incident room about tea time and asked where you were. Didn't look happy. Even less so when one of the support staff asked him who he was.'

'Christ!'

'Indeed. Where have you been?'

'Long story. It doesn't matter. I just heard the headlines on Humberside . . .'

'Yeah, Colin Ray's really fucked up. Sorry, Sarge, I mean . . .'

'It doesn't matter,' he says, and means it.

'This bloke him and Shaz brought in. All just a hunch.

Ray's gut feeling. I don't know what happened when they got him in the interview room but he came out of there with his nose bleeding and puke on his shirt. That's according to the desk sergeant, any road. Apparently Pharaoh turned up and all bloody hell broke loose. The bloke's still in the cells but they don't seem to know what to do with him.'

McAvoy feels his heart racing. Sees the headlines. Wonders how much of this almighty fuck-up can be attributed to him buggering off in the middle of the day to follow up on a feeling.

'And the fire? At Hull Royal?'

'We're here now,' says Tremberg. 'It was out almost as soon as it started but the second the fire crews ventilated the room and the smoke cleared, we got the call.'

'Why us? I mean, why you?'

'Deliberately started, no question. Top brass reckon there's no point having a serious crimes unit and then using the whole team on one case. Me and Ben were knocking off when the city DCS phoned and asked us to attend personally.'

McAvoy screws his face up. Feels the car rock as a lorry thunders by, paying no heed to the weather warnings.

'But one little fire? Sure, it's in the new unit but a uniform could clear it up with half a dozen witness statements and the CCTV . . .'

'Sarge?' Helen Tremberg sounds confused.

'Why use us? For a fire?'

Realisation dawns. 'Didn't they say on the radio? It's a fatal, sir. A murder. The man from the house fire on Orchard Park last night. Somebody broke into his room and finished the job.'

*

'I don't know where to start,' says Pharaoh, in a voice that sounds like steam escaping from a high-pressure pipe. 'You take more looking after than one of my kids.'

'I'm sorry, ma'am.'

'Will you please cut out that "ma'am" bollocks, McAvoy. It makes me feel like Juliet fucking Bravo.'

McAvoy nods. Lets her outstare him. Turns away.

They're standing in the corridor outside the incident room at Queen's Gardens. The central heating system has decided to make up for past mistakes by altering its modus operandi. The individual rooms are now as cold as the grave, while the hallways are warmer than hell.

'Do you know the kind of day I've had?'

McAvoy nods again.

It's 9.41 p.m. Twelve hours since they stood in this same spot and she told him he was her office manager. Told him to keep an eye on things while she went out to catch a killer.

And now they're back. Each having had a day they'd rather forget; their minds overflowing with information and none of it much good.

Like a naughty schoolboy, McAvoy fixes his gaze on something other than her angry eyes. Takes a keen interest in the door to the incident room. Somebody had pinned a sign saying 'Pharaoh's Palace' on the door earlier today, but it has been torn by the edge of a gunmetal-grey filing cabinet, and now lies in two neat halves by the skirting board. He can't help but wonder if it's a sign in itself.

'If I ask you to give me the bare bones on this, you'll listen to me, won't you? You won't get the wrong end of the stick and spend the next hour giving me a headache?' She suddenly sounds more weary than cross.

'Yes, ma'am. Sorry. Yes.'

So he tells her. Tells her why he left the incident room. Where he's been. What he's discovered. Tells her about Fred Stein and his important sister. Keeps it brief and doesn't look at her properly until he's finished. It takes about three minutes, and sounds so lame and fruitless that he almost runs out of energy before the end.

'That's it?' she asks, although it's a genuine query rather than an attack.

'Yes.'

She purses her lips and breathes out. 'Interesting,' she mutters, and raises her eyebrows. Her face has returned to a more natural colouring.

'You think so?'

'Come with me.'

She turns and leads him to the end of the corridor. Pushes open an office door, seemingly at random, and holds it open as he steps inside.

At a desk, lit by a green reading lamp, a man of around sixty is sitting with his feet up; a crystal glass tumbler full of whisky in one palm and a battered notebook in the other.

'Hi,' says McAvoy, and it comes out as bewildered and hapless as he feels.

'Tom's letting me share his excuse for an office until we get back to Priory,' says Pharaoh, pushing the door closed behind him. He feels her body smear against him as she angles herself into the only space not currently occupied by equipment.

McAvoy stands, unsure of himself, in the centre of the tiny room. It's not much bigger then a broom cupboard. The desk stands lengthways at the far end, home to a monitor, keyboard, hard drive and an assortment of typed and handwritten paperwork, all bathed in the eerie green light, which makes Tom Spink, in his white collarless shirt and neat white hair, seem oddly angelic.

'Now then, son,' says Tom, looking up and clearly pleased to see them. 'Welcome to my humble abode.'

'Tell Tom what you just told me,' says Pharaoh, nodding. 'About what Everett asked you to do.'

McAvoy tells the man in the granddad shirt, cardigan and soft cords all about what he has been doing these past few days. Watches unspoken signals flash in his eyes and tries to read meaning in the glances the older man throws at Pharaoh.

'What do you reckon?' asks Pharaoh, when McAvoy finishes.

'It's interesting,' says Spink, nodding and folding his lower lip back over his bottom teeth. He's addressing Pharaoh, and not looking at McAvoy. 'Intriguing, anyway. This is what we do, after all. I can see why the boy would be interested.'

'Sir, I—'

'It's Tom, son,' says Spink, turning to him. 'I'm retired.'

'Tom used to be my boss,' says Pharaoh, suddenly realising that all this must seem quite peculiar to her sergeant. 'Back in the good old days. He's all sorts of things now. Runs a little B and B on the coast. Does a bit of work for a private investigator, when he feels like he might be in danger of getting to heaven. And because he's got a nice turn of phrase and knows the funny handshakes, he's got himself a commission writing a history of Humberside Police for the bigwigs, which means I can keep him where I can see him, and he can tell me all about the days when a truncheon was designed for ease of insertion.'

'Good times,' he says, smiling. 'Nefertiti here was always hard as nails. Never took any crap from an old lech like me.'

'Nefertiti?' McAvoy can't help but repeat.

'Egyptian queen,' says Spink, with a sigh. 'Pharaoh? Get it? Honestly, and she tells me you're one of the bright ones.'

'I know—'

'That's what I thought until you buggered off,' says Pharaoh, pointedly. 'I was calling you a few names earlier on, my boy. Thought I'd pegged you wrong. Thought you were being the political animal some of the lads and ladies have got you pegged as. Sucking up to the ACC. Leaving us to do the real work. Seems I was right in the first place. ACC's more pissed off with you than I am.'

'Why?'

'Had a call from some bigwig on the Police Authority. Apparently his wife's in a right state. Some big Scottish lump has got her thinking her brother might have been murdered.'

McAvoy wants to cry. 'I never—'

'That's life, sunbeam. Get used to it. Nice to see I haven't lost it. I can still pick "natural police".'

'Natural police?'

'Get a feeling and follow it through. Listen to the little voice inside themselves and damn the consequences.'

Despite the chill in the office, McAvoy's face flushes scarlet. He realises he's being praised and wonders what the penance will be.

'Thank you.'

Spink and Pharaoh both laugh. 'It's not an asset, matey. It's a bloody curse. It means you're going to piss people off for the next thirty years and there's a better than average chance you'll lock up quite a few of the wrong people. But you'll catch some wrong 'uns, too.'

McAvoy feels his legs growing weak. He hasn't eaten since breakfast and feels suddenly empty and vulnerable. Perhaps it shows in his face, as Pharaoh looks at him with suddenly more affectionate eyes.

'This Stein case,' she says. 'You think it's important?'

'It feels wrong,' he replies. 'I can't explain it, really. I know today was a dead end with Chandler, but I just can't see this old boy planning all this. I mean, to take your own life is one thing, but to plan it down to such elaborate detail?'

Spink and Pharaoh exchange another glance. Spink gives the slightest of nods, as if he has been asked a question.

'Stick with it, then,' says Pharaoh, reaching down between her legs and pulling a half-full bottle of whisky from the drawer. She tops up the glass and takes a drink. 'I'll trust you. Like you say, it might be nothing, and the Daphne case takes priority. I won't stop you looking into something you believe is wrong but just don't dick me about. I've got enough of that with Colin bloody Ray.'

McAvoy breathes a sigh of relief. He's not sure that he actually asked for permission to keep looking into the Stein case, but he's pleased that it hasn't been denied.

'What's the situation with all that, ma'am?'

She laughs, but it's not a happy sound. 'Neville the sodding Racist,' she says, and needs a drink before she can compose her features into anything other than a snarl. 'Colin thinks he's natural police. Thinks his gut is what's leading him. But it's not. It's a load of prejudice and arrogance wrapped up in this unshakeable self-belief. According to Colin and his mini-she, this bloody old fool decided to off the first black person he took a dislike to and pin it on some tribal feud. The daft thing is, even though it sounds like nonsense, he's got some good arguments. Neville can't account for his whereabouts at the time of the attack. He's got a history of violence. He's spent time in the army so he's not going to be a slouch phys-ically. And we've seen his temper first hand. Him and Colin had a right set-to in the interview room. Was almost another bloody murder. We've got him locked up until I decide what to do with him. Charged him with assaulting a police officer, so at least he's not an official murder suspect, but when I had to go and explain where we're at to the top brass, I got the distinct impression they wouldn't be averse to us sticking it on Neville.'

McAvoy's face says it all.

'I know, son,' says Tom Spink. 'I know.'

As McAvoy gulps painfully on his dry throat, there's a faint knock at the door. Logistically, he wonders if there's actually room in here to open it.

'Get that, Hector,' says Pharaoh wearily.

McAvoy turns the handle and pulls open the door, stepping back into the room and trying not to register the faint con-nection that his backside makes with Pharaoh's stockinged knee.

Helen Tremberg stands there, looking surprised to see him. 'Sarge?'

'He's just the bouncer,' comes Pharaoh's voice from behind him, and McAvoy hears her stepping down from the desk. She appears at his side, her warm body pressed fully against his. Her perfume and whisky breath make the hairs on the back of his neck stand on end.

'Boss,' Tremberg says, relieved. 'The ID's come back on the body at the hospital.'

'That was quick,' says Pharaoh.

'Called in a favour, boss. Bloke in forensics doesn't take much sweet-talking to rush through a quick fingerprint and DNA sample. Still waiting for dental records, but the ID makes sense.'

'Well?'

'Trevor Jefferson,' says Tremberg. 'Thirty-five. Last known address was a flat on Holderness Road. Bedsit, really. Over the bookie's.'

'So how did he end up in the house on Orchard Park?' Pharaoh asks, and in her voice McAvoy fancies he hears the faint hope that there will be an easy answer.

'That's the weird bit,' says Tremberg. 'He used to live on Orchard Park. Wife, two kids and a stepson. Just a stone's throw from where he was found.'

McAvoy feels a constriction in his chest. It is almost as if he knows what Tremberg is about to say.

'So what, he got pissed and forgot where he was? Thought it was still 2003? Let himself in at the first house that looked habitable, fell asleep on the sofa with a fag in his mouth and cooked himself. Somebody heard about it, thought it was a good way to settle some old feud, and finished the job off in hospital?' The optimism in Pharaoh's voice sounds forced.

'I haven't got to the weird bit,' says Tremberg, pulling a face.

'Go on,' says Pharaoh with a sigh.

'The reason he left Orchard Park was because his house burned down. His wife and kids in it. He was the only one who got out alive. The Fire Service thought it was arson, though nobody ever got caught.'

McAvoy looks at the floor as Trish Pharaoh stares hard at the side of his face. Somehow, he gets the impression she feels this is his fault.

'McAvoy?' Her tone of voice demands explanation.

'I don't know, ma'am.'

She turns to Spink. He raises his hands in a shrug, simply relieved that he's not really involved. That he's only in Hull to write a book and that soon he'll be able to get the fuck out of here.

'Stein will have to wait,' she says eventually. 'McAvoy, you and Tremberg have got this. I want to know chapter and verse on those fires. On the suspects. On this victim. The home-owners. Helen, get McAvoy up to speed on what you know and get out to Orchard Park.'

Tremberg looks crestfallen. McAvoy realises she thinks she's being taken off the Daphne Cotton case. Perhaps she is.

'Boss, I'm swamped with the Cotton case already . . .'

'I know, Helen,' says Pharaoh, reaching around McAvoy to give her a squeeze on the arm. 'But I need somebody I can trust. Keep an eye on this lump, will you?'

Tremberg lets herself be pacified and nods. Manages a toothless smile. It's at Pharaoh, nobody else. She won't look at McAvoy. He wonders if she's angry with him, or just too disappointed to be civil.

'Right,' says Pharaoh, looking at her watch. 'It's gone ten, which means my kids will either be putting themselves to bed, or they'll have taken over the neighbourhood and young Ruby has installed herself as queen. I know which scenario my money's on.'

McAvoy takes the hint. Steps out of the office with an almost imperceptible nod and feels the heat of the hallway add another veneer of colour to his glowing cheeks. The door closes behind him, and through the wood he simply hears Pharaoh say 'fucking hell'.

'The coffee shop on the corner of Goddard,' says Tremberg, over her shoulder as she walks back down the corridor. 'Seven thirty a.m. We'll start knocking on doors while they're still snoring.'

McAvoy watches her depart.

Stands still, unsure which of the many emotions swirling in his gut to focus on.

Wonders if it's wrong to be excited.

And sinks into a sensation of delight that tonight, he'll be home in time to make love to his wife, and tell her that today, somehow, he did something important. That he is natural police. And that deep inside, a little voice is telling him that all this is connected, and the only man who can join the dots is her husband.

# CHAPTER 13

'They haven't released him yet,' says Tremberg, by way of greeting.

Her hair is damp, her face pale, and there are dark circles under her eyes.

'Neville the Racist,' she adds, in a voice still half-asleep. 'Duty solicitor's going bloody mental.'

She begins to take off her waterproof, and then changes her mind. Shrugs herself back into it and sits down on one of the padded, plastic-backed chairs that face the Formica-topped table. 'You mind? I only got out the shower twenty minutes ago. Haven't had a drink yet.'

She reaches across and wraps her hand around the large chipped mug of builder's tea that stands, half-empty, in front of McAvoy. Raises it to her lips and takes a loud gulp. Pulls a face. 'Sweet enough for you?' she asks, and her mood is far friendlier than last night.

They are the only two customers in the Pigeon Pie Café, a white-painted, glass-fronted building on the corner of Goddard Avenue. It's a proper greasy spoon, complete with laminated menus and ketchup dispensers in the shape of tomatoes. The dish of the day tends to be sausage, bacon or both, and the place is a Mecca for anybody who thinks that culinary evolution peaked with the combination of brown sauce and baked beans.

McAvoy would have loved nothing more than to order a sausage and fried-egg sandwich when he walked through the door ten minutes ago, but Roisin had knocked him up a breakfast of scrambled egg and smoked salmon on home-made rye bread before he left the house, and he knows how she would pout if she knew it had barely touched the sides of his appetite. He'd settled for tea.

'You eating?' he asks.

'Tempting,' she says, mulling it over. 'They do a belly-buster special, you know. If you manage to eat it all you get it free. Nobody's managed it yet.'

'You ever had a go?'

'What are you saying, Sarge?' She looks indignant, but then breaks into a smile to let him know she's joking. 'Sorry if I was a cow last night,' she says, taking another slurp of tea. 'Had just got my teeth into the Daphne Cotton murder and then suddenly I'm given some dead drunk on Orchard Park.'

'I understand,' says McAvoy, nodding. He feels bad that Tremberg has been lumbered with this, and worse because of all the things he has to worry about, his fear at having to make conversation with a female colleague for the day is the one uppermost in his mind.

'Two slices of toast, please,' shouts Tremberg at the big-boned woman in a blue overall working the counter. 'Butter, not low-fat spread.'

'A woman after my own heart,' says McAvoy. 'My dad used to say margarine had almost the same chemical qualities as plastic. I don't know if that's true, but it rather put me off. Like that whole thing about peanuts on the bar being full of blokes' wee-wee. Nasty.'

Tremberg pulls a face. 'Wee-wee?' she asks, laughing.

McAvoy feels the beginning of a blush and is grateful when Tremberg's toast arrives. 'Sorry. Comes from having a young son.'

'He's a handsome boy, your Fin,' says Tremberg, with her mouth full. 'Proud of you, too. Wasn't scared, y'know. He knew something bad had happened in the church and he saw you go down, but he knew you'd be getting up again. He said you'd get whoever did it.'

McAvoy has to look away to hide the huge grin that splits his face. 'That's his mother's doing,' he says, smothering his words with a big hand as he supports his head on his palm. 'Got him thinking I'm indestructible. Some kind of superhero.'

'Better than him thinking you're a knob,' she says matter-of-factly. 'That's what most kids think of their parents.'

'I don't.'

'You're weird, Sarge. Everybody knows that.'

They sit in silence for a while. McAvoy finishes the tea and watches Tremberg lick butter from her fingers. They're unmanicured and unadorned with any jewellery. They seem somehow naked when compared to his wife's, which are sparkling and dainty.

'You are, anyway,' she says finally, picking at her teeth with a finger.

'What?'

'Indestructible. Everybody knows that.'

'What do you mean?'

'Last year's palaver,' she says, raising her eyes and sitting forward in her chair. She appears to be coming to life in front of him. The tea and toast have given her some kind of sugar rush and she's suddenly full of energy. 'When you got, y'know . . .'

'What?'

'You were stabbed, weren't you? That's what everybody says.' If she thinks it's a sensitive subject that shouldn't be approached without extreme care, she does not betray the fact in her manner.

'Slashed, actually,' he says softly. 'A hacking motion. Overhand right.'

Tremberg lets out a deep breath. Feels compelled to say 'fuck'. She screws her face up in thought. 'Like Daphne?'

McAvoy nods. The thought has occurred to him too, though it is significant only to him. He knows that before her heart stopped beating, she will have felt pain. That the sensation is strangely cold. That there is a moment of dull agony, and then mere confusion. That it's a horrible thing to endure.

Tremberg cocks her head, waiting for more. Nothing is forthcoming. 'Sarge?' she prompts.

'What?'

She throws her hands up in frustration. 'You're not much of a bloody conversationalist.'

He looks at his watch. It's taken her eight minutes to find fault with his company. 'Has it occurred to you that it's a conversation I don't want to have?'

Tremberg considers this. 'Yeah.' Then she gives him an impish grin. 'Just wanted to be the one who got you to crack.'

He looks puzzled; his eyebrows almost meeting in the middle.

'Don't worry,' she says, noting his expression. 'There's no cash riding on it. Just professional pride. How are we supposed to get suspects to fess up when we can't even get one of our own to admit what happened to him?'

'People wonder?'

'Course they do. Everybody likes a mystery man, but they'd rather solve the mystery.'

'Mystery man?'

'Come on, Sarge. Big bugger like you, tiny, gorgeous little wife who cooks you gourmet packed lunches; son who thinks you're Spiderman. Then there's the little matter of Doug Roper and all that fuss last year that saw CID scattered to the four winds and you sent to some fancy private hospital in Scotland for a knife wound? You think nobody's interested in chapter and verse?'

McAvoy considers it, as if for the first time. 'Nobody's ever asked me,' he says weakly. 'Anyway, I think I like being mysterious.'

'You've got it down to a fine art,' laughs Tremberg.

'My wife will be delighted. I think she sees me as some sort of rebel, out there on the mean streets, righting wrongs, though she knows I've spent the past ten months doing nothing more than designing databases and running errands. I haven't got her thinking I'm some sort of one-man force for good.'

'She just thinks that way on her own?'

McAvoy looks into her eyes and tries to decide if she's taking the piss or complimenting him on being loved properly. He wonders if she's in a relationship herself. Whether she's had her heart broken. Where she lives, what she thinks and why she became a police officer. It occurs to him he knows nothing about her. About any of them.

'She was young when we got together,' he confides, and feels the blush spread to the back of his neck. 'And I helped her with some problems. She makes up her own mind.'

They sit in silence for a moment, and McAvoy congratulates himself on biting his tongue. For not taking an opportunity to unload his neuroses by telling his colleague that not a moment goes by when he doesn't worry that his young wife married him out of gratitude, and that some day the novelty will wear off.

'Problems?' asks Tremberg, intrigued again.

'She's from a travelling family,' says McAvoy, looking away. He's far from ashamed about the admission and knows that Roisin would not mind, but he feels uncomfortable talking about any aspect of his personal life and finds it easier not to meet her eyes.

'Gypsies?' says Tremberg, surprised.

'If you like,' says McAvoy. 'Prefers it to Pikey, any road.'

'So what happened?'

'It was a long time ago. I was barely out of training.' He stops. Can't seem to find the right words.

'Where?' she asks, helping him along as if it's an interview situation.

'Cumbria Constabulary. Borders.'

'And?'

'Group of travellers turned up in this farmer's field on the road to Brampton,' he says, sighing. Reconciling himself to the fact he will have to share.

'Popular?'

'Nice little town. Plenty of Tory voters and blue rinsers who didn't take kindly to it. Sergeant and me went out to have a chat with them. Told them there was a designated site on the outskirts of Carlisle. Anyway, they said they'd be gone before the day was out. Nice enough bunch. Maybe a dozen caravans. Kids everywhere. Roisin must have been there, but I didn't see her.'

Tremberg looks at him expectantly. 'Love at first sight, was it?' she asks, trying to keep things light.

'She was a child.'

'I'm kidding, Sarge. Jesus.' Tremberg looks pissed off. Shrugs, as if this is too much effort, but McAvoy has already started talking. More freely now. Suddenly desperate to get the words out.

'They didn't go,' he says, staring out of the window. 'More travellers turned up. Bad lot. So the landowner went down there to ask them why they hadn't moved on. He was attacked. Hurt enough to upset some of his staff. They went looking for a spot of revenge. Found Roisin and her sister walking back from the shops.'

McAvoy pauses. Tremberg notices him pick up the salt cellar and grip it hard. Watches his knuckles grow white.

'If I wasn't such a bloody idiot, I don't know what would have happened,' he says, his jaw tight.

'What?'

'I'd dropped my bloody pocketbook at the camp,' he says

apologetically. 'Sergeant sent me back to the camp on my own. Got myself lost. Found myself on this little country road a couple of miles from the camp. Pulled into a gap in the hedge to do a U-turn and get myself back in the right direction. There was an old outbuilding there. Holes in the roof. Looked like there'd been a fire a while before. Anyways, there were two cars parked up outside it. It didn't look right. There was no reason to be there. I don't know what I felt. Just some sensation that something bad was happening. So I killed the engine, and that's when I heard the screams.'

'Jesus,' says Tremberg, half wishing she'd never asked.

'I should have called for back-up,' says McAvoy, rolling the salt cellar between his palms. 'But I knew that whatever was happening in there couldn't go on a second longer. I didn't think. Got out the car and ran into the place. Caught them at it. These farmer boys, whooping and hollering and having their fun.'

'Jesus,' says Tremberg again.

'I lost my temper,' says McAvoy, staring at the backs of his hands.

Tremberg waits for more, and nothing comes. McAvoy is motionless in his seat; his usually red face now a deathly grey. She wonders if he's ever talked about this before. Wonders what he did to them, this big, barrel-chested, soft-spoken man with the scarred face and the unruly hair and a love for his wife that makes her feel almost ashamed to have ever laughed when one of her colleagues cracked a joke at his expense.

She looks down at her plate and decides there is absolutely nothing left to eat on it.

Decides, too, that whatever McAvoy did in that shed, she will never judge him for it as harshly as he appears to judge himself.

She lets out a breath. Beats a little rhythm on the table top. Tries to get them both into gear.

'Shall we make a move?'

McAvoy nods. Begins to stand. For an instant, their eyes meet. And for the briefest of moments she fancies she sees flames dancing on his pupils; a burning building, burning cars.

The double-glazed front door is already swinging open by the time McAvoy and Tremberg find themselves walking up the neat path to number 58. After spending the past hour being told to fuck off in a variety of colourful ways, and with McAvoy's face still crimson from being called 'Hoss' by the naked fat woman who threw open the upstairs window at the house that had made the original 999 call, neither detective is sure whether the opening of a front door is a sign of welcome or a prelude to the emergence of a shotgun.

'About yonder, is it?'

The man on the front step is in his mid-sixties and bald as a bowling ball. He's short but wiry, and his Merchant Navy tie is fastened immaculately at the neck of a check shirt tucked into polyester trousers with creases so sharp they could be used to slice meat at a deli counter. He stands with a straight back, and although he's accessorised the outfit with the old-man twinset of cardigan and slippers, there is something about him that commands respect. Although he's standing in the doorway of a two-bedroomed terraced house on an abandoned street on the city's worst estate, his manner puts McAvoy in mind of a country laird, opening the great double doors of a stately home.

'Jack Raycroft,' he says, offering McAvoy a liver-spotted but firm hand. He gives Helen Tremberg the same courtesy and then nods again. 'Bad business,' he says. His accent is local.

'It is that,' says McAvoy, after they've gone through the business of showing identification and introducing themselves.

'Don't know why it had to be that one,' says Raycroft with a sigh. 'Enough empty houses round here. Why pick one that somebody's taken a bit of pride in, eh? It's like pride's the crime.'

The three of them stare at the house across the tiny street. There are few signs that up until two days ago, it had been a treasured home. It is now every bit as derelict and broken as its neighbours. The front wall is smoke-blackened, and the chipboard nailed over the broken front window has already been daubed with graffiti, a canvas of obscene drawings and spray-painted tags.

'You've spoken to the uniformed officers, I understand?'

'Yeah, yeah. Not that there was much to tell. My pal Warren was in hospital with a spot of angina. Joyce, his missus, was with their lass out in one of the villages. We were inside watching some costume thing on BBC. We heard the sirens about the same time we saw the flames. Not that we pay much attention to the sirens. You hear them all day and night round here. But they were definitely heading our way. I looked out of the window to see what was going on and there was smoke pouring out the front door opposite. Even with the smoke it was the open door that struck me first. It's funny how your mind works, isn't it? You just never see an open door around here. Least of all over there. They've been here almost as long as we have. Know better.'

Tremberg reaches into the pocket of her waterproof and pulls out a sheaf of typed papers that she had printed off before leaving the office last night. It's a basic breakdown of the investigation so far, and is woefully short. 'The lock was picked,' says Tremberg, nodding, as if to congratulate herself on remembering the fact. 'Professional job, too.'

'Must have been,' says Raycroft. 'Double glazed job like that. Bought it with security in mind.'

From inside the house comes a woman's voice. 'Is it more police, Jack?'

He rolls his eyes at the two officers, who return his slight smile. 'The wife,' he says. 'Taken it badly.'

'I'll bet,' says McAvoy, nodding.

'I'd invite you in but I think she'd get upset.'

'We're fine,' says McAvoy, content to loiter on the doorstep. From the floral print on the walls of the small section of hallway he can see behind Raycroft, he imagines the living room will be a chaotic fusion of antimacassars and lace, grandchildren and wall-mounted flying ducks, and he knows instinctively that seeing all that will make him sad. He has a great admiration for people who refuse to be intimidated and refuse to move on when all common sense dictates that they should cut their losses and sell, but deep down, he knows their stand is a futile one. That when they die, the house will be flogged to whatever private company decides to clear the land and build flats for asylum seekers.

'Odd business, isn't it? Leaving the photographs and all that?'

McAvoy finds himself nodding politely, then realises he's no clue what the man is talking about. 'I'm sorry, sir?'

'I told the uniformed chap who came yesterday. On the front lawn of the house, there was a big holdall full of all Warren and Joyce's photographs. They kept them on the mantelpiece. I don't know if the victim was on the rob and chucked the stuff, then went in for a kip, but at least that's one good thing out of all this – none of their photos were ruined.'

McAvoy looks at Tremberg, who shrugs. This is news to her too.

'Where are the photos now?'

'I've got them,' says Raycroft, matter-of-factly. 'Picked them up off the lawn, still in the bag. I'll give them to the daughter when she comes round. That's OK, isn't it?'

McAvoy turns away. Looks back at the burned-out house. Tries to work out what it might mean. Why somebody would go to the trouble of saving the family pictures before setting fire to a house with a human being on the sofa. He thinks back to what had been said the day before. About the homeowner's daughter being pleased that her parents would now have to leave the area. For a moment, he wonders if her concerns for her parents' safety could be enough to persuade her to light a fire at their home or whether this was all coincidence and foolishness.

'Jack, love. Is that police?'

'Won't be a minute, pet,' shouts Raycroft over his shoulder.

'We won't be much longer,' says Tremberg, taking the lead

while her colleague stares into the distance and runs his tongue around his mouth as if he's chasing something.

'Do you know who the silly bugger was yet?' asks the old man, turning his gaze on Tremberg and surreptitiously standing a little taller, as if uncomfortable at having to look up to keep eye contact with a woman half his age. 'Why he chose that house to fall asleep in? We heard on the news that there was a fire at Hull Royal in the burns unit and that the victim had been involved. When they took him out of here he didn't look like he was ready to roll himself a cigarette . . .'

McAvoy and Tremberg exchange a glance and decide that this nice old boy deserves a little honesty.

'The fire at the hospital was deliberately started,' says Tremberg. 'Somebody came onto the ward, went into his room, doused him in lighter fuel and set fire to him.'

'Goodness,' says Raycroft, looking to McAvoy for confirmation and receiving it with the merest of nods.

'It was definitely the same man who was pulled out of the fire at your neighbour's house. The reports show he had a tremendous amount of alcohol in his bloodstream. Almost fatal amounts. So, there's every chance that he was coming home from the pub, wandered into the wrong house, lit a fag and set himself on fire. But we've managed to identify him and we've got a name. Does Trevor Jefferson mean anything to you?'

'Jefferson,' says Raycroft, coming back. 'Wasn't he the sod whose family died a couple of years back in the fire over the way? A few streets from here?'

McAvoy nods. Hopes Tremberg has the presence of mind to play this delicately and not start putting words in the old man's mouth.

'That's correct, sir. His wife, two children and stepchild all succumbed to their injuries.'

'Aye,' says Raycroft, rubbing his face with his hand. 'Few years ago now, wasn't it?'

'Yes, sir.'

'By God.' He stares over at the burned-out house and then pats the pockets of his cardigan. He pulls out a tin of rolling tobacco and with the absent-minded dexterity that always amazes McAvoy, makes himself a thin cigarette. He lights it with a match and proceeds to smoke it in the way that reminds McAvoy of his father; embers towards his palm, the cigarette held by four fingers and a thumb. Shielded from the wind and prying eyes. 'Got what he deserved, then,' he says at last.

'Sir?' McAvoy tries not to pounce. To keep his voice even.

'He was the sod who started the fire. Killed the lot of them. Never served a day for it. Only one who got out alive and he was the one playing with matches. Sounds to me like somebody punished him for it. Make sure before you handcuff him, you shake him by the hand.'

# CHAPTER 14

It's only been two hours since McAvoy and Tremberg stood on the doorstep of Jack Raycroft's home but already they are building up a pretty clear picture of the kind of man whose death they are investigating. Irresponsible, selfish, a welfare scrounger: a tabloid would need little encouragement to slap the 'evil' tag on him, though Tremberg put it best when she declared that 'nasty bastard' was a more suitable moniker for the dear departed than any of the psychological terms McAvoy suggested while poring over the limited case notes that the database had been fed.

Tremberg clicks the mouse and the computer screen fills with images of charred bodies. Both detectives sniff, and fight the urge to look away. The corpses are unmistakably those of blackened, flame-devoured children.

A rumbling belch comes from the doorway and both detectives spin round. Sergeant Linus is wrapping both of his fat, fleshy hands around a mug. He's eclipsing the light spilling in from the corridor, and the room suddenly darkens as he yawns expansively and takes a gulp of his drink. The smell coming from the container is meaty and inviting, and

McAvoy realises that the uniformed officer wedging his considerable bulk in the doorway is actually drinking gravy.

'Was a bad one,' says Linus, taking a slurp from the mug and then wiping his mouth with the back of his hand. 'Never saw anything like it. Was like Pompeii in there when the smoke cleared. Could still see the expression on the youngest lad's face. Wish I could say he looked like he was asleep. He didn't. He looked like he was in fucking agony.'

'Must have been awful,' says Tremberg.

'Fucking was.'

Tremberg waves a hand at the office, with its damp walls, out-of-date posters and threadbare carpet. 'I take it you're not missing CID. Cushy number here.'

Linus fails to spot the sarcasm and gives a nod. 'Twenty years was enough, love.'

'You got the time to fill us in?' asks McAvoy, making it sound as though the whole investigation would stumble without a few moments of Linus's valuable time. 'We just need an overview.'

'Like I said on the phone, I'm happy to help.'

Even in the first couple of hours of the inquiry, McAvoy has found it hard to escape the conclusion that the investigation into the original fire had been a haphazard affair. And he's finding it hard not to blame the shambolic, lazy bastard in front of him; a feeling not helped by the sensation that the charred bodies of the dead youngsters are staring at the back of his head from the computer screen.

'Well, it was pretty clear from the off that the dad was the one who'd pulled the trigger, so to speak. Bloke didn't have a mark on him. Was tempted to put a few there myself.'

McAvoy jerks a thumb over his shoulder at the screen. 'The forensics report suggests an accelerant was used. Lighter fluid. Early indications are that the same MO was used last night at Hull Royal. And the night before at the house yonder. You don't think that perhaps he was innocent, do you? That whoever did the fire that killed his missus and his kids might have come back to finish the job?'

Linus appears to give it some thought. 'Possible, lad. But like I said, I'm pretty damn sure that Jefferson did that fire. And I reckon somebody's decided an eye for an eye is the only kind of justice he deserved.'

The room falls silent for a moment. McAvoy nods slowly and decides to stop being so bloody nice.

'You didn't charge him, though, did you? If he's got the only kind of justice he deserved, it's because you never charged him with anything. Never even came close, from what I can see.'

Linus bristles. Pushes himself away from the wall. 'Hang on there, now,' he begins, temper flushing his cheeks. 'We did a thorough investigation. We just couldn't pin it on him.'

'Thorough?' McAvoy contorts the word into a snarl of contempt. 'The bloody *Hull Daily Mail* did a more thorough background check on this bloke. Eight fires! Eight fires at his previous addresses. That didn't strike you as odd?'

'We knew there'd been some little blazes, here and there,' says Linus, waving the accusation away with both wobbling arms. 'He'd reported them to the council, not the police. We had nothing on him except a couple of deception convictions from his younger days and a drunken assault on a copper a year before.'

'And yet you say you had him pegged from the start.' McAvoy turns to Tremberg. 'I don't know about you, Detective Constable, but when I make up my mind that somebody has killed a lot of children and his other half, I tend to be rather dogged in my pursuit of a way to lock the bugger up.'

Linus looks from one officer to the other, his many chins wobbling with righteous indignation.

He deflates slightly. Turns away. 'Look, I never said I was bloody Sherlock Holmes . . .'

Again they sit in silence. Eventually, McAvoy wipes a hand across his face and pinches the bridge of his nose. He can feel a headache starting. He feels like he's trying to complete a jigsaw puzzle and fears that more than half the pieces are still picture-side down.

'I understand, Sergeant,' he says, and hopes his face doesn't betray him. 'We all get days like that. Get weeks and months, even. We've all had cases where we just knew from the off that we were on a hiding to nothing. And it can't have been easy. Roper dumped you in it. Realised it was going to be hard to make anything stick and walked away. Hardly made you feel like going the extra mile, did it?'

Linus is breathing heavily, but the gasps are coming through a half smile. He looks relieved. Pleased that this holier-than-thou Jock bastard at least understands how it is to be running uphill with the world on your back. 'What could I do? The report said that it had been deliberately started and that accelerant was used. Fine. But Jefferson said it was the eldest boy. That he'd caught him playing with his lighters in the past. Was a case of his word against the dead.

Sure, Jefferson'd been involved in other suspicious fires, but the dead lad had been at all those properties too. Knowing something and making it stick are two different things.'

'You push him? You lay the pressure on?'

'Course I bloody did. Had him in the interview room for hours, me and Pete May. Took it in turns. Tried to make him feel guilty. Just kept sitting there, shaking his head, saying his boy did it and that was that. Couldn't charge him. Wouldn't have got past the magistrates.'

'Press gave you a roasting, though, eh?'

'That's what they do! The same papers that had been criticising us for spending a day and a night interrogating a poor grieving father went after us saying we were incompetent when they found out he'd reported eight fooking fires in the previous couple of years and that his neighbours all reckoned he was a pyro-bloody-maniac. We can't win. Wasn't easy, letting him go.'

'And the neighbours? The people who spoke to the papers. Would any of them have been bitter enough about him walking to go and finish the job?'

Linus shrugs. 'You know estates like this. Doesn't take much to get people hot under the collar. But I don't reckon I know any of the locals with the balls to walk into Hull Royal and cook a burns victim in his bed. Let alone still walk out again. I reckon you're on a hiding to nothing, son.'

McAvoy crosses to the window and opens the crumpled metal blinds with his fingers. Looks out on an estate as grey and miserable as school mashed potato. Two children of no more than seven years old are playing on the only equipment in the little swing park not to have been vandalised beyond use. The joy of seeing the two boys laughing with glee as they push each other around on the roundabout is tempered by the fact they are both smoking.

'Not exactly Tenerife out there, is it, lad?' laughs Linus as McAvoy turns away from the world beyond the glass and returns his gaze to the sergeant's sweaty, flabby face. 'Sometimes you have to wonder if these poor dead nippers got off light.'

McAvoy says nothing.

The silence is broken by the unmistakable sound of McAvoy's mobile phone vibrating in his pocket. Glad of the distraction, but concerned that it may be Pharaoh ringing for a lack-of-progress report, he pulls the contraption free. It's a number he doesn't recognise.

'McAvoy,' he says.

'It's Russ Chandler, Detective Sergeant. You came to see me . . .'

'Mr Chandler. Yes. Hello.'

'I suppose this call is a pre-emptive strike. When do you want me in?'

'Mr Chandler, I'm afraid I don't—'

'I'm not daft, Sergeant. I know how these things work. Are you sending a car, or . . . ?'

'Mr Chandler, can we start again? You and I have concluded our discussions, unless you've remembered anything further regarding Fred Stein.'

'Stein?' Chandler sounds astonished. Angry, even. 'Sergeant, whatever game you're playing, it's not necessary. I'm willing to cooperate.'

Tremberg looks at McAvoy and mouths 'What's happening?'

at him. He simply screws his eyes up in response. His mind is a mess of headaches and confusions.

'Cooperate with what, Mr Chandler?'

There is silence at the other end of the line. It sounds to McAvoy as though the other man is drawing a breath, settling his thoughts.

'Mr Chandler?'

'You must have checked his phone records.'

'Whose phone records?'

'Christ, man. Jefferson. The bloke who got cooked. I spoke to him, OK. But that's where it ends. I was nowhere near Hull when it happened. Remember that . . .'

'You spoke to him? Why?'

'The book, remember. About survivors. We spoke about it. He was one of the names I'd approached when I started researching it. Just early stages, like I told you, but he phoned me a few days ago. Wanted to know if I was still interested. Said he was short on cash . . .'

'He contacted you? When was this?' McAvoy's trying to keep his voice steady.

'I couldn't be sure. Not long after I came to this bloody place. I was out of it for the first few days but when I started picking up my messages, he was on there. He reckoned I'd tried to contact him again that week, but that wasn't true. Him and the Grimsby woman. At least, I don't think it was true. You have to remember, I was in a bad way . . .'

'Which Grimsby woman, Mr Chandler? You mean somebody from your research?'

'Yes, yes,' he says testily, dismissively, as though only the facts that he's already divulged could be of any interest.

'Angela something-or-other. Only one that the Bar-Room Butcher didn't manage to bump off.'

McAvoy is pacing now, trying to keep pace with his thoughts and fears. He knows something significant is happening. He can smell violence. Blood.

'The rapist? From years back?'

'Aye, more your neck of the woods than mine. You must remember.'

McAvoy remembers. More than a decade ago, in the Borders of Scotland, a lorry driver by the name of Ian Jarvis had got his kicks waiting in the toilets of public houses then stabbing to death and raping any woman who happened to wander in. Liked to carve his initials on their privates, too. He bumped off four ladies before some of his DNA was found at one of the crime scenes and he was picked up while at work on victim number five in the toilets of a downmarket public house in Dumfries, not five minutes from the neat semi-detached where he lived with his wife and three young children. His last victim had survived. Given evidence against him from behind a screen. Helped put him away, and doubtless rejoiced when he was found hanging in his cell less than three weeks into the first of his many life sentences. By that time, she had put herself down for a council housing exchange and taken the first offer she'd received: three rooms with no view on the seventh floor of a Grimsby tower block

'And you've been in touch with her? You've spoken to this woman recently?'

'No,' he says impatiently. 'It was just a voicemail. She said she was returning my call. But I don't remember making any bloody call.'

McAvoy is shaking his head frantically. His face has gone the same steel grey as the estate beyond the glass.

And knows, knows without question, that Angela Martindale is next.

# CHAPTER 15

The glass is empty, but she raises it to her mouth anyway. Sips at nothing. Wets her lips on the last trickle of froth and works a yellow-stained tongue around the rim.

Whispers under her breath, into the glass, misting it with her slurred prayer: 'Come on, lads.'

Puts the pint glass back down on the varnished counter with a thud. Hopes somebody will notice she's out of drink and offer to fill the void. Become one of her gentlemen and buy some of her precious time.

'Another, Angie?'

It's Porthole Bob this time. Window-cleaner famed across town for never bothering to work his shammy into the corners.

'You're a smasher, Bob,' she says, and nods at the Bass pump. 'Pint, if you don't mind.'

Bob raises his own glass at Dean the barman, busy loading bottles of alcopops into the empty fridge down the far end of the bar. 'When you get a moment, Deano.'

It's a proper pub, this. One of the last boozers on this busy shopping street on the outskirts of Grimsby town centre not to have been bought out by one of the chains. There are only half a dozen punters in today, and none are drinking together. Three old boys that Angie vaguely remembers nodding hellos to in the past are sitting in a loose triangle, each at different tables. They're talking about a boxer she's never heard of, and each has his day's budget laid out on the cracked varnish of the circular table tops. All are on their last pint of the day, and are making it last: delaying the indignity of wrestling themselves into overcoats and scarves and tottering through the wind and snow to the bus stop.

The other customer is a muscular man in a black jacket and scarf. He'd tapped on the cider pump when he walked in, and handed over his money without a word. He's barely touched the drink. Has barely looked up from the *Daily Mirror*. Angie has him pegged as a gambler, probably up to his neck in horses and debt, and decides he's not worth one of her smiles.

'Bloody freezing. I've packed it in for the day.'

Porthole Bob. He's rubbing himself warm, having just walked in through the blue-paint and frosted-glass front door, bringing with him the sound of traffic and a cold flurry of snow and wind. There would have been traffic noises, too, not so long ago. This was Grimsby's premier shopping street; a bustling community of independent traders made prosperous by their nearness to the fish market and docks. No longer. It's a dead street, all plywood and graffiti, To-let signs and metal shutters. Were she a Grimsby girl, it would upset Angie to see a once proud highway reduced to such penury, but she has only called this town her home for a handful of years, and gives the area's disrepair and ignominy as much consideration as her own.

'Today, son.'

Dean reaches under the counter and pulls out two glasses. They're still warm from the dishwasher, so he runs them under the cold tap for a moment. He's only young but is learning quickly.

'Come on, son. There's a lady dying of thirst here.'

Satisfied the glasses are cold enough to spare him any abuse, Dean turns to the pump and fills both pints. Places both on the counter. Takes the four pound coins from Bob's outstretched hand.

'Cheers, Bob.'

'No bother, lad. You showing the game tonight?'

'Nah, it's on satellite. Price of the licence is a joke.'

'They showing it in Wetherspoon's?'

'No clue. Probably.'

'Hard to compete, son.'

'We've got better beer.'

'You have that.'

Angie raises her glass in a hand that hasn't shaken since her second pint of the morning and takes a long swallow of beer. Feels the familiar trickle down her gullet; the pleasant sensation of cool liquid turning to comforting, meaty warmth in her sloshing belly. She takes another swallow. Relaxes, knowing that for the next few minutes at least, her problems are solved. That she's just another customer in a quiet old-school pub, sipping a pint and listening to a bloke talk bollocks.

Takes another drink, then makes a mental note to slow down. She doesn't know where her next drink is coming from. Doesn't know about her next meal, either, but doesn't care quite so much.

'You all right then, Angie love?' asks Bob as Dean returns to the beer fridges and begins noisily stocking them with bottles of Carlsberg.

'Bearing up, sweetheart. Bearing up.'

'You're an early bird today.'

'Had some shopping to do. Thought I'd treat myself.'

'You deserve it, love. Nice to see you.'

She looks at her latest benefactor. He's in his late forties and not much taller than her. He's wearing knock-off designer jeans, scuffed at the knees, and mucky white trainers, with a blue fleece under a faded brown suede jacket that has distinct charity shop credentials. He's not a bad-looking man. Shaggable, if that's what it takes. She tends to take a pragmatist's view of her fleeting unions. Decides on a whim whether to endure a bit of sweat and sticky knickers in the name of a few more pints.

'You had your hair done, Ange?'

'No, love. Got caught in the snow. Just dried curly.'

'It's cute. Ringlets, like. Very angelic.'

'That's me, Bob. Little angel.'

They smile and chink glasses, and she takes another gulp, suddenly confident another drink will be forthcoming. Once, she would have recoiled at the thought of comparing herself to one of the Lord's chosen seraphim, but when God abandoned her, she let Him leave, and the cross she wears around her neck is the only reminder of the fact she was once a church-going Christian who prayed only for safety and sufficiency, and offered her soul in return.

She swallows the liquor.

She's made something of an art form out of this. There are

half a dozen pubs on her daily circuit, and she can usually wangle two or three drinks in each one. She always buys her first drink in each, but rarely has to dig into her purse for the ones that follow. If she'd ever taken up the offer of the post-traumatic stress counselling, she might have analysed her need to spend so much of her time in pubs, in an environment that almost claimed her life. But Angie doesn't have time for introspection. She found out what was inside her when the man with the knife began his work. And she'd seen nothing she wanted to see again.

'Looking dapper yourself, Bob,' she says, placing a hand on the back of his. 'Pleased you came in. Was just me and the old boys for the past hour.'

Bob gives her a grin. 'I'm meeting Ken in the Bear, if you want to join us. He's all right, is Ken.'

Angie gives him a 'maybe' kind of grin, but she's pretty sure she'll pass. Although there's a small chance Bob and Ken will compete for who can be more chivalrous when it comes to keeping her glass full, there's a better chance that the crowd of old boys who buy her drinks in the Bear will take exception at seeing her with the lads best known for drinking in Wilson's, and keep their wallets closed next time she puts a hand on their thigh and tells them they're looking smart.

The door bangs again and Angie looks round. She and Bob are the only customers left. She doesn't remember seeing any of the old boys go and heard no goodbyes, but her thinking is fuzzy enough at the edges that, if asked, she couldn't swear how many punters there were when she came in. She remembers a big boy, reading a newspaper, and perhaps old Arthur, with his thick glasses and polyester trousers, but was that today or yesterday? She doesn't even have time to begin wondering whether it matters before she's decided that it doesn't.

'Did you hear about John? Silly bastard.'

'No, love. Go on. I love a story.'

She sits and listens to Bob as he begins to tell her about what John did in the Red Lion on Saturday night, and doesn't even have to make a show of finishing her drink to earn herself another one. Halfway down it, she begins to feel the urge for a smoke, but fancies she can keep it at bay. In the next pub on her circuit, she'll head straight to the beer garden and make a show of looking in her handbag for her cigarettes until one of the smokers takes pity on her and offers a fag. Then she can save her own for this evening. Smoke them in front of the telly while drinking supermarket vodka and using up her free minutes texting saucy messages to the landlord of the White Hart, who can't seem to get through a late shift without baring his soul about how he and his wife are only together for the kids, and that it's a woman like her, a real woman, who should be in his bed.

She doesn't know what he sees in her. What any of them see in her. At forty-three years old, she's not exactly pin-up material, though she does wear her purple leggings, denim skirt and loose-fitting jumper from the sale rail at Asda with a certain sassiness that, when added to the red lipstick, dark hair and large, dangly earrings, make her oddly easy on the eyes. She's tactile, too. Flirty and friendly. A good listener, apparently, though she rarely says anything other than 'you deserve better' or 'she doesn't know she's born' when roped into conversations about the failings of her gentlemen's other halves.

It wasn't always like this, of course. Angie Martindale was a miracle, once. The doctors said so. Police. Press, too, even though she was never named in any of the reports. She was the one who got away. The survivor. The one he couldn't kill. She hasn't reached the stage in her alcoholism where she will tell the story in exchange for drink but there are times, when her glass is empty and nobody is giving her the eye, that she feels like unfolding one of the newspaper clippings she keeps in her handbag and telling Grimsby's hardcore drinkers that in a pub like this, a decade and a half ago, she was brutalised and raped by a man whom a judge called 'evil' and whose dead blue eyes still stare through her on the nights she falls asleep too sober.

Her telephone vibrates in the pocket of her denim skirt. She apologises to Bob for the interruption and pointedly silences the phone.

'You could have taken it,' says Bob, trying to hide his big silly grin when he realises she's rejected the call, just so she can continue to chat.

'I'm talking to you, Bob,' she says, softening her body language slightly. She's used this trick plenty of times before. Made her gentlemen feel special, just by setting her alarm for half-hour intervals and then hanging up on whosoever had the temerity to disturb her while engrossed in conversation with the most fascinating man in the world.

She does deliver, of course. She can't get by on suggestiveness alone. On occasion, when she thinks they've earned it or she's simply too bloody miserable to face going home alone, she's invited back the occasional gentleman. Let him slobber his way on top of her and into her. Endured a few minutes of uncomfortable weight and awkward pounding, in a way that is at once her own punishment and her beau's reward. It doesn't happen as often, these days. She's become less happy with the notion of people seeing her own private space. Perhaps it is since she let the flat go to seed. The increase in her drinking has coincided with a marked down-turn in the presentability of her home, though halfway up a multi-storey block, it was never palatial.

'You sure you don't want to tag along?'

'Next time. You've got my number. Text me later and I'll see what I'm up to.'

He gives another big grin. 'I'll do that.'

'I'll probably just be at home, all by my lonesome.'

'Well we can't have that. Can we?'

'No, love.'

He kisses her cheek before he leaves. She feels his rough stubble against her skin and the tickle of his moustache against her eyelashes. Wonders if he'll want to taste her down below, like these bloody modern men always seem to. Whether his moustache will tickle her thighs. Whether he'll want the light on. Whether he'll mention the scars.

Slowly, carefully, she steps down from the bar stool. Leans over and gathers up her shopping bags. Some cheap cooked meat from the butchers. Some liver. Six white rolls. Bottle of vodka. Twenty Richmond Superkings.

'You off, Angie? Place will be dead without you.'

Dean has finished loading the bottle fridge and is standing behind the beer pumps, watching the door. It's been a quiet lunchtime, and he doesn't see business picking up again until tea. He gets a set wage, so doesn't wish too fervently for a sudden rush, but his shift passes quicker when he's busy and the owner gives him disapproving looks when the weekly takings aren't what he has expected. There are even fewer excuses at Christmas, when, according to Wilson, people have got no excuse not to be pissed.

'Think I'll go and put my feet up,' she says, smiling and feeling pleasantly unsteady on her feet. 'Taped a *Miss Marple* last night. Might give my brain a workout.'

'You enjoy yourself, love. You deserve it.'

She gives him a different kind of smile from the one she reserves for her gentlemen. It's genuine. The sort of smile she used to display without thinking. The fleeting, happy grin she once flashed at the man who carved his initials on her vagina before sticking a twelve-inch bread knife through her ribs and fucking her while she lay bleeding on the tiled floor of a pub toilet.

'Probably be in tomorrow,' she says. 'You working?'

'No rest for the wicked.'

As she heads for the door a cold draught of air works its way up her body and concentrates itself on her bladder. She looks back at Dean and giggles. 'Call of nature, I think. First of the day.'

'Honestly, I don't know where you keep it,' he says good-naturedly. 'Must be a camel somewhere in your family.'

'Ooh, you charmer,' says Angie, putting her shopping bag on top of the nearest table and heading for the toilet.

'I meant it as a compliment,' shouts Dean as she pushes open the door, but she's already out of range, and he pulls a face as he realises he might have upset her. Fears he's put his foot in it and that it may cost him a drink or two to make amends. He decides to get it over with and stoops to grab an empty glass.

He's halfway to the floor when the blow comes.

There is an instant of crushing, mind-numbing pain to the back of his neck, and then he is flat on his face; a crumpled heap of unconsciousness lying on his belly by the beer fridges, one unmoving hand comically positioned inside a half-full box of salt and vinegar crisps.

Dean doesn't hear the man stepping over his body and walking over to the front door.

Doesn't hear the soft 'snick' as the bolt is slid home or the soft sound of black boots on wooden floor as they cross the room.

Doesn't hear the door to the toilets creak open, the sound of a blade being drawn slowly from inside a leather sleeve.

Doesn't hear the screaming begin . . .

# CHAPTER 16

'You're sure?' bellows McAvoy, one finger wedged in his ear to blot out the squeal of the engine and the hum of the tyres on the concrete road. 'Well how hard did he knock?'

Tremberg changes down to fourth gear, trying to ease an extra 5mph from the one-litre engine. She finds what she's looking for, and despite the protestations of the smoking metal beneath the bonnet, pushes the accelerator almost through the floor.

'No . . . I can't say for certain, but there's a strong chance . . .'

Tremberg looks across from the driver's seat at McAvoy.

She finds herself examining the back of his hand. It's all she can see of him, gripping the mobile phone which he is pressing too hard to the side of his skull. The knuckles look as though they've been broken several times. They seem to represent the sum total of what she knows about him. That he has inflicted harm, and taken it. That the warm, protective palm and fingers in which she pictures him cradling his handsome son and beautiful wife can be turned over and balled, to create a fist capable of extraordinary, self-destructive damage.

'Kick the door in,' he's yelling. Then: 'I don't care. Trust me.'

*Why should they?* she thinks. *They don't know you. I barely knew you until this morning. I barely know you now.*

McAvoy slams the phone down. 'No answer at her flat,' he says, looking up at her from under a cowlick of damp, ginger hair, with eyes that are veined red and shining. 'They've tried the neighbours and no answer. Won't kick the door in without permission . . .'

He tails off. To Tremberg, it looks as though he is fighting with himself. Trying not to acknowledge that, throughout his career, he, too, has done things the right way. Waited for the order. Done as he was asked.

'So, where?' she asks, her eyes back on the road.

McAvoy says nothing. He appears to be biting the skin on his wrist, gnawing distractedly at it like a dog with a bone.

It's getting dark beyond the glass. There are flakes of snow in the air.

She asks again: 'Where first?'

They are approaching the industrial estate that marks the Grimsby boundary. The area smells of fish and industry, and the road beneath the tyres, with its concrete surface, is almost soporific in its brain-rattling vibration.

McAvoy lowers his arm back to his lap. Appears to make a decision.

'The uniformed officer says one of the neighbours reckons she's usually down Freeman Street from lunchtime. One of the pubs. Couldn't say which . . .'

'Freemo?'

'If that's what you call it. This is your part of the world, not mine.'

Somehow, Tremberg manages to coax another 10mph out of her hatchback, taking the needle to eighty as she screeches around the first roundabout on two wheels and roars up the flyover past the docks. She knows this area. Was a beat constable here.

'What do we know about her?' she yells, cruising past the fish-processing plant with her right foot hard to the floor. 'What does she drink?'

McAvoy looks at her as if she's insane, then gives a flustered shrug and picks up his notepad from his lap. He looks at the unfinished sentences and cryptic keywords he scrawled in shorthand during his hasty chat with the desk sergeant at Grimsby Central, as well as the vague details that Sergeant Linus found on the database and telephoned across within ten minutes of Tremberg and McAvoy running for the car park and spinning the wheel hard in the direction of the bridge.

'She's on benefits,' he reads out. 'Eligible after the attack. Admitted to Diana, Princess of Wales Hospital for a drunk and disorderly incident outside the Fathom Five . . .'

'Fathom Five? Closed down last year.'

'There's nothing else here!' shouts McAvoy, re-reading his notes in the hope that he'll see something new. A clue. An indication of what to bloody do next.

Tremberg bites her lip, swinging the car hard to the right at the latest in a seemingly endless chain of roundabouts that leads into the town centre. 'Call Sharon at the Bear,' she says triumphantly. 'If Angela drinks down Freemo, she'll know her.'

Grateful for something to do, McAvoy dials the first of the directory inquiries numbers that he can remember. Listens for what seems like an age as the Asian voice at the other end of the line reads off the welcome script. 'The Bear,' he yells. 'Freeman Street. Grimsby.'

Tremberg winces as she hears him repeat it.

'No,' he's bellowing. 'Just put me through. Put me through.'

A moment later he gives her a nod. It's ringing.

'Hello? Is that the landlady? Ms . . . ? Sharon? I'm ringing from Humberside Police. I urgently need to contact a lady who might be one of your regulars. Angela Martindale . . .'

Tremberg takes her eyes off the road for a full ten seconds, watching McAvoy's face drift through different stages of anger and frustration. She can imagine what the woman at the other end of the line is saying. Knows full well that she thinks she's doing Angie a good turn. That she's sticking by her regulars. Telling the Old Bill where to get off.

Without thinking, she reaches across and takes the phone from her sergeant. 'Sharon,' she barks into the receiver. 'This is Helen Tremberg. I arrested Barry the Bailiff when he cracked Johnno with his car-lock. Remember? Right, we need to find Angie Martindale now. I swear to God, if you find out we've nicked her for anything on the back of what you've told us, I'll pay for your beer order from my own pocket for the next twelve months. Right.' She nods. 'Good, love. Good.'

She hands the phone back to McAvoy. 'One of her regulars said he was nattering with her in Wilson's an hour or so back. Top of Freeman Street. Serves Bass.'

'Does she have a means of contacting—'

DAVID MARK

'Freemo,' says Tremberg, as she turns sharply right past the *Grimsby Telegraph* building and onto a rundown shopping street strung with dismally outdated Christmas lights. 'The place where dreams are made.'

In a blossoming darkness punctuated by neon signs and winking headlights, the boarded-up shop fronts and graffiti-covered corrugated shutters strike McAvoy as something transplanted from the Eastern bloc. He is used to this misery in Hull. This is a new town. A new imagining of recession and poverty, of apathy and pained acceptance. It hurts him to his heart.

'Top of the street,' says Tremberg again.

They see the swinging signs and ruined facades of three different pubs on their right as they pass the yawning entrance to the fish market. McAvoy tastes the air, expecting cod, haddock, perhaps turbot. Finds nothing. Not the salt of the sea. He can smell nothing but chips and petrol fumes. See nothing but snow and darkness, streetlights and shadowy shop doorways.

'That's Sharon's place,' says Tremberg as they pass a bar with a whitewashed front and black-painted double doors, inside which huddle half a dozen smokers, stamping feet, hand-rolling cigarettes, watching the traffic and spitting as far as the kerb.

'Lights are on,' says Tremberg, motioning ahead at a building on their right, sandwiched between a charity shop and a bakery. 'Good sign.'

She slows the car and pulls into a parking bay outside the bar. Closes her eyes for a second before killing the engine. Looks up and slowly turns her head. McAvoy is staring over her shoulder at the closed front door.

'She might not be here,' says McAvoy.

'No.'

'Might be anywhere. Having a drink somewhere else. Met a bloke. Gone to do her Christmas shopping . . .'

'Yes.'

'The chances of her being in there now . . .'

'Slim.'

'Almost non-existent.'

'May as well get a drink while we're here, though . . .'

'Pint of Bass?'

'Pint of Bass, yeah.'

A look passes between them as they both tell themselves they believe their lies. And then McAvoy nods.

The wind grabs the door as McAvoy tries to disentangle himself from the too-small vehicle and he feels a shooting pain in his arm as he battles with the wind to pull it shut. By the time he has got both feet on the road and slammed the door closed, Tremberg is already trying the door; rattling the rusted handle, knocking with her boots.

'It's locked,' she says breathlessly, over the sound of the wind. She locates the letterbox and pushes her fingers in, pressing her face to the gap through which a sliver of yellow light emerges. 'Police,' she yells. 'Police.'

She looks through the letterbox again. Presses her ear to it.

'Anything?' asks McAvoy.

Tremberg screws up her face as she turns to him. 'I don't know. Maybe.' Distractedly, she waves her hand at the wind, as if motioning for it to be quiet. 'I can't hear. You try.'

She moves aside and McAvoy presses his ear to the gap.

Angles his head and shouts 'Angela Martindale! Are you in there? Police. Open up.'

There is no mistaking the sound. It is human. Afraid. A guttural, animal roar of timeless, faceless terror.

Tremberg has heard it too, but her attention is distracted by sounds from down the road. The smokers from the Bear are pouring out into the street, drawn to drama like flies to shit.

She looks back at McAvoy, about to tell him to break the door in, but he is already running at the entrance.

The door comes off its hinges, smashing backwards as if ram-raided, and McAvoy spills into the foyer of the bar. There is a pain in his shoulder and he tastes blood where his teeth collided too hard on impact, but he pushes such sensations from his mind, shaking his head to clear his thoughts.

He drags himself upright, pushing down on the broken door, feeling a long, jagged splinter slide under his skin.

'Sarge!'

Tremberg takes his arm and hauls him upright. They stand on the muddy wooden floor, blinking in the light. The bar is empty. Some abandoned shopping bags stand by a bar stool. There are dirty glasses on the bar top.

'Hello.'

The word sounds comical in the abandoned space.

Then the scream comes again.

McAvoy whirls round, searching the near wall for a doorway. Finds none. Begins running for the far end of the bar. He puts a hand out and grabs the brass rail that runs along the varnished wooden top. Without thinking, he picks up a dirty glass. Almost stops as he sees the body behind the bar.

'Helen,' he yells, spotting the entrance to the toilets. 'Behind the bar!'

Without drawing breath he bursts through the swing door and clatters into a plaster wall. To his right are the entrances to the ladies' and gents' facilities. With the glass in his right hand, he kicks out at the door to the ladies and throws himself inside.

The room is bathed in blue neon, emanating from a single strip light in the ceiling. There is a broken mirror on the far wall and two cubicles, both with half open doors.

Angie Martindale is wriggling on her back on the floor. Her skirt has been pushed up to her waist. Her leggings rolled down to her ankles. In the unnatural light, the mess of blood around her pubic region looks tar-black and already clotted. Her hands cover her face, and gasping sobs escape between her fingers.

McAvoy stands immobile. The scene feels unreal, somehow. As though it is happening to somebody else. He feels suddenly cold and clammy, as if he has woken from a nightmarish sleep to find himself bathed in sweat.

'In . . . in there . . .'

Angie Martindale is raising a blood-soaked finger, ghoulish and spectral, pointing at the door to the nearest cubicle.

Instinctively, McAvoy bends to lean forward, to put his ear closer to her mouth, to hear her words and make sense of them.

A figure leaps over the cubicle door, black-clad and balaclava'd, body ducked low, leg protruding, like a steeplechaser clearing a hurdle. McAvoy looks up. Feels his world slow down, minimise and become this moment. This now. This boot, with its caterpillar tread, crashing towards his face.

At the last possible moment he jerks his head back. The boot whistles past his jaw, but the figure that comes behind the kick is too bulky to avoid and McAvoy feels all the air leave his body as the man crashes into his chest and slams him back into the wall.

The impact with the brick is sickening and for a moment McAvoy feels himself beginning to slip and sink into a black treacle of unconsciousness. The glass falls from his hand. Smashes on the tiles. His head is ringing. He can smell blood. Exploding lights dance on his vision.

And then he realises there is a figure in his arms. That in his arms a black-clad man is struggling and kicking, ramming elbows in his ribs and aiming kicks at his shins, trying to extricate himself from a bear hug McAvoy did not know he had applied.

The moment of realisation, the returning to his skin, causes him briefly to relax his grip, and in an instant he feels a strong forearm against his jaw, pushing head back against the wall as a fist slams into his ribs.

McAvoy drops his hands, pain shooting up his spine to explode in a concussive headache, and he barely gets his hands up in time to stop the next right hand that impacts with his cheekbone and forces him back against the wall.

There is no room to fight. He cannot draw his hands back to swing a punch. Cannot step forward for fear of treading on Angie Martindale.

He takes another punch to the chest.

Lashes out with a boot. Misses. Lashes out a right hand and slaps the place where his attacker's head had been a moment before.

*Christ!* he thinks, though the pain and the fog. *This guy can fight.*

He's angry, suddenly. Fucking furious. Feels himself galvanised by a rage terrible and raw.

He puts one of his boots against the wall to his rear and pushes himself forward, managing to grab his attacker's flailing arms. He propels them both across the tiled floor, slick with blood, cluttered with entangled limbs, and feels a satisfying thud as the man's spine slams back into the cubicle door. McAvoy grunts and slams him again into the hard wood. Feels his opponent weaken. Takes the man's head in his hands. Feels the wool of the balaclava. Slams his head into the door. Takes him by the throat in his left hand and slams a right into his guts. Feels him double over. Brings back his right hand to drop a haymaker from on high.

The door bursts open.

Helen Tremberg stands in the doorway. Her extendable baton is clutched in her left hand. She is holding her right up as if she is directing traffic.

She opens her mouth to speak. To tell the black-clad man that this over? To tell Angie Martindale that she will live? The words never make it to the air.

In one fluid motion, the man in black produces a blade. Whether it be from a pocket or a sleeve, McAvoy cannot later say, but one moment the man is doubled over, falling to the ground, fingers in fists, and the next he is swinging a blood-drenched blade in a great sweeping backhand arc that slices across Helen Tremberg's arm.

McAvoy's shout of anguish comes before Tremberg's scream, but in an instant the tiny space is ringing with roars of pain and despair.

The man in black lunges forward and grabs Tremberg by the neck. Spins and hurls her into McAvoy's path as he slithers and tries to find purchase on the slick floor. She hits him hard in the middle and both officers fall, landing heavily on Angie Martindale's legs.

By the time McAvoy has yanked himself back to his feet, the door is swinging closed. He staggers forward and yanks it open, running into the bar, only for a forest of arms and legs to grab him at knee, waist and shoulder height. He clatters down hard on the wooden floor and spins onto his back, lashing out with angry kicks and bitter yells at the men standing above him, trying to pin him back to the floor.

He tries to find his feet but an arm fastens around his throat and he pushes himself backwards against the brass rail, feeling the man on his back gasp as the air shoots from his lungs.

'Police . . .' gasps McAvoy. 'I'm police.'

The pressure on his neck eases in a second. McAvoy looks at the people around him. Half a dozen assorted drinkers. The regulars from the Bear. Two short, fat men, a middle-aged guy in shorts, a petite woman with too many earrings, an old man with greying Elvis hair and a tall, skeletally thin man in a white shirt who looks to be missing an arm.

'We thought . . . ,' says one.

McAvoy pushes past them. Clambers over the wreckage of the broken front door and emerges, gasping, in the street.

Frantically, he looks both ways. Left. Right. Back into the belly of the bar.

Then up to the sky, as he realises he's gone. That he had him in his hands, and let him go.

He opens his eyes wide and stares deep into the snow-filled swirling black clouds, and screams the only word that does the situation justice.

'*FUCK!*'

# CHAPTER 17

'Don't say a word,' says Pharaoh. 'Don't fucking breathe.'

She walks behind the bar and reaches up to the top shelf for a half-pint glass. She holds the glass under the optic and pours herself a double vodka, which she downs in one.

The investigation team is assembled in the front bar of Wilson's. Colin Ray is lounging in a hard-backed chair, his tie unfastened almost to his navel. He's chewing nicotine gum and looking pleased with himself. Sharon Archer, as ever, is at his side. She's got a packet of crisps open on the table in front of her, and is eating them as quietly as she can.

Sophie Kirkland and Ben Nielsen are standing at the bar, watching Pharaoh. They arrived together a few minutes ago, grumbling about the parking and shaking snow from their hair onto a floor thick with muddy bootprints.

McAvoy is resting against the fruit machine by the side entrance. Through the frosted glass he can see the fluorescent yellow jacket of the officer guarding the entrance. Two other constables are stationed at the front doors. The road has been cordoned off, but the crowd outside is still close enough to be a cause for concern. Some of the faces in the crowd had been snarling the last time McAvoy had poked his head out of the front door. He wonders whether it's even worth trying to tell them that he feels worse about Angie Martindale than they do. And he's the one who saved her life.

Pharaoh stands behind the bar. She closes her eyes. Breathes in and out for a full thirty seconds. Slowly, without saying a word, she pulls a thin cigar from a pocket of her coat, lights it, and draws the smoke deep into her lungs. She exhales precious little of it.

'She's not dead,' says Pharaoh eventually. 'This is a good thing.'

She stops. Takes another drag of the cigar.

'Helen Tremberg will be OK too. That's another good thing.'

Another drag. Another puff of smoke.

'What's not a good thing is the fact that the first I knew about all this was when I got a call from ACC Everett asking me for an update. Apparently he'd been at a funeral with the Grimsby Central superintendent when the super's desk sergeant rang for advice on whether or not to assist the Serious and Organised Crime Unit with their murder investigation, and kick in the door of a city-centre flat. Asks me how Angela Martindale fits into the Daphne Cotton investigation. Or the Trevor Jefferson case, for that matter. You remember those investigations, yes? So the ACC asks me for chapter and verse. Puts his finger in his ear and waits for enlightenment. I was a little less than impressed to get that call. Even less so when I found myself about to tell him that I'd never heard of her. That I don't know why on earth two of my officers are insisting that a poor uniformed constable kick her door in and make sure she's not dead.'

McAvoy raises his head. Opens his mouth. Closes it again.

'And now I find myself in Grimsby,' she says. 'I have an officer bleeding. I have another holding a piece of balaclava. I have a woman on her arse in a pub toilet with cuts to her foo-foo. And I have quite a lot of questions. Do you think perhaps now might be a good time for somebody to give me one or two answers?'

There is silence in the room. Colin Ray shrugs, but takes the time to turn his head and give McAvoy a wink that is in no way a gesture of comradeship. Shaz Archer follows his lead, and with a less interrogatory glare, Ben Nielsen and Sophie Kirkland also swivel. All eyes are on him.

'Looks like you've been nominated, my boy,' says Pharaoh, and there is no friendliness in her voice.

McAvoy looks up. His ribs throb like a migraine and his back teeth feel loose in his gums. He feels sick at the thought of explaining himself, and ill to his bones at having had a murderer in his hands and letting him slip away.

'There's a link,' he says, and his voice sounds like a schoolboy's. He closes his eyes again. Tells himself to just get it over with. To lay it out and hope it makes sense the way it had seemed to a few minutes before, when his fingers closed around the strong, wiry arms of the man kneeling above Angela Martindale, and he realised he had been right. Right to follow his nose, and right to smash the door in. Just wrong not to tell his boss along the way. He wonders what it says about him. Wonders if it is his own arrogance that prevents him from even considering sharing this with his superior officer. In the heat of the moment, in the rush of adrenalin, in the white-hot moment of certainty that he was about to confront a killer, it had all been forgotten.

He looks away from them all. Imagines he's talking to himself. Laying the information out on a white page.

'On the day of Daphne Cotton's murder, ACC Everett asked me to visit a Barbara Stein-Collinson to break the news that her brother had been found dead at sea. His name was Fred Stein. He was the sole survivor of one of the trawler tragedies off Iceland in 1968. He'd escaped in a lifeboat with two crewmates. They died. He didn't. A week ago, he set off with a documentary crew to tell his story and to put a memorial wreath over the spot where his ship went down. While on board, he disappeared. Got upset during an interview, went outside for some air and vanished. A few days later he was found dead in a lifeboat. Not one of the ship's lifeboats but one that had been brought on board specially. So, an elaborate suicide? Feeling guilty for being the one that got away? Possibly. But it felt wrong. Long story short, I got in touch with a writer called Russ Chandler. He's a resident at Linwood Manor . . .'

'The nut-house?' Sharon Archer is incredulous, as if he's just told her his informant is a nonce.

'He's drying out. Got a drink problem. Anyway, he telephoned me today and wanted to know when we were picking him up. Started talking about Trevor Jefferson's phone records . . .'

Several of the officers begin to hold up their hands and shoot each other confused glances. 'Trevor Jefferson? The hospital guy?'

'Yes. It transpires that as well as being the man to broker the Fred Stein deal for the TV company, Chandler had also approached Trevor Jefferson some time ago with a view to writing a book about solitary survivors. People who had been the only ones to survive.'

McAvoy's eyes find Trish Pharaoh. Her arms are crossed and she's biting at her lower lip, but she's listening, and the subtle nod of her head suggests she understands what he is going to say.

'Jefferson survived a fire that killed his wife and kids,' says McAvoy, trying to find a face he feels comfortable talking to. 'Wasn't a scratch on him.'

He stops again, waiting for somebody to ask a question.

'And how does this lead to Angela Martindale?' asks Kirkland quietly. She looks genuinely confused and her eyes are still red from the shock of seeing Tremberg sitting in the back of the ambulance, having her slashed arm wrapped in gauze.

'Angela Martindale was another person Chandler had been in contact with. She was the only surviving victim of a man the press called the Bar-Room Butcher. He raped several women in pub toilets. Carved his initials on their private parts. Stabbed them to death. Angela Martindale survived her injuries. Testified. She was the one who got away.'

McAvoy catches Pharaoh's eye. She nods again, telling him it's OK to proceed.

'Daphne Cotton was the victim of a machete attack as a baby,' he says meaningfully. 'Everybody she loved was cut up by militants. Hacked to bits. In a church. She survived. She was the only one who did.'

After a moment, Colin Ray readjusts his pose. He slides himself into a more upright position. He appears to be listening.

'Vigilante?'

McAvoy shakes his head.

'It doesn't fit,' he says. 'Sure, with Jefferson I can understand it. Especially if he's the one who set the blaze. But Stein? Daphne Cotton? Angela Martindale? What have they ever done to anybody?'

McAvoy is interrupted by the sound of the toilet door swinging open. A forensics officer in a white suit and blue face mask enters the bar, a tray of evidence bags in his hands. He looks at the assembled officers and realises he's walked in at a bad time. He puts the tray down on the nearest table. Looks at Pharaoh and mumbles 'same footprint' through his mask before ducking out the side door. An icy gust of wind and a smattering of street noise enters the room to fill the void left by his departure.

'Footprint?' asks McAvoy, gazing at Pharaoh.

'I'm sorry, Sergeant,' she says, voice dripping with sarcasm. 'I know I didn't share that piece of information with you. I hope you can forgive me. It wasn't deliberate. It's just that as senior investigating officer, I rather thought me knowing was sufficient. Frustrating, isn't it?'

'So it is the same guy, yes? The one who did Daphne?'

Pharaoh nods. 'It looks that way.'

Nielsen turns to McAvoy. 'You've seen him twice.'

'Yes,' he says, trying to show that he already feels sufficiently bad about it to be spared any abuse, however richly deserved.

'Was it the same guy? I mean, did he have the same build? Same physique?' Nielsen smiles charmingly. 'Same teary blue eyes?'

McAvoy finds himself absurdly pleased that Nielsen remembers his description off by heart. It makes him feel better to know that somebody has been paying attention.

'There's no doubt. I only got a glimpse of his eyes but they were the same. Blue. Red-seamed. Wet, like he'd been crying.'

'And the victim said the same?'

'Yes,' replies McAvoy. 'It was hard to get much sense out of her, but she was clear. He'd been crying. Sat above her for an age with his pants down and his knife drawn and did nothing but sob.'

Colin Ray turns to Pharaoh again. He appears to be coming to life. 'Money in the budget for a profile?' he asks.

Pharaoh nods without even thinking about the figures.

McAvoy, despite all that has happened, is feeling almost warm inside. It is as if his colleagues are becoming police officers in front of him. They begin to shout out questions. Theories. Suggestions. Pharaoh comes out from behind the bar and marshals Kirkland and Nielsen closer to the senior officers with a soft, stroking palm in the centre of their backs.

'Whoever it is, they're sure as hell not random acts,' says Pharaoh. 'This has been thought through. Considered. Somebody's got a bee in their bonnet about unfinished business, and we've got to find out why they think it's up to them to finish it.'

Without thinking about it, McAvoy moves away from the fruit machine and pulls up a chair. They sit together in a

rough circle and with each word spoken he feels drawn further into this sphere of energised officers. This was what he
imagined it would be like when he made the move to CID.

'So how we do know where to look next?' asks Sophie,
looking up from her notebook and her frantic scribbling.
'How the hell else do we find a sole survivor?'

Colin Ray, who has been muttering something in Shaz
Archer's ear, suddenly sits back in his chair as if he's been
shoved in the chest.

'This Chandler,' he says. 'What's the script?'

McAvoy thinks about the best way to sum up the rumpled,
drink-pickled hack. 'Typical journo, really. Out for himself.
Cuts a few corners. Ticked off at life and drinks too much.'

'Sounds to me like he's the link in the chain,' says Ray, and
McAvoy notices a few subtle nods from the others. He looks
at Pharaoh.

'You're not suggesting that Chandler could be the
actual . . .'

'Pick a prize from the middle shelf,' says Ray.

'No, I can see the connection, but in terms of his physical
capability to commit the crimes, there's no way,' says
McAvoy, and the whole idea seems so preposterous to him
that his voice is louder than he intends.

Ray gets defensive. 'Look, lad, I've known blokes with the
build of a fucking jockey who could knock over a bodybuilder
when their blood's up. There's no shame if a little fella has
got the best of you once or twice . . .'

Without intending to, McAvoy finds himself starting to
stand. 'Do you think that's what I care about?' he demands.

'Easy, Sergeant,' says Ray, not moving.

'I've met Chandler. Spent time with him. And I've met the person who's doing this. They're different people.'

'That'll do,' says Pharaoh, and waves McAvoy back into his seat. She looks from his flushed face to Colin Ray's angry one and appears to make a decision.

'What is it with you and the limbless? There was a one-armed Russian bloke shouting the odds at you when I turned up,' she says, with the faintest of smiles. 'I can live without one-legged pissheads just now.'

For a moment, he looks as though he's going to explode in anger, but he controls himself. Gives a little laugh to show he's got control of himself. Feels everybody else relax a little.

'Here's where we're at,' says Pharaoh. 'We're getting some-where, that's one thing. This morning we had two separate cases. This evening we've got four, but they're quite possibly connected. McAvoy's done some good work here, even if he has been hiding his light under a bushel . . .'

There are laughs, and McAvoy doesn't have to force it this time when his face breaks into a smile.

'McAvoy, I need you to write this up the first moment you get. I need a full report of where we're at, what you know. I need your witness statement on this afternoon's events. I'm going to make a call to the top brass and explain that we were working this all under the radar and trying to maintain radio silence. Or some such shit. Whatever makes it sound like I know what my team are fucking up to. It's early yet, so I'm afraid there's going to be no sloping off back home. Ben, you get yourself up to the hospital and get Angie Martindale's statement. The barman's too, if he's coherent. Be gentle, yeah? And Sophie, you're looking for anything that links the names in this case. Any link between Stein, Daphne Cotton, Trevor Jefferson, and now Angela. There's no doubt that this Chandler character is a major piece of the puzzle. McAvoy, he obviously feels a connection to you, so tomorrow, you and I will take a ride down to Lincolnshire and have a little chat. I want to know what else he remembers. Colin, Shaz, you speak to the locals around here. Work the pubs. Find out about Angela Martindale. Whether she had a boyfriend. Whether she talked about what had happened to her in the past. Whether it was common knowledge or her own little secret. This is a fishing community so throw out Fred Stein's name . . .'

McAvoy raises his head. Looks at her like a puppy awaiting a slice of ham.

'You've got the fun job,' she says, and in her eyes is a flicker of the warmth that has sustained him in past days. 'Use that big brain of yours. Find out who we should be protecting. Who else has walked away? Are there other sole survivors out there? We're in for a late night, and what's worse, we're in Grimsby,' she says. 'That means I'm close to home and can't pop back there to finish the bottle of Zinfandel in the fridge. This depresses me. Let's make sure nothing else does.'

They all exchange looks. Take deep breaths, as if limbering up for a marathon. Then the chair legs scrape on the floor and they are out of their seats, talking, joking, laughing, straightening ties and clicking rollerball pens.

McAvoy is last to stand. As he does, Trish Pharaoh appears at his side. He dwarfs her, but she smiles up at him like he's a giant toddler.

'I don't know if this is good work or not,' she says softly.

'But I'm sure Helen Tremberg would rather have a scar on her arm than her throat cut. And Angie Martindale's alive. Whatever gets said, remember that.'

He can't find any words, so just nods.

'You can write your report from home,' she says.

He nods again.

When he opens his eyes she's still staring at him.

And there's something more than motherliness in her gaze.

# CHAPTER 18

The air in his lungs feels gelatinous. He wants to sneeze, but fears that the explosion will make his aching ribs shatter like a neon strip light thrown at a wall, and when he tries to bring the mug of hot chocolate and brandy to his lips, his trembling hands create a tidal wave on the murky brown surface and the sloshing liquid scalds his nose.

He considers himself in the iridescent sheen of the computer screen; his face overlaid with pictures and text.

'It's the adrenalin wearing off,' says Roisin, making a garland of her thin, delicate arms and draping them around his neck. 'We just need to get you worked up again.'

McAvoy nods. Manages a smile. Feels himself about to look up and pull her in for a kiss, and angrily fights the urge. Tells himself he still has work to do. That nothing is solved. That today he held a killer by the throat and let him go.

She is sitting on his desk, perched on the edge of the sturdy mahogany apparatus that he bought for less than a tenner from a charity shop on Freetown Way and which matches nothing else in their yellow and purple-painted bedroom with its white built-in wardrobes and flimsy four-poster bed.

She is naked. Both of her dainty feet, with their dirty soles, are resting on his own bare leg; tiny toes gently massaging his flesh, digging into him as if he were made of sand. He cups one of her calves in his hand; the fingers encircling the limb, his palm registering the tiny veneer of stubble that has grown on her smooth skin since her belly became too much of an obstacle for her to be able to shave below the knees.

'Aector. Are you feeling better?'

She turns his head to face her. Gives an eager smile.

'What have we got?'

McAvoy, dressed in an old university rugby jersey and a pair of battered denim shorts, pushes himself back from the computer screen and tiredly waves a hand in the direction of the text.

'Too much,' he says, then wonders if he should correct himself. 'Not enough.'

Roisin settles herself on his knee and begins to read the screen. McAvoy watches her, up close, the tiniest of smiles on his face as he notices that she still moves her lips slightly, even when she reads in her head. It's a habit he hopes she never loses.

'Is this what you think will be next?' she asks when she's scanned the page.

McAvoy just shrugs. 'I don't see how it can be,' he says, dropping his forehead to her shoulder and taking a deep breath of her clean, fruity skin. 'I wouldn't have picked Angie Martindale if Chandler hadn't mentioned her. Or Fred Stein.'

McAvoy's mind is full of survivors. He's disabled the clock in the bottom right-hand corner of the screen because he doesn't want to know how late it is. He knows that he's been at this for hours, and has no better idea of who the killer will target next than he did when he began. He feels pathetically amateurish in his investigations. Felt a damn fool typing 'sole survivor' into Google, only to find himself reading about a movie from 1970 starring William Shatner. He'd tried to think more strategically. Used his knowledge of search commands and internet design to run a search that eliminated some of the more populist guff. Tried to focus on newspaper sites. Magazine articles. Found endless tales of misery.

Tried to narrow it down geographically. Found himself wondering what pattern could be found in the locations of the crimes so far. Sure, the Fred Stein murder happened far out to sea, but he had a link to the East Coast. He was a Hull boy. The Daphne Cotton killing took place in the city centre. Trevor Jefferson had been burned to death in Hull Royal Infirmary. The Angie Martindale attack may have happened in Grimsby, but that wasn't any more than half an hour away. Was the killer local? Did he have something against the East Coast? Had he been a sole survivor himself? Had he walked away from an atrocity. Couldn't live with the guilt. Didn't think anybody else should either . . .

'Go back to the one about the lady,' says Roisin, nodding at the mouse and encouraging him to return to a site she had read over his shoulder when she had brought him his first hot drink of this marathon session at the screen.

He retraces his steps. Opens the history of the last twenty-four hours of web surfing. Spots something down the bottom of the list. It's a story from the *Independent*, dated a little over four years ago, under the banner headline 'Brit Pays Price for Bravery'.

*A British charity worker is thought to have been the only survivor of a devastating explosion that ripped through a school bus yesterday.*

*Anne Montrose, 27, is in a critical condition in a British military hospital following the latest bomb attack in the troubled area of Northern Iraq.*

*Miss Montrose, originally of Stirling, refused to be evacuated when the region was designated an enemy hotspot six months ago.*

*Since then it has been the scene of some fierce fighting between Allied forces and insurgents still loyal to toppled dictator Saddam Hussein.*

*She originally travelled to the region with British children's charity Rebirth, which specialises in helping communities create shelters and orphanages for children bereaved by war and disaster.*

*While many of her colleagues have fled the region, Miss Montrose is thought to have stayed on to assist with rebuilding in the area.*

*Reports suggest that she was taking the children on a trip to a recently reopened play area when the bomb exploded. Up to 20 children are feared dead.*

*A spokesman for Rebirth said: 'We do not know the full details yet, but this is a tragedy simply too awful to comprehend. Anne would do anything for anybody. She wouldn't think twice about endangering her life to help others. The risks she faced on a daily basis never once stopped her being the most caring, loving person that we ever had the pleasure to know . . .'*

'Poor lady,' says Roisin. 'Is there nothing else on it?'

'Nothing,' he says. 'I've put her name in umpteen search engines and there's not a word on it after this story. Doesn't say if she even pulled through. I've emailed the reporter at the newspaper, though, to see if they have a number for her relatives. She could be up and about by now. Or dead. Sometimes the papers just lose interest.'

'They did with you,' says Roisin.

'I was never that interesting in the first place.'

'You don't really believe that.'

'It depends which way the wind's blowing,' says McAvoy, as honest as he can be. He still hasn't made his mind up whether he believes himself to be the best detective in the universe, or a big hopeless lump.

Roisin slides off McAvoy's knee and gives a large yawn, stretching her arms high and wide; her bosoms rising to reveal the two tattoos of squashed fairies that she had inked into her ribcage as a surprise for him one Saturday, and which make him laugh every time she takes her breasts in her hands and pushes them skywards for his attentions. She walks over to the bed and lies down on top of the blanket. 'Will you be much longer?'

'I've no idea,' he says, and means it. 'I've got the entire internet to read. Haven't made much of a dent so far.'

'Pharaoh did tell you to spend some time with your family,' she says, midway through another yawn. 'I'm sure what she meant was that you should come over here on the bed with me and make me feel all pretty for a little while.'

McAvoy turns from the computer screen. Lets out his breath in one fast burst. She's spread-eagled on the blanket, one hand rubbing the dark triangle between her legs, the other, thumb glistening with spit, softly squeezing the full, fat nipple on her tiny left breast.

'Roisin, I . . .'

'You just carry on,' she says breathily. 'I'm fine on my own.'

She stops for a moment. Reaches over to her bedside table and pulls out a pot of muddy green ointment. She dips her finger in it, and begins to knead it firmly into the delta of her thighs.

'What's that?' asks McAvoy, his voice catching.

'My secret,' she teases. 'It's nice.'

'What's in it?'

'Lots of things. Mostly you.'

McAvoy feels his face turn red.

'Amazing how you can still blush when all your blood's heading south,' she says, and this time there's a tiny gasp in her voice.

He begins to stand, but she shakes her head at him. 'As you were, soldier.'

She closes her eyes.

A moment later, she turns onto her side and takes a bite of the quilt, goose-pimples rising all over her body, shaking as if in convulsion.

After thirty seconds, the motions subside and she rolls onto her back, a smile on a face shiny and red with perspiration.

'Sleepy now,' she says, and one eye is already beginning to close.

McAvoy, breathless and hard, makes fists with his hands. Manages to drag his eyes away from her naked form and back to the computer screen. To the text document full of his notes. Wonders what he's learned. Wonders whether any of this has been worth his time.

Whether today he has been a good man.

He's going to have to sleep soon. His thoughts are starting to feel muzzy. He fancies he should be able to get four or five hours of sleep before he has to get himself back to the station. Before he starts getting emails back from people linked to sole survivors, and tries to put together some kind of report on who the hell they should be protecting.

Fucking reports. He's had a bellyful, this past year that began in a hospital bed, waiting for his commendation, and which, within a day, had seen his part in the capture of a serial killer hushed up, had seen promises broken, and seen the foundations laid for his speedy transfer to a job collating, sourcing, filing and inputting; dancing around the edges of real police work and trying not to let his heart burst through his chest every time the Serious and Organised Crime Unit took a call, and he was told to 'work the phones'.

He's already printed out his report for Pharaoh. Kept it succinct. Easily digestible. Kept out his hunches and theories.

Wonders whether he should have just given her it all. Handed her his mind in a manila envelope and told her to pick out the best bits.

He feels himself getting warm. Feels heat in his toes. Feet. Ankles. Can feel himself sinking into sleep. He picks up the report and shuffles it. A sheet of paper slips through his hands and he makes a grab for it. It's a picture of a one-armed, one-legged man, sketched by Fin, hours before.

McAvoy considers the drawing. Finds the energy for a smile. Finds some more for self-reproach. Should he be talking about these things in front of his boy? Is he doing him some damage by talking about death, about violence, about one-armed drunks and one-legged hacks?

He looks at the picture again. Wonders why he even mentioned the man with the missing arm. It had been one of the first things to spill from his mouth.

'You say Channler?'

The man had asked it in an accent that was pure Eastern bloc. Had appeared in front of McAvoy like some sort of ghoulish apparition as he emerged from the side door of the pub. McAvoy was putting his mobile back in his pocket, having left a voicemail for Chandler, asking him to ensure that he was going to be at the rehab centre mid-morning the following day. He hadn't realised he'd been talking at any volume.

'Chandler, yes,' said McAvoy, trying not to appear startled. Trying harder not to look at the armless shirt-sleeve, pinned across the man's chest. 'Russ Chandler.'

'Why you want Chandler? He not know Angie.'

'Miss Martindale was involved in a serious attack tonight—'

The man waved his single arm. He was tall. Wiry but hard-looking. He had a broad face, and despite only wearing a white shirt and faded jeans, didn't seem to notice the cold. There was something intense in his gaze. McAvoy placed him as one of the men from the bar. One of the men who blocked his way and got some kicks in. Bruised, cold and sick of being cut off mid-sentence, McAvoy hardened his own gaze.

'I hero. I stop bad man, yes?'

'You not stop bad man, no. You stop policeman trying to catch bad man.'

'Bullshit.'

'No bullshit.'

They stood, looking at each other, two tall men, eyeball to eyeball, angry and wind-blown.

'I mistake. Not Channler. No mind.'

The man turned to leave. McAvoy instinctively shot out a hand to stop him, and grabbed for the area where his arm should have been. He clutched at air. Then the voice of the young constable behind him had caused him to spin round. To take in the sight of the warm patrol car, its doors open, waiting to take him home. Home to Roisin, to Fin. When he turned back, the Russian was somewhere among the crowd that had gathered at the police cordon, in among the cigarette smoke and the beer cans, the chip wrappers and the wet clothes.

Somebody would take his statement. Somebody else . . .

McAvoy puts the picture down on top of the report. Looks at the stick-figure. The stump where the leg should be.

'Chandler,' he says to himself. What was the Russian talking about? Did it matter? Did any of it fucking matter?

His head starts lolling forward as the thick treacle of sleep climbs towards his mind. He staggers towards the bed, pulling his jersey off, easing down his shorts, already allowing himself to think of the warm touch of Roisin's skin as he spoons up behind her, places his large hand on the perfect orb of her belly and pictures his unborn child reaching up to press their own fingers against his, as if separated by prison glass.

His mobile phone bleeps.

Cursing, he rolls back off the bed and finds his work clothes crumpled up in a heap next to the wardrobe. He finds his mobile, and looks at the display. Notes that it's not yet 1 a.m.

Opens the message.

It's from a number he doesn't recognise.

*Colin Ray has arrested Chandler. Thought you might like to know. Tom Spink.*

Feels his heart sink as bile rushes up his throat and fills his mouth.

Wide awake in an instant.

# PART THREE

# CHAPTER 19

The snow has begun to fall. Fat, white, perfect flakes tumble in their millions from a sky a hundred shades of black, icing the kerbs, the pavements, the rooftops, the awnings; adding inches of height to the wet, damp city.

McAvoy looks but does not see. The windscreen is misted insensible from the breath that eases from his lungs in a low, icy, angry whistle. Two great dorsal fins have been carved in the snow upon the glass by wipers he has no memory of switching on. He does not register the weather. Nor the cold. Just grinds his teeth and narrows his eyes and drives the people-carrier too fast on slick, treacherous roads.

*Colin Ray*, he thinks. *Colin Fucking Ray.*

The effort of holding his jaw tight is giving him a headache and the cold is making his ribs ache. Gradually, in increments, he becomes aware of the pain. Becomes aware of his surroundings. Of the weather.

'You silly bastard,' he says to himself, for what must be the hundredth time. 'Why did you go home. Why?'

When the anger subsides he will find time to reproach himself for this. Tell himself that he lost his temper because he feared having his moment of glory taken away. Missing out on the arrest in a case that has crawled under his skin. He will find ways to loathe himself, and resolve to never let his own need for personal glory become his primary reaction when learning about an arrest in a murder investigation. But for the moment, it feels justified. He is not the lead investigator, but it feels like his case. It is he who has slotted the pieces together. He who has twice looked into the wet blue eyes of the man who is committing these crimes.

Worst of all, he finds himself wondering if he has got it wrong. Ray couldn't have gone in with nothing. Couldn't have arrested Chandler on a hunch.

Christ, what if it really is him?

Gingerly, so as not to add to the dull agony in his ribs, he turns the wheel hard to the right and pulls into the car park at the back of Queen's Gardens station. Parks in a spot reserved for visiting senior officers and finds himself quite enjoying the feeling of not giving a damn whether he gets into trouble. Kicks open the door as the wind and the snow take him in their fist.

'McAvoy,' comes a voice. 'Sergeant. Here.'

Struggling with the door, shivering as the snow spills from the brim of his hat and down the collar of his ragged rugby shirt, he glares across the car park at the dimly lit rear entrance to the building.

McAvoy leaves a trail of deep, perfect footprints as he crosses the distance between himself and the voice. The snow is ankle-deep already.

'Figured you'd come,' says the voice, and as McAvoy gets closer he sees Tom Spink, standing in the doorway, a mug of

something in one hand, dressed, as yesterday, in dark
trousers, cardigan and collarless shirt.

'I got your message,' says McAvoy, who is too wind-blown
and irritated to chide himself for stating the obvious.

Spink nods. Blows out a sigh, then holds out the mug as
McAvoy skips up the stairs and into the shadow of the
doorway.

'Fancy a nip?'

McAvoy doesn't care what's in the mug. He takes it and
gulps down a liquid that is at once warming and cold.

'Calvados,' says Spink, taking the mug back. 'They're in
interview room three. We'll talk on the way.'

Stepping through the open door, a wave of heat washes
over them both. Overhead, the motion-activated, energy-effi-
cient lighting flickers on and the corridor is bathed in lurid
green. At this hour, the station is virtually empty, with the
civilian workers long since tucked up in bed and only a
skeleton staff of uniformed officers tasked with manning the
custody suite while the patrol cars and traffic officers are
scattered across the city, no doubt hunkered down somewhere warm with flasks of tea and petrol-station food.

McAvoy is about to ask what the hell has happened in the
few hours since he left the Bear, but Spink gives him no
opportunity. He starts talking softly, rapidly, as they make
their way up the hall, past locked doors and noticeboards
overflowing with policing initiative posters, rotas, rosters
and staff news. McAvoy has never once seen anybody stop to
read them.

'Pharaoh's not here,' he says under his breath. 'She knows,
though. Spitting bullets and teeth.'

'Is she on her way in?'

'Can't. Her husband's an ill man. Wheelchair-bound, if you hadn't heard. He has good days and bad days. This is a bad day. She's trying to get somebody to watch him and the kids so she can get across, but in this weather I doubt we'll see her.'

'So this wasn't her call?'

'Are you joking? Christ, she's going spare.'

'She didn't send DCI Ray?'

'No chance. The cheeky monkey did this as soon as her back was turned. Trouble is, it's starting to look like the right move. To the top brass at least.'

'What?' McAvoy stops dead in the corridor, and then has to scamper to catch up with Spink when he realises the man isn't stopping.

'Look, I'm just an innocent bystander, son,' he says, shaking his head and then nodding to direct them down another corridor as they come to a crossroads. 'Trish knows her stuff, but she's got her enemies. She was never meant to have this job. For every woman and ethnic minority member that gets promoted to make us all look reasonable and for-ward-thinking, another twenty blokes from the old school get bumped to superintendent. If Colin Ray's gone in with his size tens and managed to nab somebody we can actually pin this on, they're not going to tell him off for going over Trish's head.'

'But it's a nonsense,' says McAvoy, the frustration apparent in his voice. 'Chandler couldn't possibly—'

'Look, I'm not the one with the answers, lad,' he says, slowing their pace and looking up from watching his footsteps to actually make eye contact with McAvoy. 'I'm just a writer these days. A writer who happens to hear things now and then and a writer who tonight, happened to be having a mug of tea with the desk sergeant when Colin Ray and Shaz Archer brought in a little bloke holding a wooden leg and asking for you. I phoned Trish. She said she'd get here as soon as she could. Told me to let you know. I have.'

'She asked you to tell me? Why?'

'I don't know, lad. Perhaps she wanted you to make them some sandwiches.'

Spink turns to walk on, but McAvoy blocks his way. 'What have they got? What has Ray found?'

Spink looks down the corridor, as if keen to make a break for it, then appears to come to a conclusion.

'I don't know how much of this is bollocks and how much they can prove, but Colin's been telling people that you and Trish have ballsed up. Failed to run a background check on a key suspect in the investigation. It turns out Chandler isn't called Chandler at all. He's really Albert Jonsson. Registered under that name at the clinic. Asks to be called Russ Chandler and people respect it, but he's a non-person. Albert Jonsson, however, is very real. And he's got a record. One count of wounding, two burglaries, obtaining money by deception . . .'

'But we were going to interview him tomorrow,' McAvoy says through gritted teeth.

'There's more,' says Spink, looking away. 'There was no chance of a warrant. Not at this hour. So Shaz Archer laid on the charm. Persuaded the night staff to do a search of Chandler's room. They found his notebook.'

Something about Spink's tone of voice makes McAvoy feel as though he is opening a final demand.

'And?'

'And Daphne Cotton's name's in there, son. Clean sweep.'

McAvoy's shoulders slump forward. His head lolls to his chest. He takes a step backwards and leans his against the wall, blood rushing in his head. Could he really have been so wrong? Could he really have sat and chatted with a killer?

'It doesn't have to mean anything,' says Spink. 'I've seen bigger coincidences.'

McAvoy tells himself to nod, but can't find the strength. He feels as though he's been kicked in the gut.

'He's not admitted it, then?' he asks, his voice suddenly weary and old.

'They're conducting the interview now. All he'll say is "no comment", or at least that was how he was playing it last I heard. But Colin's persuasive. He won't back off.'

McAvoy manages the faintest of nods. 'Jonsson? That's . . . ?'

'Icelandic, yes. Again, could be nothing.'

'But probably not.'

'No.'

He tries to pull himself together. Wishes, for a moment, that he smoked, just so he could busy his fingers with lighting something that would bring him a modicum of comfort.

'If it is him . . .'

'Yes.'

'At least he'll be off the streets,' he says, trying to make himself feel relieved that at least a murderer would be behind bars. 'At least we'll have done some good.'

'Exactly,' says Spink, and tries a grin.

The silence stretches out.

'It looked nothing like him,' says McAvoy, more to himself than anybody else. 'Different eyes.'

'I know.'

'And he called me,' he says, suddenly loud. 'He called me about Angie Martindale. Why would he do that? And he wouldn't have had time. He called, me, remember? You're getting this so wrong . . .'

'They found a mobile in his room. They've contacted the mobile phone company. Should hear back in the morning. They'll know where the signal came from. They'll know if he took a break from carving his name on Angie Martindale for long enough to give you a fighting chance at stopping him.'

'They think he was playing a game?'

Spink nods.

'Cat and mouse with me the stupid Scottish pussy?'

Spink smothers a smile by wiping his hand across his mouth. 'We don't know anything yet,' he says.

From nearby comes the sound of voices. Footsteps. Excited chatter. Without saying anything, McAvoy and Spink push off from the wall and follow the sound. They turn left at the next T-junction and carry on past the four pieces of Blu-tack that used to hold a laminated piece of paper bearing the words INTERVIEW ROOMS.

Outside a wooden door with a long narrow pane of glass at its centre stand Colin Ray and Shaz Archer. Ray is holding open a manila folder, nodding vigorously as Archer points into its depths with a chewed biro.

'. . . would make anybody frustrated,' she's saying. 'Big brain, little dick, big problems, eh Col? How many times we seen it? Can't just go out and pick a fight, because he's too high and bloody mighty for that, but he can dream up something like this, eh? Something that makes him that bit special. It's all here.'

McAvoy would have been content to turn away. To walk back the way they'd come without being seen. But Spink coughs and greets the two officers with a smile.

'Going well?'

Colin Ray's eyes flash anger. He closes the folder as if trying to squash a fly in its pages. Flares his nostrils as if preparing to charge.

'She sent her errand boy?'

The question is directed at Spink, but McAvoy knows it is himself to whom Ray is referring. Later, he will tell himself that it's a good thing, that he's now known as Pharaoh's blue-eyed boy when a week ago she couldn't even spell his name. But now, it just makes his cheeks burn.

'It's my case too,' says McAvoy, and even as he does so, wonders where the words came from.

The two senior officers share a look.

'Well, you're here just in time to watch it end,' says Ray, nodding in the direction of the interview room. 'We've got the bloody lot.'

'He's confessed?' Spink sounds incredulous.

'He's giving it all the no comment at the moment,' pipes up Archer. 'But he's getting tired.'

McAvoy looks at them both. Colin looks tired and ill, but the map of burst blood vessels in his cheeks and the vein pounding at the side of his head suggest he has enough fire in him to see this through.

'You can't seriously expect to charge him . . .'

'I bloody can,' snaps Ray, looking down at the closed folder as if it contains treasure.

McAvoy can't help himself. 'What have you found?'

Shaz Archer suddenly looks like a cat stretching out after a long nap. Her whole posture becomes preening and luxurious. 'Woke up the chap that used to be his agent,' she says though a grin. 'Interesting man.'

'And?' Tom Spink's voice has become authoritative. The DCI inside him has momentarily forgotten he's retired.

'And he says our Russ Chandler, or whatever he likes to call himself, is a bloody headcase.'

She takes the folder from Ray's hands and holds its out to McAvoy, beckoning him forward as if enticing a dog with a biscuit. He takes the file.

'Read it,' says Archer, under her breath.

As McAvoy opens the folder he hears the door to the interview room open and close. He looks up into Shaz Archer's face. Ray has gone back in to finish the job.

'Not hard to fathom when you've got all the pieces,' says Archer, waggling her fingers in the air as she mimes mystery. 'Our boy in there's spent his bloody life trying to be an author. Dreamed of it since he was a kid. Never good enough. Got his early works rejected without being opened. Got some interest when he started doing a bit of investigative work but never took off. Had to self-publish in the end. One book was almost readable, managed to get himself an agent, but it still never happened. Just lost it in the end. Couldn't keep taking the rejection. Couldn't stand writing about people who he saw as nobodies and not being a household name himself. Came up with all of this as a way of payback. Psychologically it's a neat fit. Get a shrink to sign it. Col knows somebody . . .'

McAvoy's been fighting with himself not to blurt out the word 'bollocks' but it's a battle he can't win.

'That's all just guesswork, isn't it, DI Archer?' says Spink, distracting her before she can turn on her junior officer.

'We've got his fantasies,' she says, pointing at the folder. 'We've got Daphne Cotton's name in his notebook. We've got Angie Martindale. His involvement with Fred Stein. Trevor Jefferson. He's the common link.'

'But that doesn't mean—'

'Read the letter he sent the publisher that turned him down.'

There is something about the way she says it that makes McAvoy stop talking. He leafs through the photocopied pages in the file. Notices the red felt pen circle around the page of handwritten notes. Sees the name 'Daphne C'. A phone number. Reams of shorthand. He turns the pages.

'There,' says Archer, nodding.

Dear Mr Hall,

My agent, Richard Sage, has just informed me of your decision not to proceed with the publication of my novel, *All Hands*. As you can perhaps imagine, I find this news very distressing. I have poured my heart and soul into this volume and, as sales of my previous, albeit self-published, literary efforts demonstrate, there is a market for my work. I must ask that you reconsider. In our previous correspondence I have spoken in glowing terms of the esteem in which I hold your publishing house and I have taken great personal interest in both your organisation and its personnel. For example, I know that your home address is Lowndes Square, Knightsbridge. Your wife's name is Lauren. Your son, William, boards at Rowan Prep School in Esher. I tell you this not to alarm or threaten you into offering me a publishing deal, but to demonstrate the meticulous single-mindedness of my painstaking research. Indeed, I am willing to go to almost any lengths in order to achieve my dream. As I have already mentioned, my own understanding of the criminal psyche is unsurpassed and my many interviews with convicted killers have offered me an unrivalled insight into the disordered mind. I await your response with interest . . .

McAvoy closes his eyes for five whole seconds. Imagines the correspondence being read out in court. Pictures Chandler's defence barrister telling him to change his plea to guilty and take the prosecution's offer of a reduced sentence. Sees Ray smiling as his mates slap his back.

'Open and shut,' says Archer, and for once, her words don't seem designed to pummel him. They merely state fact.

'What was the upshot?' asks McAvoy, in little more than a croak.

'Publisher threatened to go to the police and the agent dropped him,' says Archer, taking the folder from his hands and putting it under her arm. 'The agent's had plenty of emails from him as well. All in a similar tone. Totally obsessive. Sage said he's never met anybody so desperate. Somebody who would kill to see their name on a bookshelf.'

McAvoy frowns. It makes no sense. He's seen nothing in Chandler's eyes to make any of this believable.

'His eyes,' he remembers suddenly. 'The man I fought with had blue eyes. Chandler doesn't.'

'Fucking hell, McAvoy,' says Archer angrily. 'Maybe he wore contacts. That's all just detail. We've got murders, and we've got a guy with "murderer" written through him like a stick of Blackpool rock.'

'But if it's not . . .'

'Then he won't confess.'

McAvoy reaches into his coat and pulls out pages he'd printed off the internet moments after Spink sent him the message. 'Look at these,' he says pleadingly. 'There are other people at risk. Look at this woman. A charity worker blown up in Iraq. Still alive but she's the only one who made it. We can't get this wrong. The next victim could be here . . .'

McAvoy turns to Spink, but the older man is facing away from him, staring down the corridor, as if unable to meet his eyes.

The door opens and Colin Ray pokes his head out of the crack. His face is covered in sweat. The neck of his jumper is ragged and twisted. He looks at McAvoy for less than a heartbeat and then turns his gaze to Archer.

'Come in, Shaz,' he says quietly. 'Peg-leg wants to confess.'

She takes the printed pages from McAvoy's unresisting hand and walks back into the interview room.

# CHAPTER 20

8.43 a.m. Queen's Gardens. Ten days before Christmas.

A sunken area of parkland overlaid with a quilt of untouched snow, criss-crossed with hidden paths and peppered with dead rose bushes and rubbish-filled flower-beds.

One set of footprints punched deep in the ground.

A bench, missing its backrest.

Aector McAvoy. Elbows on knees. Hat pulled down low. Eyes closed.

Pulls his phone from his pocket. Eighteen missed calls.

He's hiding. He's stomped off into the snow and the solitude because it hurts too much to see somebody else shaking the Chief Constable's hand and drinking whisky surrounded by laughing uniforms and grinning suits.

Russ Chandler.

Charged with two counts of murder at 6.51 a.m.

Russ Chandler.

The man who butchered Daphne Cotton in view of the congregation at Holy Trinity Church.

Who set fire to Trevor Jefferson, then did it again in his hospital bed.

Russ Chandler. The man who answered 'no comment' for four hours, then told enough lies to get himself charged with murder.

In three hours he'll be remanded into custody pending trial. It will be months before the prosecutors begin spotting the holes in the case.

By then, the unit will probably have imploded, or been given over to Ray, and McAvoy will probably be driving a desk in some remote community nick where a man who's a dab hand with a database is a vaguely useful tool.

He puts the mobile away. Reaches down and picks up the litre bottle of fizzy pop that stands between his feet. Unscrews the cap and takes a swig. He's guzzling orangeade like a tramp downs cider. He's eaten three chocolate bars and a bag of jelly sweets. The sugar's making him feel a bit manic, and he's craving something beefy and deep.

He uncrosses his legs. Sits forward. Rubs his cold thighs. Sits back. Takes another swig. Wonders if he could just stay here for good. Make this bench his permanent home. Here, in the snow-covered isolation of Queen's Gardens; huddled inside his jacket, chocolate on his tongue, cold pain in his bones, and a feeling not unlike toothache boring into his brain, as if deliberately trying to make his thoughts hollow and painful.

It's quiet, here in the park. At this hour, this time of year, it's empty. Hull's empty. The sudden snowfall after days of frost has turned the city's network of pot-holed B-roads and winding dual carriageways into so many ice rinks and snow banks, and McAvoy fancies that the thousands of commuters who usually make their way into the city centre will be ringing in and suggesting they start their Christmas holidays early. Others will chance it. Take their old cars with their bald tyres and their too-small engines, and drive too fast on glassy tarmac. People will grieve today. Families will lose loved ones. By nightfall, forensics officers will be disentangling broken limbs from crushed cars. Uniformed officers will have broken bad news to sobbing relatives. A detective will have been assigned. A press release will have been circulated. The cycle will go on.

He wonders briefly whether anybody really gives a fuck about anything.

'Feeding the penguins, McAvoy?'

He looks up and sees the slender, elegant figure of Tom Spink crunching through the snow towards him.

'Sir, I . . .'

McAvoy begins to speak and stops again.

'Can't say I blame you,' says Spink airily. 'Does you good. Clears the head. Clears the lungs too, if you're a smoker. Mind if I join you?'

McAvoy nods at the space on the wrought-iron bench.

'It's wet,' he says, in case Spink hasn't noticed the two inches of snow icing the green-painted bench.

'It'll do,' says Spink, sitting down.

'Nippy,' he adds, as he makes himself vaguely comfortable. He's wearing a thin leather coat over his collarless shirt and soft cords. 'Suppose this is nowt where you're from, eh?'

McAvoy turns away.

'Pharaoh got as far as the Humber Bridge,' he says. 'Managed to get across despite the weather warnings. She was at the top of Boothferry Road when her mobile went and the brass told her not to risk it. To take a few days off. Colin Ray's got things under control.'

'She take any notice?'

'Yes and no. She's not going to crash the party. Diverted to Priory Road.'

'How's she taking it?'

'About as well as you'd expect. Managed to bite her tongue, but she's got to be careful how she plays this. If she keeps her head down, it could all work out fine. She'll have been lead detective on a successful hunt for a killer. If she starts shouting the odds and kicking up a stink, her card will be marked.'

McAvoy realises he's grinding his bunched fists into his knees. Forces himself to stop.

'It's not Russ Chandler,' he says through his teeth. 'I've been sitting here thinking about it. Thinking about nothing else. It's not him.'

Spink turns to him. Stares into his eyes for a good twenty seconds, as if trying to read the inside of his skull. Seems to scorch the inside of McAvoy's head with the intensity of his gaze. Then he turns away, as if making a decision.

'It often isn't.'

McAvoy pulls a face. 'What?'

'It often isn't, son. You know that better than anyone. You're going to kill yourself if you carry on like this, lad.'

'There's nothing wrong with giving a damn,' he spits angrily.

'No, lad. There's nothing wrong with giving a damn. But the price you pay for it is this. You must see it, you must see the cops who come to work, do a half-decent job, and head home without a backward glance. You must have seen them toasting questionable results and dodgy convictions. You must have wondered why you can't be that way.'

'I just think it matters,' he begins, and then stops when he feels the words catching in his throat.

'It does matter, Aector. It matters that a villain gets locked up, because that way, the public can go back to feeling all safe and secure in the knowledge that our boys in blue are up to the challenge of keeping them safe from nutters. That's why it matters. And it matters to the press, because it sells newspapers. And it matters to the top brass because it makes their crime statistics look peachy. And it matters to the politicians because voters don't want to live in a society where a young girl can get chopped up in a church during Evensong. And back at the bottom, it matters to coppers, because they don't want to get it in the neck from their superiors, and because most of them decided to become a police officer in the hope of making some kind of difference to the world. Then there are people like you, son. People who need to matter on some fucking cosmic level. People who need to find justice as if it's some fundamental ingredient of the universe. As if it's some naturally occurring mineral that you can drill for and dole out.'

Spink pauses. Waves a hand, tiredly.

'McAvoy, son, it's not like that. It should be, yeah. By Christ it would be nice if the whole world felt your outrage. If people couldn't eat or sleep or function until the balance had been redressed and the evil expunged by some act of good, or decency, or justice, or whatever you want to call it. But they don't. They read about something horrible and they say it's awful and they shake their heads and say the world's going to the dogs and then they put the telly on and watch *Coronation Street*. Or they go in the garden for a game of football with the kids. Or they head down the pub and have a few jars. And I know that it makes you sick, son. I know that you see people going about their daily business and it makes you angry and nauseous and empty inside that people are capable of such callousness and heartlessness when they should be focusing on the dead, but if you spend your life waiting for things to change, you're going to die a disappointed man.'

Spink stops. Screws up his eyes. Gives his head a little shake. Turns away.

McAvoy sits in silence. He tugs at the little patch of hair beneath his lower lip. Pulls it until it begins to come out. There's an anger in him. An indignation at being read, at being analysed, at being judged, by a man he barely knows and who has the temerity to call him 'son'.

McAvoy opens his mouth and shuts it again. He wipes a hand across his face.

'Colin Ray's got evidence, son. It might not match what's in your gut and it might just hurt like hell, but unless you've got any of that big bag of natural justice you want to sprinkle, then Russ Chandler's the man that can be tried, and maybe even convicted of murder.'

McAvoy glares at him. 'Do you think he did it?'

After a moment of trying to stare him out, Spink looks away. 'It doesn't matter what I think.'

McAvoy spits again.

He stands up. Takes a gulp of cold, fresh air.

Towers over the other man.

'It matters what I think.'

He says it through gritted teeth, but finds himself twitching into a smile, as the elation of realisation of acceptance seems to carbonate his blood, to fill his skull with endorphins and energy.

'It fucking matters.'

There's an art to walking in snow. Novices grip too hard with their feet; arching their soles, digging in with their toes, and are on their knees rubbing cramped-up calves within a hundred paces.

Others are too cautious, taking large strides, stepping onto patches of what seems like firm ground. They slip on iced concrete. Tumble, holding bruised shins – ankles twisting inside unsuitable shoes.

McAvoy walks as he was taught. Head down. Watching the ground for changes in the texture of the snow. Hands at his sides, ready to shoot out and break his fall.

He was born into a landscape harsher than this mosaic of tended grass and firm pavements, overlaid with six inches of white. He grew up on terrain scarred with crevices, with cracks, with loose shingle and shale; all concealed for eight months of the year by the relentless snowfall.

He sometimes remembers the noise the sheep made when they stumbled and snapped a leg. Remembers the silence too, in the moments after he ended their suffering. Slit their throats with a pocket knife. Pinched their mouths and nostrils closed with a gloved hand.

Remembers the artfulness with which his father could snap a neck. His acceptance of the necessity of his actions,

laced with a resolute determination to take no pleasure in
them.

Remembers, too, the damp eyes his father had turned
upon him. The tenderness with which he had reached down
and stroked the wool. The way he raised his hand to his nose
and breathed in the damp, musky scent of a ewe he had
reared from birth, and whose neck he had snapped to end
her pain.

The man at Holy Trinity Church had that same look in his
damp, blue eyes. So did the man who carved his name in
Angie Martindale. Who sat, crying, for an age before
embarking on his work.

Energised, blood pumping, thoughts racing in his mind,
McAvoy considers a killer.

'Is that what you're doing? Putting them out of their
misery? Are you ending their suffering? Are you asking me
to end yours?'

McAvoy stops. Lost in his thoughts, he has taken the wrong
path from the park.

His phone begins to ring. Number withheld.

'Aector McAvoy,' he says.

'Sergeant? Hi, this is Jonathan Feasby. I got a message to
call . . .'

McAvoy racks his brains. Puts the events of the past twenty-
four hours into some sense of order. Feasby. The reporter
from the *Independent*. The guy he'd emailed about the aid
worker in Iraq.

'Mr Feasby, yes. Thanks for getting back in touch.'

'No problem, no problem.' His voice is breezy. Southern-
sounding. Cheerful, considering the weather and the hour.

'Mr Feasby, I'm involved in the investigation into Daphne Cotton's murder and I believe you may have some information that would be relevant to the inquiry.'

McAvoy listens as the reporter gives a whistle of surprise.

'Me? Well, yeah, if I can. Hull though, isn't it? I've never even been to the North East.'

'Hull isn't in the North East, sir. It's in the East Riding of Yorkshire.'

'Right, right.'

'Are you aware of the case I'm referring to?'

'Not her name, no. But I just Googled "Hull" and "murder" and "McAvoy" and got myself about a billion hits. Process of elimination, I'm assuming it's the current one. Poor girl in the church, yes? Terrible.'

McAvoy nods, even though nobody can see.

'Mr Feasby, I want to talk to you about an article you wrote some time ago. It concerned an Anne Montrose. She was injured in an incident in Northern Iraq. I understand you were the freelance writer hired by the *Independent* to cover the incident . . .'

There is silence at the other end of the line. Pressing his ear to the phone, McAvoy fancies he can hear the sound of mental gears clashing.

'Mr Feasby?'

'Erm. I'm not sure I remember the case,' says Feasby. He's lying.

'Sir, I have a decent relationship with the local press and my colleagues make fun of me for my belief in human nature. If I talk to you off the record, will it stay that way?'

'I'm one of the last reporters who believes in such a concept.'

'Well, I'm one of the last men in the world who believes that a promise means something, and I promise you I won't be pleased if the contents of this conversation appear in print.'

'I understand. How can I help you?'

'I'm working on a theory that perhaps the man who killed Daphne Cotton may be targeting other people who have survived near-death experiences. That perhaps he or she is finishing off something that they view as an unacceptable escape from the Reaper's scythe. I am trying to work out who might be next on their list, if such a list exists. Anne Montrose fits the criterion. She was a survivor in an incident in which everybody else involved died. I want to know what happened to her after the story you wrote. I want to know that she's safe.'

There is silence at the other end of the phone. McAvoy listens out for scribbling.

'Mr Feasby?'

'If I'm off the record, then so are you, yes?' Feasby's voice has lost its lightness. He sounds pensive. Almost afraid. 'I'm not intending to incriminate myself or anybody else here . . .'

'I understand.'

The reporter lets out a whistled breath. 'Look, it probably doesn't mean much to you, but when I say that I've never done this before . . .'

'I believe you.'

McAvoy isn't sure whether he does or he doesn't, but knows how to sound sincere.

'Well, the only time I've ever taken money not to publish a story was when I tried to follow up on Anne Montrose. I had the opportunity to write one more bloody follow-up on one more bloody victim of one more bloody day of that bloody war. And I had the chance to write nothing. To call in a favour with my news desk and bury the whole thing . . .'

'How? Why?'

'I had the chance of a way out.'

McAvoy pauses. He tries to clear his head.

'After I wrote the story about the explosion, about what happened to her, a man came to see me,' he says, and his voice sounds far away.

'Go on.'

'He was the boss of a company that was making money in the clean-up operation. Rebuilding communities. Building schools and hospitals. And he said that if I did him a favour, he'd do me one in return.'

'And the favour?'

'Not another word on Anne. The newspaper would get full exclusives on everything that his company did from this point onwards . . .'

'And you?'

Feasby sighs. 'An honorary position on the board of his company.'

'You took it?'

'On paper I was a marketing consultant, helping his firm establish its media relations strategy . . .'

'And in reality?'

'I never wrote a word. Drew a salary for a few months, then went back to what I was good at.'

'You weren't curious?'

McAvoy imagines Feasby spreading his palms wide. 'I'm a reporter.'

'And?'

'And I don't think I should really be telling you any more until I've had a good hard think about what you really need to know.'

McAvoy pauses. He wonders if the reporter is fishing. Whether he is expecting the promise of an exclusive in exchange for his information.

His phone beeps in his ear. More from impulse than any conscious desire, he switches lines and answers.

'Mr McAvoy? This is Shona Fox from Hull Royal Infirmary. We've been trying to reach you for hours. It's about your wife. I'm afraid there have been complications . . .'

And nothing else matters any more.

# CHAPTER 21

McAvoy didn't sleep for the first twenty-seven hours. Didn't eat. Managed two sips of water from a cloudy, plastic beaker, then coughed them back up onto his stinking rugby shirt, mucus trailing from his eyes and nose.

Outside, Hull froze.

The excitement of a possible white Christmas gave way to fear at the harshness and severity of the conditions. The snow landed on hard ground. Froze. Fell again. Froze. The sky was a grey pencil sketch. Clouds broiled, rolled, twisted, curdled; like snakes moving inside a black bag.

The city stopped.

Later, McAvoy would tell his daughter that it was she who finally broke the winter's spell. That it was only when she opened her eyes that the clouds parted and the snow ceased its frenzied dance. That it was she who cost Hull its first white Christmas in a generation. She who brought out the sun. It would be a lie. But it would be a lie that made his daughter smile. A lie that allowed him to remember the first few days of her life with something other than a dull throb of agony.

He hears movement behind him.

Turns.

'Get back in that bed . . .' he begins.

'Well, I'm still a bit tender but if you want me that badly . . . ,' says Roisin, her face pale, her eyes dark. She's wearing a baggy yellow nightie and has a pink band holding her unwashed, greasy hair back from her face. She seems shapeless, somehow. He has grown so used to the bulge of her stomach pressing at her clothes.

'Roisin.'

'I'm bored, Aector. I need some kissing.'

He sighs. Rolls his eyes indulgently.

'Come here,' he says.

Unsteadily, she crosses to where her husband sits, his massive bulk crammed into a wooden, high-backed orange chair. He's facing the window but the curtains, with their nauseating greens and browns, are closed. She winces as she slides herself onto his knee, then drops her head to press her own clammy forehead into the mess of untended ginger curls upon his crown.

'You smell,' she says, and there's a muffled smile to her voice.

McAvoy, for the first time in days, snorts a laugh. 'You're not exactly a bowl of potpourri yourself.'

She raises her head. He feels her small, moist hand upon his cheek, turning his face upwards, angling him into her gaze.

For a moment they simply stare, a thousand conversations rendered pointless by the ferocity and tenderness of their connection.

'I was so scared,' she says, and although they are all but

alone, she whispers this admission, as if afraid that it will be used against her.

'Me too,' says McAvoy, and his truth seems to make her stronger. She leans down and kisses him. They kiss for an age. Break away only to smile at one another, to grin at the silliness of it all. To share a gleeful, knowing little glance, in the direction of the foot of the bed.

Lilah Roisin McAvoy was born on 15 December at 6.03 a.m.

Roisin had gone into labour almost as soon as McAvoy left the house, angrily reacting to Tom Spink's text; thundering through the blizzard in the people carrier with its ready-packed maternity bag in the boot.

She had tried to call him. Willed him to answer his telephone. Focused all her energies on reaching out through the cold miles between them. To come home. To help her.

Eventually, her cries woke Fin. It was he who persuaded her to ring 999. He who said that sometimes Daddy had to work and couldn't be there when other people wanted it. He who held her hand in the ambulance as the paramedics talked behind their hands about the volume of bleeding, the ice and snow on the roads, their belief that they should get time and a half for working nights in these conditions.

Roisin had tried to hold on. Tried to hold the baby in until the nurses reached her husband. But Lilah wanted out. Slithered out amid a gory rainbow of blood and mucus and was scooped up by a bald, bespectacled, Nigerian doctor, who carried her away to a waiting, scrubbed table, and performed complicated manoeuvres upon her tiny frame.

To Roisin, it seemed as if he was trying to breathe life into a dead bird.

She had turned away. Closed her eyes. Waited to be told the worst.

And then she heard the cry.

Lilah was four hours old, pink and wrinkled, with a breathing tube taped to the side of her face and oversized socks and mittens on her hands, before her father pressed his red, sweaty, tear-streaked face up against the plastic incubator and made the first of the thousand apologies he would stutter throughout the first few hours of her life.

When he took her from the nurse, she fitted perfectly in the palm of his hand.

Fin laughed at that. Asked if he had ever been that small. McAvoy told him no. That his sister had been so desperate to see him, she had come into the world early. That he was a big brother now, and it was his job to protect her.

Fin nodded solemnly. Gave her a wet, inelegant kiss upon the head. And then returned to the room full of grubby, donated toys, where he had been playing with a three-wheeled fire truck at the exact moment his sister began her wailing.

'She still sleeping?' asks Roisin.

'Out like a light. Just like her mum.'

'We've had a busy couple of days.'

'Yes.'

She tenses, as if preparing to vacate her husband's knee, and then relaxes, as she acquiesces to his firm hands and sinks back into his embrace.

'Let her sleep.'

'We nearly lost her, Aector. If she'd died . . . if she hadn't woken up . . .'

He feels her begin to shiver, and holds her tighter, shushing her sobs.

After a time, he again asks her the question he had blurted out through bubbles of snot when he raced into her room three days ago, snow billowing from his coat, a security guard dragging at either arm, almost water skiing behind him as he barrelled along the polished green linoleum.

'Will you ever forgive me?'

She answers him now, as she had then, with a perfect white smile. And for a precious moment, McAvoy feels so happy, so perfect, so loved and rewarded, that it crosses his mind to stop his own heart. To die happy.

This time, when she moves, McAvoy lets her. She stands. Winces again. Reaches out and pulls open the curtains.

'Bloody hell.'

They are four storeys up, enjoying one of the few private rooms on the maternity unit of Hull Royal Infirmary. The vantage point affords them a view of a city rendered almost faceless. Its landmarks, its idiosyncrasies, its character, all mute and anonymous beneath a thick covering of white. The streets are largely deserted. Roisin cranes her neck. Looks down at the car park. It is virtually empty. Half a dozen large 4x4s are parked here and there across the wide open space, like islands on a vast ice rink. The hospital is down to a skeleton staff. Those who were at work when the snow began to fall have largely stayed here. Those at home, with a car capable of staying right-side-up, have made it in, but the conversations on the eerily quiet wards and corridors revolve around how they will get home again; whether the car will even start when they ease themselves back behind the wheel.

'We're best off in here,' says McAvoy, pulling himself out of the chair.

McAvoy leans past her and looks out of the window. Gives a wry smile as he sees the small huddle of frail old men and fat middle-aged women, coats over their pyjamas, puffing desperately on cigarettes at the entrance to the car park; sucking the smoke into their lungs like diabetics gorging on insulin.

McAvoy looks down at the floor. He becomes suddenly aware of the mobile phone in his pocket. Feels it giving off waves of energy. Feels his fingers begin to twitch as he becomes overwhelmed by a need to switch it on. To plug himself back in. To find out what he's missed these past three days of pain and prayer.

'Roisin, do you mind if I . . .'

She's smiling. She gives the briefest of nods.

McAvoy stops at his daughter's cot. Rubs his big, rough fingers against her soft, fleshy cheek. *Apricots*, he thinks. *She has cheeks like apricots.*

Forty-three missed calls.

Seventeen text messages.

A voicemail service filled to capacity.

McAvoy stands in the doorway of the maternity unit, listening to the drone of voices.

Finds the call he has been looking for.

'Sergeant McAvoy, hi. Erm, this is Vicki Mountford. We met the other day to discuss Daphne. Look, this might not be important, but . . .'

McAvoy listens to the rest of the message. Pinches the bridge of his nose between forefinger and thumb.

Calls her back.

She answers on the second ring.

'Miss Mountford, hi. Yes, sorry. Vicki. I got your message. You mentioned that somebody else might have been aware of Daphne's essay. Is that right?'

'Yeah, yeah,' she begins. 'Well, I was talking to my sister, like I said in my message. It was a day or so after you and I talked. And anyway, I was telling her what we talked about and told her all about what had happened to Daphne and we were just gabbing about it and saying how creepy and terrible it all was, and then she remembered having told her bloke about it. Well, after I put the phone down she called me back and put me onto him and he sounded really sheepish and anyway, long story short, he remembers having a few drinks one night and telling a couple of blokes about this poor lass who's wound up in Hull and wrote this gorgeous essay about all the horrible things that had happened to her and how it would make a brilliant book . . .'

McAvoy closes his eyes. He's nodding, but saying nothing. Already he knows where this is going.

'And this was where?'

'Southampton,' she says, and from the wonder with which she says the word, she might as well be saying 'the moon'. 'He'd gone there for a job interview. He's your eternal student, is Geoff.'

'And?'

'Well, that's the thing,' she says. 'Geoff doesn't remember how it came up or what led to it, but this guy he got talking to was really interested. Said he was a writer. Well, Geoff's got a bit of a fancy for writing a book some day. So he sort of chatted this guy up. Told him what he knew, not that there was much. And he forgot about it, like. Until . . .'

McAvoy gives a cough. Suddenly feels horribly hungry. Finds himself longing for sugar.

'Until?'

'He logged on to the *Hull Mail* website a couple of days ago. The day I rang you. And he saw the man who's been charged. This Chandler. This writer. And . . .'

'. . . and it's the same man?'

There's silence again, but McAvoy can hear the nod.

He says nothing for a moment, then takes Geoff's details. Tells her she's done the right thing. That he'll get an officer to take a formal statement from her sister's boyfriend and that perhaps the lad will have to view an identity parade. Considers, for a moment, the difficulties of assembling a line-up of one-legged drunks.

When he hangs up, he catches a glimpse of his reflection in the dark glass front doors of the maternity unit.

Notes that he is smiling.

It's beginning to sink in, now.

Colin Ray's case is just waiting to be stamped on, and he knows exactly where to start.

He raises the phone again. Rings the CID office at Priory Road, where he knows there will be nobody around to answer. Leaves a message explaining that Roisin has been ill. That he hasn't been able to get away from her bedside to phone in. That he's going to be away until at least after Christmas.

Hangs up, slightly short of breath.

He's covering his tracks, now. Nobody at the CID office will think to check the time and date of the message. They'll just jot it down and eventually remember to pass it on to the brass. If it ever comes to an investigation, he'll be covered.

And he's bought himself a few days in which to find out who really killed Daphne Cotton.

He brings the phone up to his face. Rings the number that has just been breathed softly into his answering service.

It's answered on the third ring.

'Bassenthwaite House.'

McAvoy rubs a hand over his face and is surprised to discover that he is perspiring. Wonders whether this is a fool's errand. Whether this private medical centre on the edge of the Pennines has anything to do with any of this. Whether Anne Montrose matters. Whether she could be next. Whether he's just fucking wrong and Russ Chandler is indeed the man behind these deaths.

'Hello. This is Detective Sergeant Aector McA . . .'

He's met with a bright, heard-it-all-before 'hello'.

'It's concerning a private patient of yours. An Anne Montrose. I understand she's on your neuro ward receiving long-term care?'

There is silence at the other end of the line.

'One moment, please.'

Then he is placed on hold, and spends a good five minutes listening to a classical piece that, were he to really push himself, he would remember as being one of Debussy's more sombre works.

Suddenly, a deep, male, upper-class voice snaps a curt 'hello'. He announces himself as a Mr Anthony Gardner. By way of job title, he brushes over a word that might be 'liaison'.

'Mr Gardner, yes. It's regarding an Anne Montrose. I have reason to believe that she may be a patient of yours.'

After the briefest of pauses, Gardner clears his throat. 'You know I can't tell you that, Detective.'

'I appreciate your obligations to your patients, sir, but there is a chance that Miss Montrose may be in danger. It would be a huge help to an ongoing murder investigation if I was able to speak to a member of her family.'

'Murder?' Gardner's voice loses its composure. McAvoy feels oddly pleased that, even in these times, the word retains its ability to shock.

'Yes. You may have read about the case. A young girl was killed in Holy Trinity Church in Hull last Saturday. And the same person may be responsible for several other killings . . .'

'But I'm sure I read that somebody had been charged over that,' he says. McAvoy hears the tell-tale tapping of fingers on a keyboard. He wonders if the hospital exec is logging on to a news site.

'We have several loose ends to tie up, sir,' says McAvoy, with as much sinister foreboding as he can muster.

Gardner says nothing, so McAvoy plays a trump card.

'You may also have read that one of the victims was burned alive while in a hospital bed, sir.'

There is silence for a time. McAvoy hopes Gardner is considering the cost of being unhelpful. Wonders if he is weighing the angry phone call he may receive if he gives out patient details without going through the proper channels against the shit-storm that will descend if one of his coma patients gets herself immolated.

At last, Gardner gives a sigh. 'Can you leave me your number, Detective? I'll phone you right back.'

McAvoy thinks about saying no. And protesting that he'll stay on the line while Gardner does what he needs to do. But his approach seems to be working, and he doesn't want to push things hard enough to make them fail. Not yet. So he leaves his number and hangs up.

Paces for a while. Texts Tom Spink and Trish Pharaoh. Tells them Roisin is much better. That Lilah is thriving. Asks about Helen Tremberg.

His mobile rings. Anthony Gardner, sounding like he's giving out the combination to his safe, is curt and quiet, as though afraid to be heard. He's on the phone less than twenty seconds, but he gives McAvoy what he needs.

McAvoy gives a little nod to himself. Says nothing as he hangs up and immediately dials another number.

The call goes to voicemail.

'This is Sergeant McAvoy. Many thanks for those details. I'm sorry if we got off on the wrong foot the other day but I appreciated your change of heart. You were right. Anne Montrose is indeed a patient at that centre. And you won't be surprised to learn who's paying the bills. I think there may be a story in all this. Give me a call if you're interested.'

He ends the call. Counts to twenty. Enough time for Feasby to listen to the message. To mull it over. To give a sigh and give in to his hack instincts . . .

McAvoy's phone rings.

'Sergeant,' comes a voice. 'This is Jonathan Feasby.'

# PART FOUR

# CHAPTER 22

The clock on the dashboard reads 1.33 p.m. It's getting dark. Perhaps it never got light.

McAvoy is eighty miles from home, somewhere that the road signs claim to be the heart of Brontë country.

In the distance, the moors of West Yorkshire scream with bleak foreboding. Although the grass is damp and green, he would only be able to draw this picture with charcoal. It is a rain-lashed, empty and menacing landscape, fighting against a constant wind beneath skies the colour of quicksilver.

The track veers left. McAvoy follows it.

He steers the car through black, wrought-iron gates onto a gravelled drive. The driveway opens onto a large forecourt, which borders an immaculate green lawn, lush with dew and fine rain.

Against the darkening sky sits the house. Broodingly wealthy and eccentrically frayed around the edges.

'Take it easy,' he says to himself, as a prickling patch of sweat forms between his shoulder blades. Wishes he looked more like a police officer. In his stinking rugby shirt, threadbare jeans and increasingly ragged designer coat, he looks more like a tramp who's robbed a fancy-dress shop.

A movement behind him makes him turn. Another car is pulling into the driveway.

McAvoy does his best to fasten his shirt by its one remaining button but concedes defeat as it comes off in his hand.

He approaches the other vehicle, which is occupied by two men. One is perhaps in his fifties. He has greying hair and sharp, hawk-like features. The other is a younger man. Big, with a GI Joe-style crew cut.

He spins as a sound comes from the house.

A curvy, middle-aged woman in an expensive dress, black raincoat and leather boots emerges from the large oak double doors beneath the granite portico at the front of the house. She has blonde hair running to grey, cut into a layered bob. She is striking, though there is a sagginess to her face that suggests a melted beauty; that if she could just be twisted tight from the scalp, she would be vivacious and desirable once more.

The older man comes round from the driver's side. He is wearing a pair of jeans, an expensive pink shirt and a tweed jacket beneath a padded coat. A pair of glasses hangs on a chain around his neck and his face is so closely shaven that the skin looks raw and painfully abraded.

He extends a hand as he approaches and a gold watch glitters at his wrist. He jerks his jaw out a little, as if to say hello.

'You McAvoy?'

'Detective Sergeant Aector McAvoy. Humberside Police Serious and Organised Crime Unit. Lieutenant Colonel Montague Emms, I presume?'

The other man gives a grin. 'Not any more,' he says. 'Not the rank, anyway. I'm still Montague Emms, but I hate that, so call me Sparky. Everybody else does. Even the lad Armstrong, here.'

Emms extends a hand. McAvoy finds a calloused, rough palm and fingers. Gives a subtle roll of his thumb upon the back of the proffered hand and feels a set of knuckles that have been broken and inexpertly set.

Emms gestures in the direction of the house. 'Shall we?'

The woman in the doorway retreats inside as they approach. Emms makes a show of having forgotten something obvious and turns back to the soldier. 'Get your stuff, son. The boys will be back soon to show you where you're going. There's a barn and stables down that track to your left if you want to keep warm.'

He turns back to McAvoy before Armstrong can even snap off a salute.

'New recruit?' asks McAvoy as they pass through the doors.

'Possibly,' says Emms, who, up close, is taller than McAvoy has realised. He walks with a straight back and firm, confident steps.

'Lovely place,' says McAvoy conversationally as they pause in the hallway. A few steps ahead, the woman is opening a wooden door set in an oak-panelled wall. She smiles at them both, pushes the door back as far as it will go, and then steps back.

'Guess we're going in my study,' says Emms lightly. 'That's the wife, by the way. Ellen. Looks after me. Don't know where I'd be without her.'

'I've got one of those,' says McAvoy, before he can help himself.

'A good woman's worth her weight in gold,' says Emms, and the two exchange a look that suggests they share a wisdom and truism that not many other men have learned. McAvoy finds himself warming to the man.

'Right, I'll just go rustle us up a pot of tea. You make your-self comfortable in my study and I'll be back in a jiff. Tea, yes? You don't strike me as a coffee drinker.'

'Is that racial stereotyping, sir?' asks McAvoy, with enough of a smile to show he's joking.

'Ha!' says Emms, throwing his head back.

Emms is still laughing as he strides away, turning left at a door opposite the study and leaving a trail of muddy boot-prints on the wooden floor.

McAvoy has to bow his head slightly as he enters the study. The house must be at least three centuries old, and he knows from experience that doorways then were built for a smaller race.

It's a modest, rectangular room, with a large sash window taking up almost the whole of the far wall. Two computers and three telephones sit on an antique desk, which is littered with typed documents and what look like haphazardly folded architectural blueprints.

On the desk, in an ornate gold frame, is a pen-and-ink drawing. McAvoy has to squint to make it out. A face or a form? A landscape? It seems to have been scribbled and scrawled, but upon closer inspection he sees that each and every line has been individually etched. It is a bewildering piece of haphazard beauty that McAvoy wishes he better understood.

The light from the window is insufficient to illuminate the

room, so McAvoy reaches up and flips an old-fashioned metal light switch. The bulb flickers into life.

McAvoy finds himself staring at an entire wall of photographs. Squares of corkboard have been nailed up and their surfaces are adorned with snaps of smiling, grinning men in military fatigues. McAvoy examines the images. There must be hundreds of men here. Sitting on tanks. Giving thumbs-up on dusty, sun-baked runways. Overloaded with packs and guns, helmets and radio equipment, lounging in the backs of open-top Jeeps or stripped to the waist and greasy with exertion, a football between their legs and sand on their boots. Some of the images must be thirty years old. In some, the moustaches of the officers and the poor, grainy quality of the images put McAvoy in mind of footage he has seen of the Falklands War. He wishes he'd done more research on Emms's military career before he asked Feasby to arrange this meeting. Wishes he knew what the fuck he was doing here.

'Ah, my wall of shame,' says Emms, making McAvoy turn round sharply as he emerges in the doorway holding two mugs of tea. McAvoy doesn't know why, but he'd rather expected a pot on a tray, positioned between elegant cups and saucers. Instead, into his hand is thrust a mug bearing a company logo. Magellan Strategies.

'I was just admiring . . .'

'Yes, yes,' says Emms, happily enough. 'Those are the boys and girls who've served under me. Mostly boys, if I'm honest. And not all of them. But as many as I could find. Ellen thinks I'm daft. Tells me that I should have pictures of the grandchildren up in here, but I can't bring myself to take them down.'

'You must miss it.'

'Soldiering? Yes and no. I did twenty-eight years. Enough to scratch any itch. And I'm still on the scene, as it were. Still got plenty to keep me busy.'

'You set up the company when you were discharged, did you?'

'Just about. Made the right contacts while I was working towards retirement, so to speak. But things just landed right. And it's not just me, you understand. I had partners at first. Board of directors now we're established. All very proper and above board. I don't even think they need me any more. I've got an honorary title and they still ask me to oil a few wheels, but we're not doing so badly.'

'You're still involved in recruitment, though?' asks McAvoy, gesturing back towards the door, where he imagines Armstrong to be standing rigidly at attention, as the fine rain that has begun to drift past the window soaks him to the skin.

'Oh, he's the son of an old pal of mine,' says Emms, plonking himself down in the armchair and taking a swig of tea. 'Didn't really take to the regular army. Some don't. He lost a couple of mates first tour. Insurgents. Opened fire while him and two pals were handing out sweets to a bunch of kids. Armstrong ran. His mates didn't. There was a video on the internet for a while of what happened to them. The worst. Not a mark on Armstrong but it hurt him. Pointlessness of it, you see? I'll never understand it myself and we make a living as experts in these places. Managed to get him a discharge and we're going to try him out. I've got our assistant head of recruitment up here this weekend with a couple of the other new boys. They're out on a training run right now.'

'You didn't let Armstrong in the house,' says McAvoy, turning away from the photographs to fix Emms with a deep stare.

'If your wife looked like mine, would you fill your house with soldiers?' Emms says it with a laugh, but McAvoy can tell he is serious.

'Good point,' he says.

After a pause, Emms shrugs and appears ready to get down to business. 'So,' he says, as McAvoy takes a seat in the wooden chair. 'You wanted to talk about Anne.'

McAvoy looks away from the older man's friendly, alert face. Suddenly, the silliness of it all hits him like a fist. He wants to be able to tell him something with substance. Something that justifies this man's time. Justifies his own decision to drive into the middle of bloody nowhere.

'Mr Emms . . .'

'Sparky,' he corrects.

'About that . . . ,' he says, grateful for the reprieve.

'Long story, told short. When I was a young officer I came up with a brilliant time-saving device ahead of a night out. Decided to dry my hair while still in the bath. One day, dropped the bloody hair-drier. Danced like a bloody fish on dry land for about five minutes until a pal switched the thing off. Almost cooked myself. Been Sparky ever since.'

McAvoy breathes out, impressed and appalled. 'Ouch.'

He starts his explanation again.

'Anyway, as I'm sure Mr Feasby said when he called, I'm involved in the investigation into Daphne Cotton's death. Are you aware of the case?'

'Bad business,' says Emms, closing his eyes. 'Poor girl.'

'Yes.'

McAvoy pauses. Decides to plump for honesty.

'I was there when it happened. I heard the screams. Got there a minute too late. Got knocked down by the man who did it.'

Emms simply nods. His eyes speak volumes.

'In the wake of that crime, I've been looking into several other incidents. Not obviously connected, but certainly with a link that bears examination.'

'Oh yes?' Emms looks interested.

'The link between the victims is their survival,' says McAvoy. 'Survival of an incident that killed everybody else. A former trawlerman who made it home alive when thirty-odd mates drowned was found dead in a lifeboat off the coast of Iceland just over a week ago. A bloke who set fire to his own house and killed his family was burned to death in a room at Hull Royal Infirmary. A woman who was almost butchered by a serial killer was attacked in exactly the same way in Grimsby.'

McAvoy drops his head to his hands.

'I just don't want Anne Montrose to be another victim.'

Emms says nothing for a while. He takes another slurp of his tea. Looks up at his photographs and then gives a nod.

'I see where you're coming from. Did I not hear they had somebody for that, though? Some writer bloke. Pissed off at the world, and whatnot.'

'Russ Chandler has been charged, yes.'

A slow smile spreads across Emms's face. 'But you're not convinced.'

'I believe there are still avenues to be explored.'

'I bet you're going to be popular.'

'I don't care about being popular. I want to make sure the right person is locked up. I want to make sure nobody else gets hurt.'

'Very commendable,' says Emms. 'Why Anne?'

'She's one of many,' says McAvoy, looking through the glass as the landscape darkens and the rain begins to billow like unfastened sails. 'But it fits, I suppose. I don't know how he's choosing them. I don't know why he's doing it. But . . .'

'But . . .'

McAvoy balls his fists as he blurts out to this virtual stranger the one thought that makes him a better policeman than those around him. 'Because if I was doing it, she'd be the one I'd do next.'

'Method actor, are you?'

'What?'

'You know, De Niro and Pacino. Put yourself in the mind of the character, yeah? Live like them. Think like them. Get inside their heads, and whatnot.'

'I don't know if I—'

'Makes sense,' says Emms. 'Well, at least I can put your mind at rest.'

'I'm sorry?'

'Anne Montrose. If you're right about this bastard, he's out to get people who survived properly. Cheated death, or however you want to see it. Anne didn't. Anne's never woken up. She's been in a coma since it happened. She's not a survivor. She's just got a pulse.'

McAvoy nods, rubbing his face with his hands. He realises how unshaven he is.

'Could you at least tell me a little about the background? What happened. Your relationship. Why the bills come to you.'

Emms raises his glasses from the chair around his neck and puts them on. Examines McAvoy with a collector's gaze.

'I barely knew Anne,' he says, and shrugs. 'She was a nice woman, from what I'm told. Loved kids. Real sweetheart. Wouldn't get out when it made sense to. Thought she could do some good. Wrong place, wrong time. Arranged a trip for the school where she was helping and the bus blew up the second the driver turned the key. Anne was still in the open doorway, waving to the other teachers. The blast threw her clear but she hit her head. Never woke up.'

'But why you? Why did your company get involved?'

Emms blows a long, sustained sigh that turns into a raspberry on his wet lips. He stands up and crosses to his picture walls. Pulls down an image that has been pinned in the top right corner of the boards.

'Him,' he says, showing McAvoy the picture.

McAvoy looks at an image of two smiling men. One is stripped to the waist, sweat greasing a boxer's torso, and one beefy arm thrown round the neck of a tall, rangy man in combat fatigues. McAvoy squints and turns to Emms.

'That you?'

Emms nods. 'A younger version, anyway. Balkans. Ninety-five, maybe? I should really date these things.'

'And the other man?'

'Simeon Gibbons. Major, by the time he got his discharge. Trained as a chaplain but joined the front line.'

McAvoy waits expectantly.

Emms cocks an eyebrow. 'Anne Montrose's fiancé.'

'And your relationship to Major Gibbons?'

Emms gives a rueful laugh. 'Call it brothers-in-arms. He was my best officer. Best friend, if such a thing can exist. I wanted him to come into the security business with me but we had a difference of opinion over all that. Call it a clash of ideals. He said he wouldn't be a mercenary. I told him that we were helping people. Building something special. Saving lives. He said Anne would do that for free. It was an argument neither of us was going to win. So he stayed in the army. I set up Magellan.'

'And Anne?'

'He met her in some godforsaken hole in Iraq. Fell head over heels. He's not the sort to do that, Simeon. He's a controlled sort of chap. Keeps it all in. Has his beliefs and won't change them. Christian man. Fell for Anne like you wouldn't believe.'

'So when the explosion happened . . .'

Emms shrugs. 'I heard about it from another old pal. Thought the least I could do for an old mate was to keep the press away. Easily done, to be honest. Don't expect me to feel bad for paying off a journalist, Sergeant.'

McAvoy shakes his head. 'I don't. I understand.'

'Gibbo lost his mind over it. Couldn't reconcile it. It's hard to describe to people who have never been there. To war, I mean. Over there. Under the sun. The remoteness. You start questioning everything. You start seeing the world differently. People find religion, or lose it. Happens to the best of us, and when he lost Anne, it kind of broke him open. I don't know what filled him up. He wouldn't speak to his old mates. Wouldn't go home. Even when I had her flown back to the

UK . . . even when I got her in the private facility, got her round-the-clock care . . .'

Emms looks down at the photograph in his lap. Looks into the face of an old friend who lost his mind when his heart was broken.

'Was he discharged?'

'Didn't get the chance,' says Emms, looking up. 'Chunk of metal from a roadside bomb tore through his throat not long after. He bled to death on the side of the road in Basra. Should never have been cleared for active service in the first place.'

'I'm sorry.'

'It was such a waste. Such a beautiful man.' He reaches back. Picks up the pen-and-ink drawing from the desk. Holds it up to show McAvoy. 'Talented, too.'

He unclips the frame and pulls out a piece of expensive, cream-coloured card. It's signed on the back. Emms closes his eyes as he regards it and McAvoy suddenly feels intrusive and out of place.

'I'm sorry.'

'You said.'

Silence falls in the small room. It's only mid-afternoon but the darkness is sliding towards the floor like a blind.

'And you still pay her bills?'

'Wouldn't you?'

McAvoy doesn't have to think about it. He knows he would bankrupt himself to care for a stranger.

'I'll put two of the boys on a guard detail at Anne's bedside. Just to be on the safe side. Phone me when you think this is at an end.'

To break the air of misery that's fallen, Emms turns to the window. 'Never stops,' he says.

'Sorry?'

'The rain. I bought this house for Ellen. She always wanted to be lady of the manor. Grew up reading the Brontë sisters and fancying Heathcliff. Had this romantic notion about windswept moors and rain-lashed hillsides. And she's got 'em. Just bloody depressing, if you ask me. She's wanting a horse next. I think she's got a fancy for meeting some dusky chap in riding breeches out on a hillside. She's got a lovely mind for that kind of thing.'

McAvoy gives a smile and enjoys the feeling. 'My Roisin's like that. Head full of lovely pictures.'

'Hard to measure up, isn't it?'

McAvoy nods, and both men share a moment of something that feels uncannily like friendship.

'Armstrong will be shivering,' says McAvoy.

'He's been through worse. We'll work him hard but there's good money in it if you play it right.'

'And you think his mind is right? After what happened?'

'He won't be in the firing line, so to speak. He'll be overseeing one of our freight contracts. Going to meetings. Providing a bit of muscly reassurance for building contractors. Once he gets in with the lads, he'll lose himself in the banter. Your mates are what matters, places like that.'

In the way he says it, McAvoy catches a need for something he recognises. Perhaps better than anybody else, he understands the need to be told that he's done the right thing.

# CHAPTER 23

The snow that fell in Grimsby earlier in the week has melted away. Somehow, it has endeavoured to clean the streets with its departure, and the town has a scrubbed appearance that puts McAvoy in mind of a dog emerging, blinking and bewildered, from a bath it has unwillingly taken.

The evening air is infused with the kind of subtle rain that can soak a man to the skin before he's even realised he should put on a coat.

McAvoy didn't expect to be back here so soon. Not back on the street where so recently he wrestled with a killer, and saved a life.

Perhaps to spare him the sight of that bloody and painful struggle, or perhaps just to tuck her beloved vehicle away somewhere slightly better protected, Pharaoh parks the sports car several streets away from the Bear.

'Cheer up,' she says, opening the door and filling the car with a gust of chilly, greasy air. 'We're on expenses.'

McAvoy pulls his collar up as he extricates himself with difficulty from the compact two-seater. His head is reeling.

Suddenly, as he wanted all along, the investigation is being done the right way.

He focuses on the barrage of new information that Pharaoh has poured into his ear on the half-hour journey from Hull.

'They speak bloody good English,' she says, impressed. 'Very respectful people. Actually wanted to help. Very refreshing.'

She is suddenly a fan of the Icelandic State Police, having spent a pleasant fifteen minutes charming the pants off a couple of young detectives in a rural station – massaging their egos and explaining that their information could help catch a serial killer.

They were only too happy to help. And the information they divulged was going to make Colin Ray very unhappy.

One of the containers on the cargo ship which had been chartered for Fred Stein's documentary had indeed been tampered with. When the vessel docked, and the missing man was reported, two officers from a small-town police station had interviewed the captain and first mate. They had taken photographs of Fred Stein's cabin. They had interviewed the TV crew and requested copies of their film. And they had taken a brief look around the cargo bay. Even to their somewhat inexpert eyes, it was clear that one of the containers at the bottom of the stack was not in the same condition as the scores of others that towered above and around it. A ragged hole, perhaps four feet by three, had been carved into the metal door. A torchlit examination of the interior showed it to be empty, save for a dirty sleeping bag and three empty bottles of water. They questioned the captain again. Asked what could have caused the damage. Whether it looked to him, as it did to them, as if had been made using with an oxyacet-ylene torch. He had shrugged. Said that stowaways were a problem. There was a serial number on the side of the con-tainer that Tom Spink had managed to trace to a haulage company based in Southampton. The woman who answered the haulier's phone was the same person who had, a little over a week before, taken the initial freight order that booked the container's passage.

'Sometimes it's just joining the dots,' says Pharaoh, as they begin walking up Freeman Street, pressed close enough together to be mistaken for a mismatched couple. 'Sometimes you just get lucky. Sometimes, it really is that bloody easy.'

The woman at the haulage company remembered the booking. It had been made by a man she knew well. Used to drive the cherry-picker that loaded the containers onto the cargo ships at Southampton docks. Lost his arm when a stack toppled over in high winds and crushed him under enough cargo to kill most people. Had moved up north, last she heard. Was nice to hear from him again. Apparently, he was working as a stevedore up on the Humber somewhere. They'd been asked for a reference and been happy to oblige, and he sounded pretty well when he said his hellos and booked pas-sage for the container which, bizarrely, he had insisted be stowed towards the bottom of the stack. She put it down to a peculiarity caused by his accident. Perhaps she'd misheard what he'd said. It was sometimes difficult, due to the thick Russian accent . . .

Pharaoh nods at the open front doors of a dark-painted,

old-fashioned bar that takes up the space of three shops in a small arcade that faces onto the main street.

A bouncer, mug of tea in his hand and earpiece trailing down a thick bullish neck, lounges against the brick front wall. He glances at Pharaoh's breasts, impressively visible despite her leather jacket, and then gives McAvoy his attention. He appears to straighten slightly, as if suddenly realising that, for the first time in a long time, he is looking at a bigger man.

'Evening,' he says. 'Last orders in fifteen minutes so you better sup quick.'

Pharaoh reaches into her cleavage and pulls out her warrant card.

'Oh fuck,' says the bouncer with a sigh.

'It's nothing heavy,' she says, putting her hand on his arm. 'I need to talk to somebody who drinks in here. And I think you would like to help me. A big chap like you has "protector" written all over him. And I know you want to spare me the bother of walking the streets on a night like this.'

The bouncer gives a scowl, but it's a token gesture. He still seems keen to be in Pharaoh's good graces.

'Who?'

'Russian chap,' she says, moving close enough to him that McAvoy has no doubt his nostrils are filled with her scent, and the warmth from her body will be permeating his jacket and resolve. 'One arm.'

The bouncer raises his eyes. 'Zorro, you mean?'

'Eh?'

'He went on a fishing trip with some of the lads,' he says, by way of explanation. 'When he was casting a line the wind caught his rod. It was like he was carving a load of letter Zs in the air. Like Zorro. Y'know?'

'So? Where might I find him on a cold winter evening on Freeman Street?'

'He was in earlier,' says the bouncer with a shrug. 'Left around eightish with a couple of the lads. Heading into Top Town, I think.'

'And where would you suggest I start looking?'

The bouncer eyes her again. Weighs up his options, and decides he's not doing his acquaintance that much of a disservice by exchanging a small piece of information for the affections of this nicely rounded and very sexy older woman.

'Lives over the tanning salon down by Riby Square,' he says, nodding in the direction from which the police officers have just come. 'Won't be back until late, I wouldn't have thought.'

'And if I wanted him now?'

The bouncer smiles and Pharaoh holds his gaze.

'I could phone him for you.'

Pharaoh smiles, reaches up and gives him a kiss on the cheek, as though he is a good boy who has just done a really lifelike drawing of a dog. He gives a grin in return that is more childlike than lustful, and appears to correct himself by giving a leer.

'People can be so friendly,' she says to McAvoy, and then threads her arm through his. 'Come on. You can buy me a drink.'

Pharaoh is almost at the bottom of her second round of vodka and Diet Cokes.

They are sitting at a round, mahogany-coloured table. To

McAvoy, the pub is grotesque; a pastiche of better. A broken mirror gleams grubbily from behind a long dog-leg of a bar stocked with own-label spirits and cheap beer.

'You take me to the most glamorous places,' says Pharaoh, draining her glass. Then adds: 'We're on.'

McAvoy looks up and sees the bouncer pointing them out to a tall, wiry man with flat, clearly Eastern European features and an empty sleeve in his leather jacket. He approaches, looking less than delighted.

'Algirdas?' asks Pharaoh. 'Lads call you "Zorro"?'

'Yes,' he says, and turns his attention to McAvoy. 'I see you before?'

McAvoy nods. 'After the business over the road. You came to talk to me.'

The Russian narrows his eyes as if trying to remember.

'You the copper my friends hurt?' he throws back his head and gives a bark of laughter. 'They fuck up, yes?'

'Yes,' says McAvoy.

'Was terrible,' says Algirdas, shaking his head. 'I know Angie. Nice lady. Lonely lady, I think. Was my friend.'

'She's not dead,' says McAvoy, before Pharaoh can speak.

'No, no. Not the same though, eh?'

They consider this for a moment. Wonder what sort of person will emerge from the hospital. How many years Angie will live in fear of another man finishing the job, before the booze and cigarettes pitch her into blessed release.

Pharaoh takes over. She fixes him with soft eyes and taps the back of his hand as it sits, blotchy, pale, and inked with something indecipherable across the fingers and knobbly knuckles.

'I hope you appreciate us coming over like this,' she says, smiling. 'We had a lot of things we could be doing tonight, but when my sergeant here told me about you, I dropped them all in an instant.'

Algirdas closes one eye, as if trying to focus better, then swings his head in McAvoy's direction.

'Chandler?' he asks, and withdraws his hand from the table to start kneading at the place beneath his jacket where his arm ends in a stump.

Pharaoh nods. McAvoy sits motionless.

'You know him?'

Algirdas looks around again, and Pharaoh marches to the bar. She has a swift discussion with the barman – leaving him in no uncertain terms that the last orders bell has not yet rung – and returns with a pint of bitter and a double vodka for the Russian, another pint for McAvoy, and a packet of pork scratchings for herself.

She tears open the bag and starts shovelling the snacks in her mouth, never taking her eyes off Algirdas as he takes the top off his pint. He downs the vodka in one, then presses his sleeve to his mouth and breathes in through it.

Pharaoh gives McAvoy a sly look, as if asking what he's doing.

'It accentuates the hit,' says McAvoy. 'Russian thing.'

'Fuck you,' says Algirdas, conversationally. 'I'm Lithuanian.'

'Fuck you, sunshine. I'm a policeman.'

They sit quietly for a moment, eyes fixed on one another.

'Are you aware that Russ Chandler has been questioned in connection with two murders?' asks Pharaoh over the noise of the barman chucking empty bottles into a plastic bin. 'Probably charged by now.'

Algirdas sits back in his chair as if he's been pushed in the chest. He's bolt upright, suddenly, hand squeezing at his stump in a manner that looks almost invasively painful.

'Murder? Who murder?'

'A young girl called Daphne Cotton,' says McAvoy quietly. 'And a man called Trevor Jefferson. Those names mean anything to you?'

Algirdas takes a large pull of his pint. Taps his pockets and withdraws a pouch of tobacco and papers. Skilfully, with his one hand, he begins rolling a succession of cigarettes. He places one in his mouth.

'No smoking indoors these days,' says McAvoy, and, with a suddenness that surprises himself, reaches across the table and plucks the roll-up from the other man's mouth.

'Chandler,' he says again.

Algirdas looks to Pharaoh. He seems to lose his temper. 'Barry. Bouncer. He tell me police want to see me, I come. He says nice lady, big tits. I say no problem. I come here. I talk to you. I think it Angie. I think, maybe witness statement, yes? Not Chandler. Not murder.'

'You were the one who mentioned his name to me,' says McAvoy, slowly dismantling the cigarette and returning it to its component parts on the wet, sticky table top. 'You heard me on the phone. You heard me say his name. And you asked me about him. That's why we're here.'

Algirdas sucks at his lips. Starts biting his lower one. He reaches inside his shirt and pulls out a dull metal pendant on a chain. He puts it in his mouth like a pacifier.

'Your saint?'

Algirdas snorts. 'Change from my first English pint,' he says. 'Two pence. Nine years ago. In a bar like this one.'

'Touching,' says McAvoy, and takes the sudden moment of pressure against his leg as a sign from Pharaoh that he should step off.

Algirdas finishes his drink. He looks to Pharaoh. He appears to be wrestling with something, then gives a little growl of acceptance. 'I not illegal,' he says. 'I have papers. I have right to be in Grimsby.'

Pharaoh pops the last pork scratching in her mouth. 'I couldn't give a damn about all that, matey. Anybody who wants to be in Grimsby must be fleeing something bloody terrible. You're welcome as far as I'm concerned.'

Algirdas nods, as if having come to a decision.

'I meet Chandler in bar like this. Southampton, yes? Five years? Six? We drink. We talk. He listen my story. He writer. Great writer. He tell me.'

'He going to write your story, was he? Make you famous?'

Algirdas hits the table again, and it's hard to tell if he is angry or excited. 'In Lithuania, I singer. I make record. Big hit. Not just my country.'

Pharaoh seems to be trying not to laugh. 'You on Lithuanian *Top of the Pops*, were you?'

'I on TV. Radio. Posters on bedroom wall. Big star.'

'Yeah?'

'Yes. I good.'

'What went wrong?'

'Fucking politics. I want more money. They not pay. I think I star. They not. I walk out. Wait for phone to ring. Take real job. Pay bills until all get better. Never got better. Real job become real life.' He stares at the table top with eyes that contain bitterness and regret.

'And Chandler . . . ?'

'He love story. Say there could be book. Say could be hit. Tell my story. How pop singer become dock worker in Southampton. Then I hurt my arm. Chandler visit me. Says it make book more real. More human, he says. Says he call. Arrange interview. Speak to publisher.'

'And he called?'

Algirdas looks away. 'He start writing other book. Always writing. Always working. Sometimes drinking, yes. Likes the drinking.'

'So what brought you up to Grimsby?'

'I come for work. I have friend here. Offer me job. Not many choices for one-armed man.'

McAvoy pinches the bridge of his nose. 'He contacted you again, though, yes? Recently.'

Algirdas nods. 'He call, maybe month ago. Find my number. Say he has book in mind. Not forgotten me. Wants to meet.' He closes his mouth, unsure if he should continue. McAvoy soundlessly pushes his only drink across the table and the Lithuanian takes it hungrily.

'But first . . .'

'He need favour for friend. Friend moving Iceland. Need booking on container ship. Asks can I arrange it . . .'

'And you could?'

Algirdas shrugs. 'Docks busy places. I got friends. Know system.'

'And Chandler knew that?'

'He must remember. I tell him. Tell him how easy to get people in and out. How police, how security, no fucking point. People come and go as they please.'

Pharaoh turns to McAvoy, but he doesn't look at her. Keeps staring at the man who, any moment now, is going to tell him how Fred Stein ended up dead in a lifeboat.

'And you said yes?'

'Chandler tell my story. Show people who I used to be.'

McAvoy understands this overwhelming need to be appreciated, how a miserable little scribbler like Russ Chandler could pour honey in the ear of stronger, more capable men.

'What were you asked to do?'

'Chandler's friend call me. Say he need container to stay shut. Need on bottom deck. No inspection. No sealed behind other. No top of stack. I book for him.'

'You spoke to him?'

'Short call. Two minutes. Matter-of-fact. You know this phrase? He to the point. I think talking hurt for him. Voice sound like he being strangled . . .'

McAvoy closes his eyes. He can smell blood and snow.

'I wait for Chandler to ring . . .'

'Has the phone rung?'

'No,' he says quietly, and then suddenly raises his head. 'But he in jail, you say. He not ring me. How he write book now? Chandler not killer. He small man. One leg. Drunk. How he kill anyone?'

McAvoy's temper flares. 'He didn't, you stupid gullible bastard. And he's never written a book. Not a proper one. He's a miserable little failure who's just got his hands on a bloody best-seller!'

Running his hands through his hair, McAvoy stands up, knocking his chair over and bumping the glasses. Suddenly standing at his full height, Algirdas looks up at him as if he is a giant. His mouth opens and closes like he's a dying fish. Pharaoh reaches up to put a hand on her sergeant's arm, but he shakes her away and storms from the pub, oblivious to the stares and the meaningless words of the bouncer.

The cool air hits him like a slap.

He hears Pharaoh's heels clatter on the wet pavement. Realises she'll have to sprint to catch him, so slows his pace to allow her to talk him out of storming off.

'McAvoy!' she shouts. 'Hector.'

He turns, face flushed, hair damp, sweat pooling in the well at the base of his neck.

'McAvoy, I don't understand . . .'

'No,' he snaps. 'You don't.'

'But it all points to Chandler, doesn't it? I mean, it looks like he's guilty . . .'

'Oh, he's guilty,' he says, tipping his head back to stare up at a sky utterly devoid of stars. 'Guilty of playing games with people. Guilty of preying on people's conceits and fears. Guilty of a huge amount of anger. But pulling the trigger? Stowing away on a bloody boat with a welding torch and a lifeboat? Hacking up Daphne in a crowded church? Putting me down twice? No, that's not his style.'

He feels Pharaoh's hand on his forearm and this time he doesn't shake her off.

'So what is his style? Tell me.'

McAvoy breathes out. Looks down the deserted main road

with its random constellations of blinking neon lights and broken shop-signs.

'He can tell you himself,' he says angrily. 'We're going to see him.'

Pharaoh looks up at him. Her breasts are heaving with the exertion of running, and her smell is ripe in the small pocket of air that seems to contain them both.

He pulls back.

Looks at his feet, and then fills himself with Daphne Cotton.

With Fred Stein.

With Angie Martindale.

Even Trevor fucking Jefferson.

He finds himself suddenly aware that 'good' and 'bad' are not the same things as 'right' and 'wrong'.

And he knows that the reason he has to catch the right man, has to reset the scales by flinging the right murderer into the right cell, is the same reason he will not let himself kiss this sexy, passionate, powerful woman.

It's because somebody has to give a damn about the rules.

And because nobody else really gives a fuck.

# CHAPTER 24

McAvoy and Pharaoh are forty miles from Hull when the call comes through. Forty miles from Wakefield Prison, too. A little under an hour from a private meeting room, a table, three chairs, and an hour in the company of the only man who can tell him if he is right.

Pharaoh, in the driver's seat, pulls the mobile from between her thighs and answers with the word 'Tom'. She gives a few brief grunts and curses. Her face darkens as she hangs up.

Silently, one hand distractedly silencing McAvoy's questions, she pulls onto the hard shoulder.

'I think we're at the end of the road,' says Pharaoh.

'What? It's miles yet . . .'

'Chandler. He tried to kill himself.'

McAvoy feels like he's been punched in the stomach.

'How?'

'Had a razor in that false leg of his. Nobody checked. Found him in his cell, bleeding from the throat. The wrists. The ankles. Well, the ankle . . .'

'He knew we were coming,' says McAvoy flatly.

'He didn't, Hector,' she says, and her voice is barely audible over the sound of the articulated lorries that tear past, inches away. 'We were off-radar, my love. The warden was doing us a favour. We were going out on a limb. If his solicitor had found out . . .'

'He knew.'

'Hector.'

'He fucking knew.'

There is silence for a moment.

He knows what she will say next. Knows that Pharaoh has gone as far as she can. That she, Spink, Tremberg, all of them, will begin to convince themselves of Chandler's guilt. That they will begin to do what needs to be done to ensure Colin Ray's case remains watertight. That they are all seen to get their man.

'You know he didn't do it,' says McAvoy. 'Not properly, I mean.'

'I don't know what to think, Hector. These are the actions of a guilty man.'

'A guilty man who happens to be innocent.'

Pharaoh shakes her head.

'We haven't really got anything, have we?' she says, half to herself. 'Not you and me. Not Colin. We've made a bloody pig's ear of this from the start. Serious and Organised? Which one do you see me as?'

McAvoy looks out of the window. Watches the angry sky.

'What do you really think?' asks Pharaoh.

McAvoy sighs. 'I think what Chandler saw as an idea for a book, somebody else saw as something more. Something that made sense. I don't know . . .' Raps himself on the forehead with a bruised knuckle, furious at his inability to unravel the

DAVID MARK

angle of thoughts that were messing up his mind. 'This isn't
random. I know that much. This isn't a crime for love or
money or revenge. These are deaths that only make sense in
the mind of one person. Somebody is redressing the balance.
They're taking away their second chances at life. People who
survived when nobody else did. They're being bumped off in
the same way that somebody thinks they should have died.
That means something. They're replicating the conditions.
They're trying to take the miracle away. The only reason I
could see Chandler doing that is to get himself a book out of
it, but I met the man and there's anger and self-loathing in
those eyes but there's no . . .'

'Evil? McAvoy, it's not always about—'

'I know, I know. Most crimes are just about anger or drink
or hitting somebody harder than their head can take. But I've
looked into evil eyes and the eyes of the man who's doing this
aren't like that. This is about sadness and despair and having
to do something you don't want to do. It's about paying the
price. It's . . .'

Pharaoh reaches out and puts a hand on the back of his
own. She nods at him.

'Who do you think is killing these people, Hector?'

'Someone like me,' he says.

'You'd never do this,' she says. 'You'd never hurt people.'

'I would,' he says to the floor. 'For my family. For love. I'd
send my soul to hell for the people I love. I'd cry while I was
doing it, but I'd do it. Wouldn't you?'

Pharaoh turns away. 'Not everybody loves like you.'

'So we need to find a man who does. Somebody strong
enough to fight me. Somebody capable of cutting their way

out of a container and killing an old man. Somebody close enough to Chandler to use his connections. To make him call Algirdas. We're looking for a man who loves like me.'

His face is angry, his gestures manic. Pharaoh, involuntarily, seems to shrink back a little in her seat, and McAvoy instantly realises the intimidating picture he must be presenting.

'I'm sorry, guv, I just . . .'

Pharaoh shakes her head slowly, the tension breaking only when she gives a half smile. She follows it up with a punch to his shoulder.

'You should come with a bloody manual,' she says. 'Your Roisin must be a saint.'

McAvoy gives the faintest of laughs.

'She's better than all of us,' he says, gesturing, his vague wave taking in the street and its drunken occupants, its boarded-up shops and litter-strewn doorways. 'Better than all this.'

Pharaoh regards him, holding his gaze. Eventually, she nods, a decision apparently made. 'Keep making her shine, Hector. See if any of it rubs off.'

# CHAPTER 25

McAvoy is lounging against one of the red brick columns that make up the elegant portico framing the glass sliding doors.

'Detective Sergeant McAvoy?'

He turns and sees a tall, slender, short-haired woman in a Puffa jacket over a white coat and trouser suit. The woman extends a pale, ringless hand which disappears entirely as McAvoy closes it in his own and takes care not to squeeze.

'Megan Straub,' she says.

McAvoy smiles and is pleased to see it returned.

'I'm Anne's doctor,' she says, gesturing for him to follow her back into the warm embrace of the modern hospital. 'I think some of our executives and pencil-pushers are a bit upset about all this,' she adds brightly as the double doors swish open and they begin walking down a long corridor laid with gleaming polished wood.

'Well, as I explained, this is a murder investigation . . .'

'Yes, they said something like that,' says Doctor Straub carelessly, then laughs and adds: 'I can't imagine Anne's a suspect.'

'No, nothing like that,' begins McAvoy, and then halts abruptly as he notices that the doctor has stopped by a door and is standing with her fingers on the handle.

Doctor Straub opens the door.

The room is lit by a glorious rectangle of light which scythes down from a high, undraped window set in a wall painted in deep crimson and adorned with black and white sketches in chunky gold frames.

In the centre of a wrought-iron, four-poster bed, lays Anne Montrose. Both of her arms rest above the smooth, cream and gilt bedspread and her blonde hair puddles on the pillowcase like a pool of molten gold.

The drip that feeds her, and the other that takes away her waste, are discreetly hidden behind two tall, rococo lamps, and McAvoy's eye is drawn to a hand-carved, pine bedside table and matching bookcase that stand against the near wall, beneath a giant mirror which makes the room seem even bigger and more opulent than it is.

'She looks like a princess,' breathes McAvoy.

Behind him, Doctor Straub laughs. 'The families of our patients sometimes like to decorate the rooms. Whether it's for them or the patient, I couldn't say, but this one is a definite favourite with the staff.'

'The light that comes through . . .'

'There's a set of bulbs up there,' explains Doctor Straub. 'Even when the weather is shocking, it's like a summer's day in here. That's how it was set up.'

'Can't have been cheap.'

'Her bills are always paid very promptly, I'm led to believe,' says Doctor Straub, cautiously, crossing to the bed and smiling at the figure in its centre. 'And there are never any problems when we want to try new techniques that may cost that little extra.'

'I'm sure Colonel Emms is very generous,' says McAvoy, staring into Doctor Straub's eyes.

'I wouldn't be able to discuss that,' she says with a smile that tells McAvoy all he needs to know.

Curious, he crosses to the bed and leans over Anne Montrose's sleeping body as if leaning out over a ravine. Her skin is perfect. Her face unwrinkled. Her hair full of lustre and life.

'It's like she's . . .'

'Sleeping? Yes. That's the difficult thing for loved ones to understand. They're grieving for somebody who's still here.'

'Is she still here?' he asks, dropping his voice to a whisper. 'Do they come back?'

'We get some of them back,' she says. 'Not always as much as was there to begin with, but they can come back.'

'And Anne? Will she . . .'

'I hope so,' says Doctor Straub with a sigh. 'I'd love to get to know her. From her records we would appear to have lots in common, though I fear that the work she did abroad would have been beyond my generosity.'

'You know about her charity work?' asks McAvoy, stepping back from the bed.

'I'm her doctor,' she explains. 'It's my job to try whatever I can to get a response.'

'You remind her of who she was?'

'Of who she still is.' She stops herself and purses her lips. 'What's this about, Sergeant?'

McAvoy opens his mouth and begins to tell her it's just routine, but stops himself before he has made a sound. 'I think somebody is killing people who have survived atrocities and disasters,' he says, 'and I think Anne is involved somehow.'

'You think she might be in danger?' asks Doctor Straub, pulling a face and raising a hand to her mouth.

McAvoy shakes his head. 'Perhaps,' he says.

'But . . .'

McAvoy just shrugs. He's too tired to go through it all, to explain the thought processes that have brought him into Doctor Straub's world.

'Does she get many visitors?' he asks gently.

'Her mother,' says Doctor Straub, and there is more animation and excitement in her gestures now. 'Her sister occasionally. Obviously, we have visiting doctors and students . . .'

'I understand she was in a relationship at the time of her death,' says McAvoy.

'Yes, her personal effects were brought here when she was transferred to this facility and I have spoken to her family as much as I can to get some details of her life. She fell for a soldier she met while working in Iraq. I'm led to believe he may even have been a chaplain with his regiment. A grand passion, it seems. Such a tragedy to have it cut short.'

'You use this in the therapy, do you?'

'We use whatever we can.'

'You read to her?' asks McAvoy, nodding at the bookcase.

'Sometimes,' she replies. 'I've read her the odd romance. Some poetry. Talked to her about the political situation in Iraq.'

She smiles at McAvoy's expression of surprise.

'Things she was interested in, Sergeant. I've got a patient downstairs who appears to become more withdrawn when we don't tell him how Sheffield Wednesday got on. They're still people. They're just trapped in there. We're looking for whatever it is that unlocks them. We're trying to disentangle a miracle . . .'

McAvoy runs his tongue around his mouth. He looks again at the figure on the bed. Closes his eyes. Looks inside himself. Grits his teeth and presses his large hands to his forehead as he tries to make sense of what he thought he understood . . .

'Sergeant, are you OK?'

His vision is blurring. The room is starting to spin. His legs feel weak, as though unable to support the weight of his thoughts.

'Wait there,' says Doctor Straub urgently, as she lowers him into a sitting position on the floor. 'I'll get you some water.'

The door swings open and McAvoy is left alone in the room, his huge body folded into a schoolboy pose, cross-legged, heavy-headed on the wooden floor.

He finds the strength to look up.

Focuses on the bookcase.

Romances and poetry, fairy-tales and myths.

He reaches out and takes a book at random.

The title swims in his vision. He blinks. Focuses.

Holy Bible.

Gives a half laugh and opens it.

The pages fall like leaves from a dead tree.

McAvoy finds his lap covered in pages of text, torn into confetti, ripped into angry strips and shards.

He stares at the hardback binding.

Scrawled in angry, jagged letters on the inside cover of the empty book he holds in his hands, McAvoy makes out five words, scrawled again and again; deep enough to be fatal if etched in human skin.

### The Unjust Distribution
### Of Miracles

And in the centre of the mantra, amid the mass of angry letters and ferocious scribbles, a piece of scripture, dug into the page in the same furious hand.

*On that day I will become angry with them and forsake them; I will hide my face from them, and they will be destroyed. Many disasters and difficulties will come upon them, and on that day they will ask, 'Have not these disasters come upon us because our God is not with us?' (Deut. 31:17).*

McAvoy forces himself to his feet; torn pages of the scripture falling from his body as he yanks himself upright.

He is breathing heavily, trying to make sense of this rage, bitten deep into the Holy Bible.

He stares again at the figure in the bed.

He scrabbles through the pages; creasing and crumpling leaf after leaf of mania.

Holds up a page of artful lines. Another. More.

Among the scrawls, the furious words, are half a dozen pen-and-ink drawings; vague and abstract, beautiful and unreal.

The tears in his eyes, the blue tinge to his gaze, make the images suddenly swim into focus.

The pictures are all of Anne Montrose. Intricate, loving, detailed images of her laughing, smiling face.

He has seen such penmanship before.

He stares at the images in turn. They are poems to the feeling she has evoked in the artist. Smiling. Laughing. Sleeping . . .

McAvoy holds up the last image. It has been daubed on a torn-out page of a notebook.

It is a picture of Anne Montrose, asleep, in a wrought-iron four-poster bed; her arms above the bed-sheets, her hair puddled on the pillow.

It is smudged with tears.

McAvoy turns it over.

It is signed and dated a little over a week ago.

He runs for the door.

Pulls his phone from his pocket.

Calls the only person he knows with the skills to raise the dead.

# CHAPTER 26

Three hours later, and McAvoy is pulling up outside Wakefield Hospital. The snow hasn't reached this outpost of West Yorkshire yet. It's bitterly cold and the air feels like it has been breathed out of a damp, diseased lung.

McAvoy pushes his hair out of his eyes. He straightens his back and stands his collar on end.

He takes a last breath of outside air, then steps through the automatic doors and strides across the tallow-coloured linoleum. Somebody has made an attempt to put Christmas decorations up in reception, but they look somehow obscene against the peeling plaster of the walls or hanging from ceiling tiles mottled with brown damp.

He endeavours to look like he knows where he's going. Passes the reception desk without a glance. Picks a corridor at random and finds himself following the signs to oncology. He decides that the direction feels wrong, and spots another corridor leading right. He takes it, and almost immediately has to pin himself to the wall as two burly female nurses with round backsides and bosoms that strain their blue uniforms all but take him out as, side by side, they push two tall cages stacked with linens.

'Coming through,' says the older of the pair in a thick West Yorkshire accent.

'Narrow squeak, eh?' says the other, who has proper ginger hair and the sort of round spectacles that went out of fashion a decade before.

'Well, if I was going to get run over today, I couldn't have asked for a nicer pair of assailants. Can I just check, am I going the right way to ICU . . . ?'

Five minutes later, McAvoy is stepping out of the lift on the third floor. His nostrils fill with the scent of blood and bleach; of flavourless food; of the squeak of trolley wheels and rubber-soled shoes on the scarred linoleum.

A fat prison officer is leaning back against the front desk, sipping from a plastic beaker. He has a head shaved down to guard number two, and small, slightly cauliflowered ears sit like teacup handles on the sides of a misshapen, potatoesque face.

McAvoy makes eye contact with the man as he approaches. For the first time since the rugby pitch, he tries to make himself look big. Hopes he looks like somebody to be reckoned with.

He pulls out his warrant card and the guard straightens up.

'Chandler,' says McAvoy, businesslike and official. 'Where are we at?'

The man looks confused for a moment, but the warrant card and the managerial tone are enough to show him his place in the scheme of things, and he makes no attempt to ask McAvoy why he wants to know, or who has sent him.

'On a private ward, yonder,' he says in an accent that sounds to McAvoy's practised ear as though it originated in the Borders.

'Gretna?' he asks, with an approximation of a smile.

'Annan,' says the guard, with a little grin. 'You?'

'Highlands. By way of Edinburgh and just about everywhere else.'

They share a smile, two Scotsmen together, bonding in a Yorkshire hospital and feeling like they've just enjoyed a taste of home.

'Bad way, is he?'

'Not as bad as thought at first. There was so much blood. Parts of his neck were just flapping off. He must have done it himself. He was in solitary. Nobody was near him.'

'Is he conscious?'

'Barely. He's had an emergency op but there's talk of microsurgery if the stitches don't do the job. He was dead to the world a minute ago, face bandaged up like a mummy. I just popped out for a coffee. There's another guard gone for his lunch will be back soon. Nobody said to expect visitors.'

McAvoy nods. Ploughs straight on through the other man's growing cynicism.

'I need five minutes with him,' he says, eyes boring into the guard's. 'Asleep or not.'

The guard appears to be about to argue, but there is something in McAvoy's gaze that seems utterly rigid in its devotion to purpose, and he quickly tells himself that there is no harm in stepping aside.

McAvoy thanks him with a nod. His heart is thumping, but he stills it with deep breaths and closed eyes. His shoes are surprisingly quiet on the linoleum floor.

The silence is eerie. Grim. It makes him wonder about his own final days. Whether he will die amid noise, surrounded by bustle and chat. Or whether it will be a solitary gunshot, and then nothing.

He steps inside Chandler's room.

The curtains are the same yellow as the drapes on the maternity unit at Hull Royal, but everything else is a washed-out and joyless blue.

Chandler is lying pathetic and motionless on the bed. His false limb is propped next to the single bed, leaving his pyjama leg empty. Nobody has bothered to tie a knot below the severed knee, and the garment is twisted, slanting left, so that at first glance, it looks as though the leg is pointing at an obscene angle.

Chandler's throat is wrapped in bandages. A tube connected to a bag filled with clear fluid runs into a needle in the back of his right hand. Another, thicker tube runs into his mouth and down his throat. It has been taped to the side of his face, and already a crust of drying salvia has begun to form over the adhesive strip.

McAvoy reaches inside his coat and removes the bottle from his inside pocket. Roisin had warned him to put gloves on while handling it. Had said that the stink would eat into the skin of his fingers and never wash out. He pulls down the cuff of his shirt. Wraps it around both hands. Holds the vial in one hand and carefully unscrews the lid with the other.

The stench is extraordinary. Even at the remove of an arm's length he feels his nostrils flare, grows instantly dizzy as the raw ammonia courses into his brain.

He crosses to the bed in three strides. Holds the bottle under Chandler's nose.

One . . .

Two . . .

Three . . .

The bandaged figure on the bed begins to thrash. There is movement beneath the wrappings as his eyes fly open and what's left of his face begins to contort. His hands fly to his mouth and begin tearing at the breathing tube, at the bandages, as muted, rasping coughs escape his lips with a hiss.

His solitary leg kicks out and drums on the mattress.

McAvoy leans forward. Takes the breathing tube in one hand and pulls. It emerges wet and vile from his open mouth and McAvoy drops it to the floor.

Chandler hauls himself upright and heaves bile into his own lap. Coughs and begins clawing at the bandages.

McAvoy's face is impassive. He merely watches. Allows Chandler these few moments of panic. This agony of fear and confusion as he awakes in the dark.

He listens as Chandler finds his voice. Watches the serpentine tongue lick dry lips beneath the sick-stained dressings.

McAvoy leans in. 'You survived, sir.'

'Sergeant . . . ?' The voice is dry and sore. 'Sergeant McAvoy?'

McAvoy replaces the stopper and deposits the small vial of clear liquid back in his inside pocket.

'I'm sorry to have done that, Mr Chandler,' he says, settling his large bulk on the bed at Chandler's side. 'I just need yes and no from you, sir. You've been through quite an ordeal.

You are in hospital. You attempted to end your own life.'

Chandler's eyes begin to open. He's swallowing painfully, and McAvoy pours him a beaker of water from the jug on the bedside table and lifts it to the writer's lips. He takes a few sips and then collapses back on the pillow.

'You worked it out, didn't you,' McAvoy says, locking eyes with the pitiful figure in the hospital-issue pyjamas. 'You know who and why.'

Chandler gives the faintest of nods. 'My fault,' he says. 'My big mouth . . .'

'He would have done it anyway,' says McAvoy, and means it. 'He'd have found a reason. The thing that was inside him would have come out no matter what.'

'But he was a good man,' stutters Chandler. 'I was just talking. It was just drunken bollocks. I wasn't telling him to change everything he believed . . .'

'Grief is a terrible thing,' says McAvoy.

'So is murder,' says Chandler.

They sit in silence for a moment, then McAvoy stands. Turns away from the bed. Walks to the window to compose his thoughts. Looks past the yellow curtains at the damp car park with its swaying trees and rain-lashed vehicles and scampering, stick-insect figures. Perhaps it is the elevation, the sense of looking down upon them, but he has never more felt that it is he, and he alone, who carries the burden of protection and justice. He turns. Wants to end this.

'Simeon Gibbons,' he says. 'Where is he?'

The name hangs heavy in the air. Chandler's lips close. The tension in his body seems to ease a little. McAvoy watches as he licks his lips afresh.

'I wish I knew.'

'When did you last see him?'

'About ten minutes before they arrested me.'

'He was there? At Linwood Manor?'

'He's a permanent resident. His room's paid for by an old army mate of his.'

'Colonel Emms? Runs a private security firm in the Middle East?'

Chandler nods.

'Deep pockets, has Sparky.'

Chandler looks away.

'He made me his confessor without telling me a thing.'

McAvoy hopes that Emms is now confessing all to Pharaoh, who had set off for Brontë country as soon as he'd told her what he'd found in Anne Montrose's room. 'Tell me how it happened,' he says. 'How you worked it out.'

'It was Chief Inspector Ray. During the interview he was reeling off a list of names. People Simeon may have hurt. I think it was your research. He mentioned a young woman in a coma. Anne Montrose.'

'And you recognised the name?'

'I knew she was called Anne. The rest sort of made sense.'

'He told you her name was Anne? In rehab?'

'He would cry out in his sleep.'

'Did he tell you what happened. In Iraq?'

'He told me about his life. People do that, tell me things. They think I'm going to make them famous. They think I'm going to write a book about them and they'll somehow matter . . .'

'But Gibbons didn't want that?'

'He just wanted somebody to talk to. He was a mess. Did you see him, when you came to visit me? No, he'll have been covered up. His face, Sergeant. It's a mess of burns and scars. From the explosion. The one that nearly killed him.'

*Nearly, but not quite*, thought McAvoy. Was Emms paying for his treatment as well? Almost certainly.

'I'm a writer, Sergeant. I ask questions. When we were paired up, we got to talking.'

'You became friends?'

'Yes, I would say so. It was boxing that got us started. I was telling him about my book. The journeyman one I told you about. He mentioned he used to box in the army. That was how it started.'

'Was he in there for alcoholism too?'

'He wouldn't touch it, Sergeant. Whatever it was that kept him going, he didn't want it dulled.'

'So, depression? Post-traumatic stress disorder?'

'Perhaps. I just knew he was very, very sad.'

'And Anne?'

'We got to talking about past loves. I didn't have much to say, but he told me he'd only ever been in love once. That she'd been hurt in an explosion. He'd walked away but she'd never woken up. Thought he meant she was dead. He didn't. It came out she was in a coma. That she was in a private health-care centre. I didn't know what to say. Made some crack about Sleeping Beauty. He liked that. Smiled for the first time since I'd known him. Seemed to come out of himself a bit. Started talking. Telling me about the things he'd learned over there. In the desert. How his mind was opened.'

'Opened to what?'

'To everything.' Chandler closes his eyes. 'Have you ever wondered about pain? About who it afflicts? About why some are lucky and others aren't? Have you ever wondered if you take one person's pain away, whether that pain goes somewhere else? Whether there's an agreed amount of agony in the world? That's what he used to talk about. That was what used to torture him. I suppose I indulged him. Let him talk. He used to bring me bottles . . .'

McAvoy nods. 'You told him about your work? The people you've interviewed? Funny stories?'

Chandler closes his eyes. 'It was just chat.'

'Fred Stein?'

Chandler nods.

'Trevor Jefferson?'

Another nod.

'Angie Martindale?'

Again.

McAvoy swallows hard. 'Daphne Cotton?'

Chandler says nothing. Just keeps licking his lips. His hands, without a pen and pad to hold, are lifeless, feeble things.

'Sole survivors, eh?'

Chandler nods.

They sit in silence for a moment, listening to the wind and the rain kick listlessly at the grubby windows.

'When did he decide to kill them all?' McAvoy asks, staring unblinkingly into Chandler's eyes. The writer screws up his face like a tissue and begins to cough. McAvoy helps him to more water and then sits back, all without ever breaking eye contact.

'We were talking one night,' he says, more to himself than to McAvoy. 'He liked to hear my stories. Remarkable people, you know. I said that it made you think. Made you ponder the big picture. What's it all about. The nature of existence.'

'And Gibbons was a Christian man, yes?'

'Middle-class boy. Went to church every Sunday and said prayers before bed when he was at boarding school.'

'But did he believe?'

'I don't think he'd ever questioned it until the explosion. And then none of his life made sense any more. And he found a religion of his own.'

'Did he still pray at Linwood?'

'Not in front of me.'

'What did it, Chandler? What did he fill himself up with?'

For a moment there is no sound in the room save Chandler's wheezing breath. Finally, he says: 'I mentioned miracles. Cheating death. Cheating God, I suppose. I said something clever. It might even have been a title for the book. It was just a phrase . . .'

'Which was?'

'The Unjust Distribution of Miracles.'

'And Gibbons liked that?'

'It was as if he'd just found the head of John the Baptist under his bed. I've never felt so fucking worthy in all my life.'

'Worthy? He took your words and made a religion out of it. He found a cause. A mission! A way to bring her back.'

'I didn't know,' says Chandler, shaking his head and sniffing back snot. 'I didn't know what he was planning.'

'But he spoke to you about it,' says McAvoy, biting his lip. 'He ran his ideas past you. Asked his preacher's opinion.'

Chandler flashes him a look of anger but just as quickly bites it back. 'I liked the attention.'

'What did he ask you?'

The answer comes from the pit of the writer's stomach, and reeks of bile and regret.

'He asked me whether I thought mercy was a finite resource. He read me passages from the Bible. From books he'd found. About righteousness. About justice. About miracles.'

McAvoy can already see the answer to his next question.

'He asked you whether you thought taking away one miracle would leave room for another,' says McAvoy, with his eyes closed. 'Whether cancelling out an act of mercy would create another.'

There is silence in the room.

'And you said yes.'

'I said it might do.'

'And then you phoned the Russian for him. The one-armed bloody pop star.'

Chandler looks confused. He shakes his head as if not understanding and then slowly stops as a drunken memory emerges from his ruined, pickled mind.

'I was pissed,' he wails.

McAvoy shakes his head. He can feel his throat closing up. The old wound in his shoulder begins to throb with an icy pain.

'Who's next, Chandler? Who else did you tell him about?'

Chandler licks his teeth. Raises his hands and begins to rub at the crusted saliva on his chin.

'I'm sorry,' he says, and turns away.

'Chandler?'

'It was just talk. Just chat. I didn't think . . .'

'What is it, Chandler? What have you done?'

'After we spoke,' he sniffs, between the sobs. 'I told him about you. About your wife. About how strong she was. About how she endured so many miscarriages and still kept trying . . .'

'What do you . . . ?'

McAvoy stops. It feels as if fingers made of ice have closed around the nape of his neck and begun to squeeze.

'I'm so sorry.'

Adrenalin surges through McAvoy's body. All he can see is Simeon Gibbons, smothering his newborn daughter between Roisin's thrashing, bloodied legs . . .

He runs. Sprints for the exit, pulling his phone from his pocket, blood rushing in his ears, boots squeaking on the floor; Chandler's sobs echoing down the hall.

The prison guard sees him. Begins to push himself away from the desk where he lounges with his plastic cup. Sensing something wrong, he moves to slow him but McAvoy clatters into him and through; pulling open the door and thundering down the steps three at a time.

He looks at his phone. No signal. No fucking signal.

*I'm so sorry, I'm so sorry, I'm so sorry . . .*

Tries to find a way to make himself believe that what is happening to his wife and children is not a direct result of his own vile vanity.

Runs through all he knows about the man who intends to kill his child. Recalls the physical strength, the ease with which he had avoided McAvoy's blows.

That boxer's gait . . .

McAvoy stops. Pulls up short on the green linoleum; a statue of sudden, horrid comprehension.

Chandler's protégé. The boxer. The room-mate. The guy with his face in shadows . . .

He tears through the lobby, staring at the screen of his mobile. He tries the home number, but the damn thing won't ring. He presses the wrong digits with his shaking, frantic fingers.

Finds himself listening to the message Trish Pharaoh had left after her meeting with Monty Emms:

*. . . he's alive, McAvoy. You were right. There are messages from Gibbons in Emms's phone going back weeks. I left the Lieutenant Colonel sitting in the Fleece, halfway up the hill in Haworth. Can't hold his drink, can he? Got his phone without a squeak. We need to get it officially because it's going to be exhibits A to bloody Z. It's dynamite. Apologies and gratitude, to begin with. Thank yous for getting him out. For putting some Iraqi in a body bag and telling the world he was dead. For setting him up with a new life. A new home. For taking care of Anne. Paying her bills. And so many 'I'm sorrys'. Sorry for letting him down. Sorry for not being able to pay for Anne's care himself. Sorry for the things he's done wrong. They change, though. Maybe a month ago, if the dates are right. Starts talking about making sense of it all. About having a way to change it all. Monty's too pissed for any more but I'm going to work him. We'll mop this all up later. If you're still sure about seeing him, you're going to need a confession . . .*

McAvoy slams the phone closed to silence it and opens it again. He almost exclaims with joy as he sees that he has a full signal. Sprinting across the car park, pulling his keys from his pocket, he dials Roisin's mobile.

Three rings . . .

'Hi, baby, how did it go?'

Relief floods him. His wife sounds tired, but very much alive.

Safe.

They are safe.

Breathing heavy, sweat running down his face, he pulls open the car door and slumps heavily into the driver's seat.

'Oh darling . . .' he begins. 'I thought . . .'

He looks at himself in the rear-view mirror.

Too late sees the movement in the back seat.

And then the blade is at his throat.

A face, turned to melted plastic and charred meat by flame, eases out of the darkness, and a hand partially covers McAvoy's own, closing the phone.

McAvoy stares into the wet, blue eyes of Simeon Gibbons.

Feels the knife move down his body.

Feels the pressure as it slices through his coat, his shirt. As it nicks at his skin.

Feels Gibbons lean forward, and part the ruined clothing with his hand. Sees him stare at the wound left by a murderer's blade a year before.

Realises, too late, that he, too, is a survivor. A man who walked away.

He closes his eyes as he realises that Chandler has misled him. That his wife and children are safe, but that it is he who will be dispatched in the manner that he survived twelve months ago.

There is a thud. A sudden dull pain as a rigid thumb rams into his carotid artery with an expert swiftness and precision.

And then blackness.

# CHAPTER 27

McAvoy wakes into nothingness. He can't move. The pain in his throat, his neck, is the centre of his being.

He tries to lift his head. Fails. Tries to move his arms. He can't seem to send the message to his limbs.

He listens. Tries to focus. He senses the hum of car tyres.

He is crumpled in the passenger seat of his own car, moving at speed.

There is a voice near by. A soft, sibilant, animal whisper. It sounds as though it has been talking for an age.

'. . . just this one, my love. This one, then wake. Wake for me. Wake for me. Take it back. Please. Take it back . . .'

McAvoy tries to will himself back to his limbs.

He manages to lick his dry lips. Moves his head the tiniest fraction.

'He survived. Survived when you didn't. Survived like me. Like all of them. We'll take him to where it happened. Cut him like he should have been cut the firssst time . . .'

Through the fog, the haze of his thoughts, McAvoy understands. Understands that Simeon Gibbons is taking him to where it all began a year before. Where Tony Halthwaite slashed him with a blade for daring to discover that he was a killer of young girls. Where he became the one that got away.

McAvoy shifts his head. Catches a glimpse of the road. Of dark trees, swaying in a wind filled with slashing rain.

Recognises the familiar silhouette of the Humber Bridge.

Half an hour from home.

Five minutes from the spot where, a year ago, he'd caught a killer, and almost bled to death for his trouble.

'. . . Sparky let us down, didn't he? The room. The bed. The best money could buy. And you still asleep. Asleep and beautiful, but no more than a picture in a frame. He said he was our friend. But they couldn't fix you. Couldn't make you wake, could they? It was beyond that. Beyond medicine. We needed somebody's miracle, didn't we? The writer knew. Made it make sense. There's only so much justice. Mercy is finite. It falls like rain but the sky is dry. Only so much luck. People lived when others died. Why not you? Why did they steal your mercy?'

McAvoy feels the car swing round a roundabout. Sees the density of the tree cover begin to change overhead.

McAvoy thinks of Roisin. Remembers the last time he kissed her mouth. Pictures her in the kitchen, grating and mixing and chopping like his good little white witch . . .

Remembers the potion in his pocket.

The glass vial of ammonia.

He opens his eyes. Turns his head.

Looks into blue eyes set in a face of pulped skin; of molten flesh and risen welts.

Reaches into his pocket and, with an arm that tingles and throbs, closes his tingling fingers around the glass.

Turns.

Lashes out . . .

Smashes the glass vial into the ruined features of the man who killed them all.

Tries to grab the wheel and flicks his head to look at the road . . .

Doesn't even have time to exclaim as the vehicle ploughs at 60mph into the brick and glass building at the edge of the car park and explodes in a ball of flame.

The heat is intense against McAvoy's cheek as Gibbons pushes his face against the window of the buckled passenger door. The windscreen itself is so much shattered glass, and the flames from beneath the bonnet are starting to curl, like flapping laundry, into the vehicle.

McAvoy brings his fist up short beneath Gibbons's extended right arm, feels something break as the punch slams into his elbow.

For a moment, the connection is broken, and McAvoy grabs at the door handle. He pushes, but the door refuses to give.

He takes his eyes off Gibbons and spins in his seat to face the door. He brings both feet back and kicks at the window. Once. Twice. The glass explodes outwards, and as fresh oxygen rushes into the car the flames are given fresh fuel; tongues of red and orange heat flutter and tear over the steering wheel, the dashboard and the two men in the front seat.

McAvoy feels the flames catch at the trousers. Scorch his hands. Kiss his face.

He kicks at the door this time. Kicks with everything he has.

Creaking, hurting, the door folds outwards, and McAvoy scrabbles for the gap.

Hands close around his boots. Strong arms encircle his legs.

He slithers forward, pulling Gibbons behind him, until both men slide and thud onto the wet car park.

McAvoy kicks his legs free and instinctively rolls away from the vehicle.

He tries to stand.

Then Gibbons is upon him. In the light of the flaming car, his scars are monstrous. There is no moisture in his eyes now. The black of his pupils has almost engulfed the blue of his irises.

They are twenty yards from the burning vehicle. Gibbons is hauling him to his feet. The wounds at the ex-soldier's throat seem to be reopening.

McAvoy feels himself being dragged towards the dark shadow of the wood that stands at the edge of the car park.

He struggles for purchase on the wet tarmac. Tries to tear himself from Gibbons's grasp. The other man seems to sense what he is doing and swings another pointed thumb in the direction of McAvoy's neck. He sees it coming and yanks his head back, lashing out with two swift right hands that catch Gibbons on the side of the head and send him reeling backwards.

McAvoy falls. Tries to stand and slips again.

Everything hurts. He watches Gibbons shake his head, as if trying to clear it. Sees him bunch his fists. The glint of a blade in his hand. Sees him turn his head and look down on McAvoy's sprawled, vulnerable body.

McAvoy drags himself to his knees. Puts one hand on the wet tarmac and pushes himself to his feet, righting himself just in time to see Gibbons pounce like something feline and beautiful from five feet away.

The punch is instinctive. McAvoy's vision clears for a moment. The pain subsides just for an instant. For a heartbeat, he is a strong, big man, a man who could have been a boxer if he had been able to inflict pain without remorse.

The punch swings upwards almost from the floor. It catches Gibbons just below the chin.

His trajectory changes. He flies backwards like a tennis ball struck by a racquet.

McAvoy, the last drop of energy draining from his body, falls backwards onto the wet earth.

And then the car explodes.

Flame and metal and jagged glass fill the night air.

Gibbons is still staggering backwards from the force of the blow when the blast tears his body into offal.

McAvoy doesn't see the moment of release. Doesn't see the killer shredded and cooked and smeared across the earth.

He is lying on his back, staring at the sky, wondering whether the clouds above will give Roisin and his family snow for Christmas.

# EPILOGUE

*Wake up, wake up, wake up . . .*

The glass of hot milk and cinnamon is going cold on Doctor Megan Straub's bedside table, a thick skin forming on its untouched surface.

*Too wired to switch off. Too energised to let go . . .*

She is sitting up in bed, reading by torchlight so as not to wake the skinny, Asian-looking man who dozes next to her, here in the largest bedroom of this modest apartment on the outskirts of Keighley, forty-five minutes from the hospital where her patients lie in a sleep that mocks her own insomnia.

'Mercy,' she reads. 'From the Latin word for "merchandise". A price paid.'

She frowns, and wonders at the mercenary origins of a word associated with divine intervention. Could it be bought? Could the centuries have dulled people's understanding of the true nature of the concept? Could there be a way of influencing the seemingly random, scattered distribution of the Almighty's pity?

She feels troubled. Confused. Finds herself analysing

concepts that seem too big to unpick. Wonders, for an instant, if prayer is ever anything more than a desperate plea for favour.

Doctor Straub is suddenly unsure whether she should have taken the book. Whether she should have left it untouched, sitting among the scattered snowstorm of papers on the carpeted floor around Anne Montrose's hospital bed. Would the bull-chested policeman with the soft eyes and the easy blush be returning to gather up the gospel that had sent him sprinting from the room?

Despite the heat rising from the naked man at her side, Doctor Straub shivers and tucks herself more firmly inside the expensive quilt. She angles the torch to better illuminate the ruined pages of the holy book. Tries to make sense of the scribbles and jagged graffiti. Wonders why she cannot put it down.

She turns the book slowly, like a wheel. Through the mess of violent scribbles, there is some sense to what at first appears to be muddled hieroglyphs. She wonders if it is her own long experience of reading other doctors' handwriting that allows her to make out a meaning in the blocks of ink.

*Prayer indeed is good. But while calling on the gods a man should himself lend a hand.*

She looks away. Screws up her eyes and attempts to locate a memory. She remembers the quote. Hippocrates? Yes. The man whose oath marshals her profession.

Doctor Straub peers closer. Locates another strand of meaningful writing.

*Whatever a man prays for, he prays for a miracle. Every prayer reduces itself to this: Great God, grant that twice two be not four.*

296

She finds herself wondering who might have written these words – at the venom and fury that had caused them to drive the pen into the paper with the force of a knife.

*The creator who could put a cancer in a believer's stomach is above being interfered with by prayers.*

Doctor Straub closes the book.

She has given up on sleep. Is surprised she even went to the trouble of going to bed. She shouldn't be here, really. Should be back at the hospital, waiting for news. Should be stroking Anne Montrose's hand. Should be urging her to try again. To open her eyes . . .

She had already been on her way home when the call came through. It was one of the nurses on the ward, her voice breathless with excitement.

This evening, Anne Montrose had stirred. Her eyelids had flickered, and the read-out from the monitor showed a spiked increase in brain activity.

A dream? Dr Straub has often wondered what her patients see. What goes on behind the eyes.

Here, now, she wonders whether, wherever she is, Anne Montrose is happy.

Wonders, too, whether she will ever get the chance to ask her. To talk to somebody who has come back.

She locks her teeth and feels a tension in her jaw. She does not want to let herself get carried away. Is trying to contain her excitement. But somewhere, in the unscientific part of herself, she fancies that, before dawn, Anne Montrose may experience a miracle.

Softly, so as not to wake the man at her side, she slips out of bed and pads across the varnished, hardwood floors. She opens the bedroom door and makes her way into the living room, with its white leather suite and tasteful black and white photographs.

She switches on the large plasma TV that dominates the imitation chimney breast and lowers the volume as she flicks through the news channels. The clock in the corner of the screen declares it well past midnight.

Drowsily, Doctor Straub settles on one of the twenty-four-hour rolling news stations. There are hundreds of homes in Scotland without electricity owing to the storms. A police officer has been taken to hospital with minor injuries following an incident at the Humber Bridge Country Park which saw a vehicle explode and destroy a nearby administration block. One person is believed to have died in the incident. In other news, a decorated British army colonel has been arrested in West Yorkshire by officers looking into the death of Daphne Cotton, who was murdered several days ago in Hull's Holy Trinity Church. Officers say he is not being questioned about the murder, but about withholding vital evidence linked to this and several other cases . . .

To her left, nestled on a tower of books, Doctor Straub's telephone begins to ring.

Quickly, for fear of the noise waking her partner and robbing her of these moments of thoughtful solitude, she jumps up from the chair and answers the call.

'Doctor Straub?' The voice is breathless and excited. 'Doctor, this is Julie Hibbert. I'm sorry to call so late, but I thought you would want to know . . .'

'It's no problem, Julie,' she says, and there is a tremble in her voice. Could her patient be awake?

'It's Anne Montrose, Doctor Straub,' says the nurse.

'Yes?'

'I think it must have been an anomaly. She's stabilised. Returned to her standard brain function. Heartbeat regular. Whatever caused her to flicker, it's gone.'

Doctor Straub thanks her. Replaces the receiver.

Settles into the chair and leans her head against the cushion.

She gives an almost imperceptible shake of her head, and then closes her eyes.

*Miracles.*

# ACKNOWLEDGEMENTS

Thanks go to Oli Munson at Blake Friedmann for being generally ace and putting up with my endless questions, and also to Jon at Quercus for much the same reason. Thanks, too, to Sarah Jones and Sarah Morgan for being the people you are. More than anything, thanks to Nik and the kids. You give me a reason.

I am also grateful to Ottar Sveinsson, whose terrific book *Doom in the Deep* proved invaluable in researching the Triple Trawler Tragedy.